I0737130

HER DEVIL   1

Let me introduce you to the new blood.

The
SECT
A PENDLETON PREP NOVELLA
H.L. PACKER

Copyright © 2023 HL Packer

All rights reserved. Without limiting the rights under copyright reserved above, no part of this publication may be reproduced, stored in or introduced into retrieval system, or transmitted, in any form, or by any means (electronic, mechanical, photocopying, recording or otherwise) without the prior written permission of both the copyright owner and the above publisher of this book.

This is a work of fiction. Names, characters, places, brands, media, and incidents are either the products of the author's imagination or are used fictitiously. The author acknowledges the trademark owners of various products referenced in this work of fiction, which have been used without permission. The publication/use of these trademarks is not authorised, associated with, or sponsored by the trademark owners.

Editor – Lindsey Powell Editing
Cover Designer – LJDesigns
Formatter – LJDesigns

# ONE

## Nick

The cold seeps into my bones from the concrete, the rope digging into my wrists as I attempt to move my arms far enough to wipe the blood dripping from my nose, but it won't reach.

Breathing in, I blow it out through my nose, the blood splattering messily in front of me, before I'm jostled once again, another body landing with a groan.

I don't know how many of us there are or how long we've been waiting, all I know is that right now I'm cold, fucking tired, and just about every bone in my body hurts.

"Welcome," a voice booms from in front of us, my head snapping to attention. "Welcome all."

Fabric rustles behind me, but any chatter fades out almost instantly, a sweet smoke drifting past me.

"I love this." He chuckles, the rich sound echoing around the room, something passing between him and those who can see him before he turns serious. "I'd like to take this moment to officially welcome you to the elite, to The Sect. Here we have the start of a new year, a new intake. Ten fresh-faced hopefuls with not enough time to prove their worth."

I thought she was crazy, our mother, when she sat me and my twin brother down and told us that Pendleton Prep and The Sect were expecting us. We thought she'd finally lost what little marbles she was holding onto in the wake of our father's death. But apparently not. Apparently, she wasn't as crazy as she sounded.

Liquid sloshes in a glass, and he swallows loudly before placing it down, every sound amplified by the lack of sight. "This isn't going to be easy, certainly no walk in the park. We're going to test your loyalty, your patience, and your trust, amongst other things. And not just your loyalty to The Sect but to each other too. Ten of you kneel here, three will stand at the end. I'm interested to see who makes the cut."

A few rumbles of agreement ripple from behind me, or us, as we wait quietly for further instruction.

"Stand." The command echoes around the space, and as I push to stand, someone knocks into me from the side, forcing me to my feet unsteadily. Placing my foot out to stop my fall takes me out of the line for barely a second, but it's enough.

The collective hissed intake of breath ensures I know how badly I've fucked up before the recompense even comes, a lump forming in the pit of my stomach. I straighten back up, sliding myself in place and hoping like fuck this isn't three strikes and you're out, because I know for damn sure I'm one down already.

The sound of a knife being flicked open rings out to my left, shuffling swiftly following until its directly behind me, the blade sliding through the rope at my wrists like butter.

Pulling my arms to my front and rubbing where the skin is raw doesn't do much to ease the tension threaded through every muscle, the silence ominous.

"Left hands out," is commanded from the front, and I hold mine out, palm up, automatically.

The anticipation builds as more than one hiss of pain rolls from my right, some pussy letting a near whimper tumble from them. And then there's a blaze of fire slicing across my palm, and my hand closes instinctively against it, catching the edge of the blade as it draws back.

My eyes narrow behind the blindfold and my lips purse, but I'm not willing to give them any more ammunition against me, and I bottle down any other response as the guy moves down the line, continuing on to the next person until it all falls silent again.

"We are the elite. We are The Sect. And once your blindfold is removed, you'll be privy to some of the names and faces running this great country from the inside. And that's why you'll take blood oaths right now."

Understanding rolls over me. This isn't just an introduction to the induction process, this is it, the start.

"You'll repeat after me. I hereby swear my life and my loyalty to The Sect."

The words echo back to him as the ten of us reply

confidently.

"I understand there is no way out from here, except by death or excommunication."

They may as well be the same thing. But for those that don't make the cut, I guess it helps. The words roll off my tongue easily, and I can't help but strain my ears, listening for my brother, hoping against hope he's here too.

"Gentlemen, let's make them some space. Blindfolds off."

I reach up to remove the thick cloth, only someone slices through it from behind and it tumbles to the ground at my feet. I take a quick look to my left and right, getting my first look at the competition and seeing Jacob further down the line.

He smiles and winks my way, letting me know he's okay, if a bit worse for wear.

# TWO

The jerk to my right shoulder checks me as he barges back into place, unfortunately not knocking the chip off his as he does. He looks me up and down with disdain, running his tongue over his teeth. *Fuck boy.*

His dark hair sits perfectly as he runs his hands through it, pulling the longer layers back and smoothing down the sides. His hazel eyes pin me with irritation, and I can't help the smirk that tumbles from me in reply. He thinks I pushed him on purpose. Like I need the fucking help. No, that came from further down the line. I was just lucky enough to keep my feet under me where he clearly didn't.

Some blonde sashays along the line, swapping the bloody cloths pressed into our hands with clean ones and keeping them all in order. Mine isn't the only gaze that follows the length of her legs from one side to the other, and when two claps ring out upfront, it's clear the distraction was intentional.

"Ten begin, three will end, and one of you won't see out the night." The guy who's been talking the whole time is none other than the deputy mayor, his balding hair and mid-life paunch not quite what I was expecting from our induction leader, but whatever.

He nods his head and the men gathered around us part, showcasing the three boxed in squares. Hay bales make up the border of each, and I can only ponder their use.

"Before loyalty, before trust, there's protection." And then the penny drops. They're rings. Three fighting rings. "If you can't protect yourself, how can I expect you to protect your brothers? Us? Me?" He raises an eyebrow and looks down the line, making eye contact with each one of us and making sure we understand the seriousness of the place we find ourselves.

"Nicholas Daniel Barratt." The guy to my left tenses. "Because of your transgression, let's start with you." I see him nod in my periphery, his fists tightening and releasing at my side. "Actually, let's make this interesting. Leopold Miles Windsor and Jacob Atticus Barratt, you're up."

Whoops and hollers call out from behind us, and as I turn, I recognise more than one face there. The question is, are they cheering me on or him?

Stepping forward, I follow the deputy mayor's outstretched hand, guiding us to the furthest ring. He calls out other names, pairing some more up as I wait for whoever this other guy is.

The spitting image of the guy next to me, Nicholas, walks towards me, all the way down to the cocky swagger I'd expect him to have, and suddenly the names make sense. Nicholas Barret. Jacob Barret. Brothers. Twins. And the punishment will be watching me kick his brother's ass. Now I get it.

A grin splits my face and I crack my knuckles in anticipation. For once, I'm glad I don't sleep well, the jeans I'm still wearing likely to protect me better than the soft sleep shorts hanging low from his hips. The ones that incidentally match his brother's. Not that I noticed.

He absentmindedly rubs the edge of his lip, disturbing where blood clings to the broken skin. A little oozes out, and he wipes it away with the back of his hand. He pays no mind to it, smearing it across his chest before flexing his wrists and closing the distance between us.

He holds his hand out to me, shaking it with a nod before the two of us begin to circle. No one calls out any rules or tells us how long to go for, so I guess it's just a free for all.

His hands go up, a guard I know more than one way to evade as he throws an easy combination of punches in my direction, more than one hitting its mark. An ache seeps through my shoulder where he managed to land it squarely, but it's all textbook. Moves he learnt in a controlled environment, with no-one looking to do him any real damage.

I might have grown up with a silver spoon, but my best friends came from the wrong side of the track. Neither of them are shy about throwing a punch, and I learned quickly how to take one, how to give one, and how to land it to make the most impact.

As he steps in to close the distance between us, I pull back, thrusting my leg forward and hitting him squarely in the chest, his momentum giving it more force than I could have managed alone. He crumples, his chest caving in as he gasps for breaths that won't come, the air knocked cleanly out of his lungs.

The crowd goes wild somewhere behind me, could be for this, or it could be something going on in one of the other rings, but I can feel the heat of his stare burning through my side, and I can't help but smirk. The watery green of his hazel eyes hold a plea I'm not going to heed, no matter how much the darker hue of his brothers gets my dick hard.

He sucks air in as I wait for him to get to his feet. I might be able to fight dirty, doesn't mean I'm going to though. Stepping back, he gets his hands back up, but I know he's hurting. We circle each other slowly, the rest of the world and everything going on in the room falling to the wayside.

He launches forward, landing a solid shot to my jaw, throwing me off balance and snapping my teeth together as the reverberations bound around my head. He'll need more than that for me to go down though, and as I parry, shaking the shot out, I wait for the second his guard comes down and throw my weight behind the punch, twisting my body to give it everything.

My knuckles split with the force, pain radiating up my arm as my chest heaves, the adrenaline kick like nothing else in this world.

# THREE

## Jacob

There's nothing I can do but watch it come.

It's like a car crash you can see happening but have no way to intervene before it does, except this is my body, and I ought to be able to move, to react. Apparently, my reaction times suck under pressure, and I don't even get to use any of the groundwork I spent years practicing, because like that car crash, there's nothing I can do to get out of the way of the doom that's coming my way.

There's no bracing myself before it lands, darkness sweeps over me, and that's it. Lights out.

The world comes back patchy, the sounds and scents the first thing my brain registers—damp haybales that edge around the makeshift ring, and blood in the air.

"Jake. Jake. Wake the fuck up," Nick screams from

a million miles away. But the more he says it, the closer it gets, until my eyes fly open, everything snapping back into focus as the ringing in my ears gets lower and the light floods back in, my body registering the way he slaps me *gently* in the face.

I'm not sure there's a gentle way to wake someone up, and just about every bone in my body hurts. Fuck. *Did he just knock me out?*

The world rushes back in with startling clarity as I rub the side of my head, looking around. Embarrassment creeps over me as I push up, using Nick's shoulder to steady myself as I try to stand, but it's the guy who hit me that holds his hand out, catching me before I face plant, again.

"Woah there," he says, amusement laced through his tone. "You went down pretty hard. You good?"

But it doesn't seem like he's laughing at me, there's genuine concern lining the dark brown of his eyes as his gaze checks me over. Or it does, until Nick flies to his feet, shoving his hands in the guy's chest and growling at him to, "Back the fuck up."

"I leave you alone for two fucking minutes and this is what happens," Nick growls, turning to look at me over his shoulder.

The couple of guys that were loitering around disappear as something seemingly more interesting catches their attention.

"Don't worry about it," I reply. "I'm fine."

"Better pull it together, man. You've got another round," whoever the guy is I just fought adds from the other side of my brother. Turning and walking away, he runs his fingers through the thick of his hair, scraping his nails down the short sides. I can almost feel the action against my own head, hear the rough catch in my ears, despite the raucous sound around us.

"What the hell was that?" Nick hisses, shoving me in the shoulder. "Too busy checking the guy out to watch your guard, huh?"

"What did he mean, another round?" I ask, shaking the last of the ringing from my ears and ignoring the fuck out of his question.

"It's last man out," he adds sadly, checking me over again. "Which means, the losers fight until there's only one remaining. He's out."

"Shit," I hiss. "Take it you didn't lose?"

"Of course I fucking didn't," he clips, looking at what's going on behind me. "I didn't expect you to, either." He rolls his eyes as we make our way back to the rings.

Apparently, they hauled my ass out of there and carried on regardless. Good to know.

"Jacob Barrett," a voice booms over the cacophony of the room. "I'm looking for Jacob Atticus Barrett."

"Here," Nick calls, the two of us making our way to the ring he silently gestures to.

"Do not fuck this up," he growls. "Do not drop that guard." He pulls my fists together and places them by my jaw, the amber of his eyes boring into my slightly greener matching ones. "Do not stop. Do not give him chance to recover. This is not sparring. This is war."

"This is war," I repeat, testing the words on my tongue. "This is war," I say again more confidently, heat pouring through my veins as the knockout wears off and the adrenaline kicks back in. I bounce from one foot to the other, checking out the lone guy on the other side.

He looks worse for wear, and I guess, I probably do too. Not just from the beating we've both just taken, but the brutal way I was dragged from slumber and the punches taken to get me here. If this is an easy start, I can only imagine the hell we have yet to go through. We'll do it. We always do.

Nick massages my shoulders as I mentally get myself together for this fight. It's my last one for the night. It has to be. *No retreat, and no surrender.*

# FOUR

## Wyatt

The bloody mess of a man wobbles opposite me. He attempts to rally, to circle, but his eye is swollen shut, blood still pouring from his obviously broken nose, but none of that is my problem. I just have to get through this.

I limp on my left leg, the knee more than smarting where the last guy crushed the shit out of it, but I can't focus on that. I drop my shoulder, doing my best to run, driving it into his stomach as I force him backwards, taking us both down to the cold blood-spattered concrete.

There's no fight left in him as the air whooshes out of his lungs. It's a matter of process to get the arm-bar in place and claim the submission, marking my spot in the safe zone. Someone coaches encouragement loudly behind me, and I can't help but feel good that someone isn't alone in this hellhole. Friends, allies… they're going to be important here over the next few months.

Submission isn't my favourite way to get the win, but I'll take it. There was fuck all fight left to the guy, and I'd rather not be responsible for finishing him off.

"Come on, kid. It's almost over," one of the other recruits says from behind me, making me jump. My mind had been a million miles away, watching two guys drag the bloody mess of my opponent away.

My blood cools as the crisp air of the night wraps itself around me, my boxers doing absolutely nothing to help. But when you're dragged out of bed in the middle of the night, what else is to be expected? Something, if the soft blue denim of his jeans is anything to go by.

Following him, the final fight ends, and we're all lined back up, some of us significantly bloodier than others and more than one missing as we're jostled into some kind of order. The guy in the jeans is at the top end, barely a hair out of place or a mark on him as the bigger guy next to him flexes his shoulders.

"Seven of you stand," the deputy mayor calls out in front of us, drawing my attention back to him as the rest of the room falls silent. "And nine will continue. Try not to take tonight too personally though, and get to know your fellow recruits."

I adjust the cloth over my hand, the split skin a stinging reminder of what we all agreed to just an hour ago. Two guys appear, handing glasses to each of us from behind plain black masks, another one appearing with an unlabelled bottle and pouring a healthy amount into each one before topping up the deputy mayor.

"Get to know each other. Drink, and have fun tomorrow, because on Sunday, you're moving into the Big House." A ripple of excitement travels over me and throughout the line-up. The first challenge is done, onwards and upwards we go.

"Salute," he says, holding his glass up in toast before taking a drink, the rest of us following suit.

The scotch burns as it goes down, heat racing through my veins and dulling the pain, just a little. It'll take a lot more than that to piece me back together though.

"The cars will be leaving in thirty minutes. If you need checking out or stitches, the doctors are at the back of the room."

We all turn to look, more than one guy heading straight there. The guy beside me is one of them, his friend appearing and looping his arm around his waist as I watch them go.

"You shouldn't need stitches." My head snaps to the side, the winning guy in the jeans stood beside me and inspecting the cut above my eyebrow. "But you might want to get that leg checked out."

"I can walk on it, so it's not broken," I brush off. "Soft tissue damage at best."

He nods, scratching some invisible itch on the centre of his chest before declaring, "I'm Leo."

"Wyatt," I reply, accepting his outstretched hand. Looks like making allies might be easier than I anticipated.

"And that," he says, gesturing to the two guys I was watching walk away. "Is Nicholas and Jacob Barrett."

"Yeah?" I ask, having heard of the spoilt as fuck twins

from London, not really all that surprised they made their way to The Sect, I suppose.

"I think he was right, this year is gonna be fun," Leo adds, an interested twinkle in his eye as he watches them.

I don't know whether or not his support will work in my favour, or what his interest in the brothers is, but I'm excited to see where it goes...

# Her DEVIL

A PENDLETON PREP NOVEL

## H.L. PACKER

Copyright © 2023 HL Packer

All rights reserved. Without limiting the rights under copyright reserved above, no part of this publication may be reproduced, stored in or introduced into retrieval system, or transmitted, in any form, or by any means (electronic, mechanical, photocopying, recording or otherwise) without the prior written permission of both the copyright owner and the above publisher of this book.

This is a work of fiction. Names, characters, places, brands, media, and incidents are either the products of the author's imagination or are used fictitiously. The author acknowledges the trademark owners of various products referenced in this work of fiction, which have been used without permission. The publication/use of these trademarks is not authorised, associated with, or sponsored by the trademark owners.

Editor – Lindsey Powell Editing

Cover Designer – LJ Design Services

Formatter – LJ Design Services

# PROLOGUE

The silence is pronounced. More so in the wake of the screaming. Whiskey runs down the wall four foot to my right, and I'm reasonably sure I've been stunned silent. *Well, that's a first.*

"This isn't up for negotiation," my father clips out. He stands, smoothing down the wrinkles in his shirt as he does so, sparing half a glance at the cut crystal now shattered on the floor, before taking the seat beside me.

He's never raised his voice to me before, his cool and calm demeanour sliding back over him like a familiar jacket. The warmth slides back into his eyes, a smile teasing the edge of his lips as it does so. But I've seen it now— the crack. This is just another mask that he wears, another persona he becomes; doting father.

The walls around my heart build quickly, quicker than I ever expected they would. And it's strange, this silence. The absence of his genteel and placating tone, infantizing and demeaning, should one choose to take it that way, but it's also empty of the sharp prickly way he spoke just moments ago, the glass hurtling through the air so swiftly after.

How quickly he turned from one person to another. *That's never happened before.*

But then, how rarely do I refuse him something, anything?

I've been his good little girl for a long time—too long. I've smiled at the cameras and doted on the perfect daddy, the one I thought I had. But that ideal lays shattered on the floor, along with the glass I bought him just a few birthdays ago.

"It's one year, that's all I'm asking," he says, the mask back in place as he reaches for my hand, pulling it into his lap.

But I snatch it back. He's not asking, he's demanding, just with a pretty spin. And I can't bring my gaze to his, my eyes focused on a small blemish on his desk, a bruise in the wood, perhaps, a spot where the varnish didn't take as well, or maybe it's something different, something darker. This version of my father could be capable of many things I've never considered. Until now.

"You can go and do whatever you want after." He sighs, resigned, dismissing the tension that crackles between us with the wave of his hand. "Give me one year at Pendleton Prep and then you can go and do whatever psychology major it was you wanted to do."

My eyes narrow as his words sink in. He's never commented about what I want to do before. Yes, he knew that university was always going to be in the future for me, why wouldn't it be? But this is the first time he's ever commented about something specific, and something the two of us have never openly discussed.

"And why can't I go now?" I ask, crossing my arms over my chest. It's a defensive position, I know, already subconsciously preparing for the verbal blows that will come my way, for the rejection.

"It's bad timing. With the elections coming up next year and all the political instability that's hanging around at the moment, I need you close and available. If you're at a university at the other end of the country somewhere, that's a problem."

There is a stack of conditional offers hidden in my drawer upstairs. I've got the results required in the bag, there's no doubt about that, and I can have my pick of places, once they're confirmed.

There's no logical reason I can see for him to send me away to a preparatory school. What kind of draconian ridiculousness is this anyway? It's just an excuse to control me for a little longer.

"And if I say no?"

I throw the proverbial gauntlet down, testing how it feels.

He's been my safe space, my solace. The rock I never realised I needed. And now, the entire house is shaking around me, metaphorically speaking, and all because I chose to say no.

I must have refused him before, for something or other. I'm sure I'm not a complete doormat for him, am I? But the anger that flickers over his features briefly makes me reconsider. Maybe I have been?

"Those offers might just disappear." His eyes narrow and the words tumble from him idly, without thought, like rocking my entire universe is nothing more than a minor inconvenience to him.

"You can't do that." I gasp, my horror clear as I turn to face him. *Well, he has my attention now.*

"I don't have to." He smiles, all the warmth gone from his eyes. "Because you're going to be a good little girl for one last time and spend twelve months learning the basics at Pendleton Prep. You're going to make the contacts that will secure your position for years to come, and anything else I decide. That way, I won't have to do anything drastic with your credit cards."

My mouth slams shut, anger surging through me as I stand, walk out, and slam the door behind me.

It's more than clear I'm not going to get any movement with him. There's no negotiating allowed here. It's his way or no way. And no way leaves me penniless and alone. My mother isn't going to fight my corner any more than she already has, she's going to stand by and watch him take everything from me, one thing at a time.

"Well, it was a pleasure doing business with you," he calls loudly, the sound echoing down the corridor from his home office, his satisfied chuckle following my every harried step as my blood boils.

# ONE

## Ivy

"Do you think there's a Starbucks on campus?" Tamsin asks from the passenger seat, disinterestedly flicking through the Pendleton Prep brochure. "Or do you think they're going to have one of those bougie places with like forty different kinds of tea?"

I don't need to answer, instead I concentrate on the road ahead of us as she continues to ramble.

"What if they don't have avocado toast for lunch?" She gasps. "I know technically it's a breakfast food or whatever, but who in their right mind has time for that of a morning?"

"I dunno, Tam. You're the one with the info literally in her lap. You tell me." I roll my eyes, turning down the music, because now she's started, she's not going to stop. The fifteen minutes of quiet contemplation is over and now it's time for full-on Tamsin.

"Eurgh, this thing is for parents. It doesn't tell me anything useful at all." A scoff of a laugh falls from me before she continues undeterred. "Class type and co-ed, blah, blah. Exam results and the best University selection process… who even cares about this rubbish?" She throws the booklet in the door panel, grabbing a sip of her strawberry-infused water.

"Uh, I do."

"No, you don't. It's all going to be fine," she placates gently. "You've already got the results you need for the courses you want to take. The offers will still be there next year."

They fucking better be.

"And look at it this way, you get to spend the whole year with me." She grins excitedly. "We can party and get drunk without anyone breathing down our necks, for a change."

"Like anyone has ever been watching over your shoulder."

Tam's father is an international diplomat, he comes and goes from this country to that one, being the face of the beautiful country we live in, and it's one of the reasons our parents are friends. And as much as I love my family, or rather, loved them, I always coveted the freedom my best friend has been afforded.

"Yeah, well, now they're not looking over yours either. I don't know why you're so against this. It's gonna be fun!"

"Just tell me I don't have to share a bathroom with anyone and there's somewhere I can get a decent coffee. That's all I'm interested in right now."

It's not like I had any choice in this, not really. Might as well take what I can get. But we're not a million miles from home, a full fifty minutes in the Range Rover. Far enough to feel safe. Except, there's a reason he wanted me to come here, there must be.

This is about more than just being available for the

occasional photoshoot; I can feel it. He lost it way too quickly for it to be something so trivial. For a man who's known for his poker face, he showed me a lot at that moment, more than he probably meant to.

No, there's more to me attending Pendleton Prep than convenience. I just need to work out what it is.

"As far as I can tell, we're in apartment-style housing."

"What does that mean?"

Our six-bedroom detached house in the quiet gated neighbourhood with security gates feels like a long way away right now.

"That means," she starts, grabbing the brochure out with a sigh and flicking through, scanning the pages for the info she wants. "Blah, blah, blah. Oh, here we go. Three luxury twin rooms, complete with stylish fittings and lavish bedding, adjoined with communal kitchen and living spaces."

"So, three people to a bathroom?"

That can't be right.

"No, gimme a minute. There's a picture somewhere. Ah, here," she says, turning the page and thrusting it in my face.

"I'm trying to drive," I grumble, glancing briefly and shoving it out of the way. "Words, Tam. Use your words."

"Fuck, you're grumpy today," she comments. "So, twin rooms for two people with an en-suite."

"So, I just share with you. I can do that." I nod my head, my relief more evident than I expected it to be.

The chuckle that falls from her tells me she knows exactly how horrified I was at the thought of sharing bathroom space with complete strangers. But she knows me far too well to comment on it, thank God.

"We share the kitchen and living room with four other girls, so let's hope they don't have shit taste in television preferences. I am not down for watching those house of whatever-it-is fantasy things right now."

"Hey, you might like it," I argue with a smile. "Don't knock it 'til you've tried it."

I've never had to share my space with anyone other than Tamsin and her sisters, and I'm excited about the challenge. And if they drive me nuts, I'll push daddy for an apartment nearby. He said I had to attend for the year, he never specified that had to be on campus though.

And despite this being thrown at me from left field and my original hesitation, if I'm going to be spending the year here, then I'm going to make it the best year I can. I need to get as much out of this diversion as I possibly can to make it worthwhile, there's no way this year is going to be wasted.

"I am not here for all that make-believe '*doing your uncle because he's hot*' bullshit. It might get you hot under the collar, but, girl, just wait until you see what the real world has to offer. We're going to Pendleton Prep, the maker of world leaders."

"Do you really believe that?"

"Absolutely. Did you not check out any of the alumni? No, of course you didn't. You're still in denial that you're even attending."

"Whatever," I grumble, following the sat-nav directions off the main road.

The campus signs are small and understated. Not the

*'look at us, we're the best'* kind I was expecting. The high drystone wall and black metal gates are though. *We're going into a glorified prison.*

The driveway leads us past four main residential complexes. And, yes, that's complex, not dormitory. With in-house cleaning, swimming, spa facilities and a gym, this is a little more than just somewhere to rest your head. *Not that I looked, obviously.*

There's parking everywhere, plenty of it already in use as I follow the signs towards the main administration buildings.

"Well then, bitch. I guess we made it," Tamsin says excitedly, sliding her feet back into her Jimmy Choos and flicking her thick dark hair over her shoulder. "Come on, let's get this started."

She jumps out with much greater enthusiasm than I can muster, rounding the car and sliding my arm through hers as she pulls me out. "Whatever this year brings, we're in it together, right?" she asks, looking at me for confirmation before opening the door to the Pendleton Prep offices.

"Of course," I reply with a roll of my eyes. "As if you even have to ask that question."

"Better safe than sorry," she says with a shrug of her shoulders. "This is gonna be fun."

"Ladies," a woman excitedly greets us from behind the desk, her gaze flicking to the clock above the door. "You're cutting it fine, aren't you? Classes start tomorrow."

I know. It was intentional.

I don't plan on spending one second more here than I have to.

"Well, let's get your welcome packs together and find which buildings you're going to be in."

"Buildings? As in, plural? Like, we might not be placed together?" I ask, my heart rate picking up.

I can share a bathroom with Tam. I can deal with four random strangers, so long as she's by my side. I can *not* do this without her.

"Let's take a look, shall we?"

# TWO

## Nick

"**I** told you coming here early would bite us in the ass," I mumble under my breath, shoving a handful of trousers back into the case I unpacked just weeks ago.

"You did," Jacob agrees with a smirk. "But you were more than happy to pack your ass up and get out of that house."

A shiver ripples over me as I think back to the empty mausoleum of a home we left behind ten days ago.

Our mother is still traipsing around dressed in black, like she ever gave a fuck about our father—you'd think she was the one dying. Andrew does nothing but antagonise her further, and with Sophie flitting between London and Italy, you could never be sure there would be anyone around to run interference. Being home was a drag, and neither of us wanted to be there.

So, at the first opportunity, we packed our bags and made our way to Pendleton Prep, never expecting the events of the last twenty-four hours. We both thought she was off her head and having some kind of mental breakdown, but we both bear the marks to prove this is real, Jacob more than me.

"True," I agree. "Still said it'd be a problem though, somewhere down the line."

"One day you're going to be more positive about life. You're going to see all of the good that comes and you'll smile more," he decides with a nod.

"Why? When I've got you for all that." I smirk, looking at him over my shoulder.

"Just admit it. You've enjoyed being away from The Manor, and you've been having fun getting to know Matthew, James, Richard and Ian."

"Fat lot of use that's going to be now we're moving out," I add.

"You might have classes with them, or I might," he argues. "Not everything has to have an obvious use right in the present moment, you know?"

"Sure. Whatever." I shrug, grabbing a handful of textbooks and carefully placing them in the moving boxes we picked up earlier.

We didn't have half the things we'd need when we turned up here, but the guys in our apartment have been cool. Matthew showed us around the local town, and the best drinking spots are now firmly stored in our heads, we even tested them out to be sure.

James dug out a copy of the reading list for us and managed to get a replacement set of our schedules after ours magically disappeared. My money is on Jacob throwing them in a box or bag and unintentionally throwing them out, but what do I know?

They've mostly done a reasonable job of working out

which one of us is which, most of the time. Not that it's hard to tell, in my opinion. But then, I'm not likely to mistake myself for someone else, am I?

Now we get to do it all over again, in a house full of guys that are our competition, if what we learned the other night is anything to go by. Only three will make it through, and I'm going to do whatever I have to do to ensure Jacob and I are in the final three. How could I not? How could *he* not?

We couldn't seriously be expected to go forward in our lives without the backing and support of the other, could we? I can't imagine closing the door as he walks away into a life of power whilst I figure out what to do on my own. It doesn't bear thinking about.

That shit might have worked for our brother Andrew, the golden boy, but he was always going to fall on his feet at Barrett Enterprises. The two of us, not so much.

"You guys nearly ready?" Ian asks as he pops his head around the doorway. "There are some people here to give you a hand."

I look as confused as Jacob does as one of the guys from last night ambles casually through the doorway, pushing his surf boy locks back as he does, raising his chin in greeting.

"Figured you might need a hand," he says by way of an explanation, dropping onto what was my bed and throwing his feet up like we've known each other half a lifetime. I don't even know who the fuck he is.

"Oh, I think we're good," Jacob replies, fastening his case and straightening up the boxes of books.

"We're here now." He shrugs. "Might as well make use

of us.”

“Oookay,” I reply, the guy clearly not taking the hint. I close up the box, marking a large 'N' on the outside of it. “Let me do one last sweep to make sure there aren't any errant charger cables, but I think we're ready.”

He whistles loudly twice and another guy comes through, the two of them grabbing boxes and making their way out. *What the hell?*

“Do they know where to take those?” Jacob asks as we both search the bedside cabinets, checking through our usual secret spots and making sure everything is packed and ready to go.

There's not a lot, a couple of suitcases and a couple of boxes of books. The plan has always been to get what we need as we go. *Good job really, I guess.*

“I fucking hope so.”

No sooner have we lugged the last few bits out to the living area and said our brief goodbyes to the guys than they're back, double-checking everything before following us out.

“Are you guys excited?” one of them asks as we wait together for the elevator. I still have no idea who either of them are. I wasn't paying much attention to anyone last night, well, other than the guy that hit Jacob, and the rest is more of a blur. “We're staying at the Big House and making it through the first round. Nice fight, by the way, man. You were a beast.”

He awkwardly offers me a high-five as the four of us wait. Someone asks about a football match and that's all we need for the ice to be broken and the conversation to flow. By the time the elevator finally arrives, it's like we've known each other for weeks rather than minutes. We load the car up, meandering our way through the campus to the main reception.

"You need the office upstairs," the receptionist smiles. "First floor, second door on your right."

With a nod, we make our way to the elevators down the corridor, the glass-fronted building streaming full of light. *We didn't need to do this when we got the card to the apartment.* And just as that thought sinks in, the elevator arrives and the four of us file in. If it wasn't for the lull in the conversation, I'd have missed the girl's yell.

Slamming my hand on the button, I hold the elevator for her, the door sliding back open on two red-faced brunettes. They're both laughing as they thank us and squeeze into the elevator, an interested look being sent more than just my way by the shorter of the two. But it's the leggy one that catches my attention.

Her jeans are practically sprayed on, and the heels she wears bring her almost to my height. Raven-coloured curls trail down her back, but the gaze that flicks around the cramped space is indifferent at best and frozen at worst. If I hadn't seen the light in her eyes and the laughter on her face just moments ago, I wouldn't have thought it possible.

She dismisses us with a turn of her shoulder and a flick of her hair, drawing her friend closer, like she'd be any protection in an enclosed space with four guys at least double their size. *Nice try.*

"Do you need a hand?" I offer, noting the welcome pack she presses against her thigh. Not that I looked at her thigh, honest. "With your suitcases and stuff."

"I think we're all set, but thanks," the shorter girl, her friend, replies with a smile, turning to get a proper look at me.

"It's a one-time offer," I add, popping the dimple on my cheek and raising an eyebrow. If I can't get the attention of the one I want, this one might work as an introduction. *If only I can get their attention.* "We're on our way out right now, and we won't be back if you change your mind."

A blush covers her cheeks, mischief twirling in the light blue of her eyes, but it's her friend's attention I want, and she's not giving it. All too soon, we hit the first floor, the doors open, and they're released into the fresh air of a large open corridor.

"No thanks, we've got this," the tall one clips out, pulling them both away without so much as a second glance.

"Thanks, anyway," the smiley one adds as she's dragged along, clearly as interested in getting to spend some time with us as the guys at my side are, if the looks they're giving are anything to go by.

"Well, it was worth a shot," Jacob agrees with a shrug of his shoulders. "And never say never, we might see them at the welcome mixer tomorrow night."

"Good point," the surfer guy says. "I'm Wyatt, by the way. You're Nicholas and Jacob, right?"

"Yep," I agree. "But just call me Nick, and he's Jake."

"Jasper," the other guy adds, leading us to the directed doorway, the girls disappearing around a corner and out of sight.

The administrator behind the desk looks us over twice.

"Nicholas and Jacob Barrett, I assume." It could be a question, but it's not. I nod as he pulls two small envelopes from the depths of his desk, my interest piqued. *I wonder what other things he's got in there, and what he might know about what's to come.* "The garage is programmed to your licence plate, the keys are individual, please only use your own." He hands the named envelopes to each of us before dismissing us with nothing more than a wave of his hand.

"This place gets weirder by the minute," I grumble, following the guys out of the office and back to the elevators. Those girls we saw are nowhere to be seen as we leave the building and cross the car park. "This is mine," Jasper says, gesturing to a sleek silver BMW. "Are you guys okay following me around?"

"Sure thing," I agree, heading to my M4 and flashing it open, Jacob and I throw our envelopes into the back seat, everything else already loaded as the engine roars to life, Jasper and Wyatt idling in front.

I follow them around the building, away from the residential units, past the library and the administration buildings, the lecture halls and the academic spaces, and down a single lane that tracks through the woods, no signage to be seen, as we follow the 8 Series down the winding lane, the tree coverage thick.

It doesn't thin out, not a gentle parting of the trees. No, they just stop. One second you're in the dark, hidden by trees, and the next, the mid-day sun is beating down on the car. And, granted, in September it doesn't carry that much heat, but it's like stepping into another world. The fountain in front of the main entrance spits water twelve feet in the air before cascading back down over a series of shelves.

We pass it, heading around the building to an oversized garage that opens automatically as we approach. Parking behind Wyatt, the doors close slowly behind us, encasing my baby and plenty of others in security. The lineup of cars is impressive as I skim over them, our two making eight of the ten spaces filled.

The garage must have been for display purposes rather than actual use at some point; the glass display cabinets along one wall feel out of place with so many vehicles stuffed in here, but it fits us all in, so I can't complain. There's no chance some cheap-ass hatchback is going to be banging its door against mine in the car park now either. Bargain.

"We'll grab your stuff in a bit, let's give you the grand tour first, eh?" Jasper says, holding an internal door open.

Following him through, we make our way into a boot room, jackets lined up along one wall before we head through into the main entrance. This must be the front doors, if the heavy-set wood is anything to go by, the stained-glass window above sending coloured patterns across the wooden floor.

"So, kitchen, dining and movie room to the left, den and games room to the right, bedrooms are upstairs. There's a washroom and changing space tucked under the stairway for guests."

"Changing room?" I ask, looking around the opulent space and taking in the food laid out in the kitchen. *Nice.*

"For the pool and steam room, and there's a sauna out there too, but I'm not here for that dry heat," Wyatt adds. "It makes me cough."

Jacob and I both nod. *Impressive.*

"So, we're having a party here soon, right?" Jacob asks excitedly. "It'd be a waste of the mild autumn weather not to."

"How about we get you guys moved in first, huh?" Jasper laughs, grabbing a petit-four as we pass the food-laden island in the kitchen. "Let's go get those bags and find your rooms."

"We're not together?" I ask with a tilt of my head.

"It's in your envelope, the room allocation is all pre-arranged. There's a note on each door with our names on," Wyatt says with a roll of his eyes as we head back through the entrance. "Nick, you're with me."

My gaze collides with Jacob's, my irritation reflected in his eyes.

Is this how it starts? Separate our rooms, break the bond between brothers, pitch one against another in a competition for something more important than money, than women. Power.

That might have worked on other people, but it won't work with us.

# THREE

*Ivy*

"This is where we're staying?" I ask, looking at the not-so-small self-contained unit. The house we passed was impressive enough, dark stone with vines growing up the side and a fountain out front, but to come around that and find this cute glass-sided pool house at the back is more than a little surprising.

I park the Range Rover alongside the other cars in a neat row opposite the main door, the huge stone house looming ominously to the right of the building on the other side of the lagoon-style cascading pools. *So extra.*

"This is not what I was expecting when you said *apartment-style living*," I comment.

"This is not apartment-style living," Tamsin replies, looking around excitedly. "It looks like your daddy got us upgraded."

Whatever he's done, it's intentional, and not likely to be for our benefit. He knows more than well that I'm only here because he gave me no choice, backed into a corner with no way out. So, if he set us up here, it's with purpose.

I don't have time to explain all that to Tamsin, because

the front doors open, and four over-enthusiastic women head straight for us. *Here we go.*

***

"Are you being serious right now?" I ask exasperatedly, dropping onto the soft comforter at the foot of her bed. "I thought you'd be almost ready by now."

"You can't rush perfection," she replies, holding the mascara wand steady before finishing off. "Besides, it's only the first day. It's not like we'll be missing anything important. It's all an introduction to the tutor and the course, making sure we know what we've signed up for and what's expected."

"What *have* you signed up for?" I ask, conscious we didn't pick classes together. *Daddy* wanted to make sure I got a good mix of things and not just what I wanted, shocker. Plucking her schedule from the bedside cabinet, I lean back and get comfortable, knowing her makeup is going to take more than a minute to finish.

"I honestly can't remember," she replies. "Nothing too strenuous, I'm sure."

"You're in sociology with me, good choice. But philosophy, really?" I ask with a disbelieving raise of my eyes.

I'm not in the slightest bit convinced that isn't reading a billion old books by men that died a lifetime ago, and then sitting on the fence whilst discussing it. It might not be academically hard in the same was as Maths or Physics, but it's not exactly going to be plain sailing either.

"Sounded interesting." She shrugs, knowing full well she's going to end up married to some rich boring guy with abs of steel and the personality of a placemat and spend the rest of her adult life sipping cocktails with her personal shopper. Philosophy, or any of this, is going to be no good to her really.

But, I guess, at least she'll be able to do it whilst contemplating the good versus evil dichotomy of the wealth she lives in.

"Fair enough," I reply, checking the time on my phone again. "We're going to be late."

"I'm almost done," she placates, blending her blush with the roll of her eyes.

You'll never see Tamsin sans make-up or with her hair anything less than perfect, at least at the start of the day. She doesn't rush for anyone or anything, and I think going for that elevator yesterday was the first time I've ever seen her run, outside of the gym anyway.

Finding out she wasn't going to be able to bring her PT and nutritionist was an issue. One we solved with bi-weekly zoom sessions, but she wasn't happy. I, on the other hand, am quite content to leave that torment behind and hope for a gentler approach in the gym here, maybe a Pilates class or something.

"Seriously, Tamsin. We can *not* be late for our first class on our first day. I'm sure that's bad luck."

"Is the coffee ready?" she asks, picking up a lip gloss tube before placing it back and grabbing another one out of the rack. Clearly not the colour she was looking for.

"Yes, Penelope showed me how to do it last night and then left instructions out this morning, as if I'd forget. This is coffee, the life blood of the masses. I'm not going to forget."

"Helpful of her though, just in case I was attempting to make it, because I was absolutely not paying any attention yesterday."

"We noticed," I reply with a roll of my eyes. I drop the schedule into her lap and head to the kitchen, grabbing our named travel mugs from the side, already filled. Apparently, the nice lady in the office gave them our details so they could have them made specially, so we all match. *Cute.*

A white envelope catches my eye, placed perfectly in the middle of the dining table, a single blood-red rose laid beside it. A shiver ripples over me as I look around. None of the other girls are up yet, and this definitely wasn't here before we went to bed. *Someone was in our house.*

"Tamsin," I call, picking the envelope up and turning it over.

It's not sealed, and my curiosity gets the better of me as I slide it open, pulling the heavy cardstock out.

*Angels.*
*You are cordially invited to the first official party of the year.*
*Friday 13th*
*7pm*
*Main House*

The gold calligraphy is handwritten and there's an embossed logo in the corner I don't have time to make out before Tamsin comes bursting through the doorway, finally ready to go.

"And here I was thinking you were patiently waiting for me," she says with a roll of her eyes. "What've you got there?"

"Some invitation," I reply, dropping it back to the table and sliding my bag over my shoulder. The ten-minute meander to class is quickly becoming a five-minute march, or less, as each precious second ticks by—I don't have time for her to dissect this right now. "I swear to God, if we turn up to this class a hot, sweaty mess, I'll never forgive you."

"You totally will." She smirks as I close the distance between us, heading for the front door and thrusting her mug in her hand.

"Do you have your key?" I ask as we leave, knowing mine is safely tucked in the back of my purse.

"Of course. Not that I'll need it, because I have you." She smiles, wrapping our arms together as we make our way into the fresh morning air. "Hey, this coffee is pretty good, you know?"

"Better than the stuff from that tea shop, that's for sure," I agree. We found the bougie tea place yesterday. It's safe to say, if you like your coffee thick and dark roasted, that is not the place to be.

She peeks over our shoulders as we pass the house, the feeling of someone watching us creeping over my skin. *Maybe we should have taken the car.*

It takes until we're part way down the driveway before the dam breaks, the thoughts running rampant through her head finally breaking the surface. "Do you really think they were moving out yesterday? The day before classes start. Why would they do that?"

"I don't know."

This is Tamsin's thing, how she processes. She doesn't

need a reply from me, just to talk her way through whatever is on her mind.

"They couldn't have been kicked out before it started, surely? And, if they'd done something worthy of being kicked out, everyone would be talking about it, wouldn't they?"

"Probably," I add as we near the academic buildings, the sparse car parks and boxed hedges giving way to a softer, gentler flow of flower beds.

"So, was he just trying it on then, or what?" she asks exasperatedly, like the thoughts have been running through her head all morning. *They probably have.*

"If you're that interested, ask the girls. They're going to know." It seems like they know everything else going on around here.

"You think?" she asks, pulling open the heavy doors as we search out the right lecture hall.

"Absolutely," I agree, spotting someone familiar. "Otherwise, you could ask them right now."

A blush creeps over my cheeks as the taller dark-haired guy from the elevator and two of his friends head straight towards us. I barely got a glimpse yesterday, but it was enough.

He's the all-American boy next door; broad shoulders, a dark shirt that hangs sinfully well across his chest, sliding over his narrow hips to his long legs. Legs that make it here quicker than I expected as the distance is eaten up by his long strides.

"Holy mother of..." Tamsin whispers, jolting me out of whatever ridiculous stupor we found ourselves in.

Hurrying our steps, I attempt to get there first, hoping to slide in unannounced and find somewhere to quietly observe. The lecture, of course. Not the boys; we're not here for that. But I don't manage it.

One of his friends holds the door for us, his hair clipped short at the sides but longer on top, clearly spending as much time as Tamsin has this morning making sure it's picture-perfect. I smile and whisper a "thank you," sliding through the doorway and hoping to be unobtrusive about it. Except…

"Well, I'm glad meeting you was more than a one-time thing," Tamsin says, devouring the three of them before making eye contact with the guy from the elevator.

"Ah, the elevator girls." He nods, clicking his fingers. "I couldn't work out where I'd seen you before. You look different this morning."

"Is that a compliment?" she asks with a raise of her eyebrows.

Conscious we're blocking the doorway, I sigh, linking my arm back through hers and attempting to move us away and find a desk before the lecturer arrives. We were late enough leaving as it is, the last thing I need is to miss the opening notes because she's busy flirting.

And as hot as he is up close and personal, the spark that sizzled under my skin being trapped in that enclosed space with him yesterday isn't there. *Maybe it was all in my head?*

"You were practically glowing," he adds with a smile, that dimple popping with perfectly charming timing. I'm completely over the cheesiness of the entire conversation and ready to drop the lot of them and go, but I tug Tamsin along regardless.

His friends continue their conversation, oblivious as the three of them follow us, finding a row of seats just by the two desks I find for me and Tam. Any hope I had of getting her attention back where it's supposed to be is lost as they slide into the seats.

His hazel eyes come to mine as he takes the seat slightly to my right and below me. Staggered seats, of course. I make a mental note not to wear a short skirt to this one, thinking of the view he'd get from there. He's charming and attractive, and no doubt women flock to him. He'd know exactly what to do with the length of my bare thigh at his shoulder level.

"Ivy, say hello," Tamsin says loudly and slowly next to my ear. She's clearly already said it more than once if their gentle laughter is anything to go by. Here's hoping it wasn't as obvious where my mind went.

"Uh, hey. Sorry about that, my mind was… somewhere else. I'm Ivy, and you've clearly already been introduced to Tamsin. You guys are?"

"Jacob, Taylor, and Emmerson," Tamsin explains, pointing out each one.

"Well, it's nice to officially meet you." I smile, dropping down into the chair and reaching for my notebook and pens.

"So, did you get everything moved in okay?" Jacob asks, turned in his seat, his forearm resting against the back and his attention fully on me.

There's something easy in the way he smiles at me, despite the early hour and the frosty reception I gave him yesterday. Not that it stopped him from hitting on Tamsin, because she's a gorgeous girl, so why wouldn't he? I nod my reply, looking at Tamsin for some back-up, but she's busy in discussion with one of the other guys, animatedly talking about who knows what.

"Did you?" I ask. "Get everything moved out, I mean."

"Yeah—" he starts, but gets cut off by the lecturer storming in, the door slamming behind him.

"Some people think this is an easy start to the week," he declares, his heavy bag landing on the desk with a thump. "It's not. Books out."

A whirring noise comes from above us as the projector springs to life, notes showing up almost immediately on the huge screen behind him.

"Ladies and gentlemen, I hope you came prepared, because we're going to start as we mean to go on and hit the ground running. Are you ready?"

The stunned silence is clearly not what he expected as Jacob slides around in his seat, other people still logging in to their laptops or pulling books from their bags. *Well, at least we weren't late*, I ponder. Imagine how much worse that would have been.

"Come on, people. Are you ready?" he asks animatedly.

The half murmur-come-mumble that comes back to him is apparently enough to appease, as I look at Tamsin with an amused smile. This is going to be an interesting way to start the week.

He's not wrong, and he doesn't hold anything back. The nearly two hours we're there fly past and I'm left reeling and with a reading list half as long as my arm. Hopefully, they've got one or more of these in the library here.

"Well, that was..." Tamsin says, attempting to form words, her overwhelmed brain well and truly in need of more caffeine.

"Yeah," I agree. No further explanation required, I totally get it.

"Are you ladies going to the mixer tonight?" the guy, Emmerson, I think, asks from the other side of Tamsin. "We might see you there if you are."

"Uh, yeah, I think so," I reply, unsure because we haven't talked about it yet. Yes, the other girls from our apartment said they'd be going, but we were going to see how today went and decide from there. But I guess the hot guys and their interest might sway that.

"Then absolutely." Tamsin nods as he slides a stack of paper out, dropping them on his desk before putting his laptop away. "What's that?" she asks, pointing at the dark flyers.

"We're having a housewarming on Friday night," the guy who held the door open says, picking out a couple and handing them over as the rest get stashed away. "You guys should come."

"Yeah, it would be cool to see you there," Jacob adds from my side as the guys climb out of the row, clearly waiting for Tamsin and me to be ready.

"Well, consider us there," Tamsin says, plucking her bag from the back of her chair and sliding her arm through Jacob's as she passes me. "I told you we were going to have some fun this year."

"Oh, I'm sure we can accommodate that," Taylor replies, following the two of them down the stairs.

"I'm not sure that we're free," I comment idly, thinking back to the invitation I left on the table and the fact I still haven't mentioned it to Tamsin.

"You don't have to make excuses, you don't have to come if you don't want to," Emmerson says, clearly picking up on my hesitation as he gestures for me to go down the stairs, waiting patiently. "There'll be plenty of other opportunities, I'm sure."

"Oh, no doubt." I smile, knowing there'll likely be plenty of parties around these first few weeks. "Is it not really your scene?" I ask, noting his lack of enthusiasm.

"Not usually," he admits. "But it's time for a change."

"Fair enough." I shrug, catching the hint of a black eye as we head out into the fluorescent lights of the corridor.

I don't make any comment about it. Who knows what his life was like before he came here, and who am I to judge?

"Right, come on you," I say, pulling Tamsin from the two guys and the drunken antics they're likely planning. "Let's go find the library in this place."

"It's in the main office building," Jacob replies as I peel Tamsin away, an amused smile on his face. "The double doors at the end of the main corridor."

"You'd better not be sending us on a wild goose chase," Tamsin replies light-heartedly, her gaze tracking their movements even as we walk in a different direction.

"I would never," he replies as I give them my back, more than done with listening to the guy flirting with my friend.

I don't know why it irks me, why it's under my skin, but I could practically feel the heat of his intense gaze locked in that elevator with them yesterday, and today, nothing. I know there were other people there but I couldn't tell you a single thing about them, it was him I could feel. The energy vibrating from him was something else entirely. And now he's laughing and flirting with Tamsin like he didn't feel it, and it's irritating.

I'm sure women fall to their knees in his presence, but I won't be one of them.

# FOUR

## Nick

"You're a lifesaver." I sigh, dropping into the seat opposite my brother and wrapping my hands around the steaming hot mug. "I don't know what he did to piss off the Gods of heating, but that hall was fucking freezing."

"Yikes," Emmerson comments.

"Here's hoping it's fixed next week because I could barely feel my fingers to make notes. Not that he said much of anything that needs to be remembered, but still…"

The warmth of the coffee starts to thaw through my frozen digits, heat pooling around me in the warmth of the little coffee shop. Signs and posters with silly sayings cover the dark green walls, where you can see them, hidden behind shelves of tiny ceramic houses painted in various bright colours.

The barista bangs the coffee behind me as a steady stream of customers enter and leave, my brain finally thawing out enough to be able to take in my surroundings.

"Hopefully your morning went better than mine?" I ask.

"Yeah, actually, it did," Jacob replies with an interesting

smirk.

"We invited a dozen or so people for Friday night," Emmerson interrupts, placing his mug down on the table and leaning back in the chair. "Including some girl you met yesterday, apparently."

My eyebrows raise as Jacob continues. "Apparently, Ivy and Tamsin are in our Monday morning Sociology class, and we'll be seeing quite a bit of them." My interest piques. But which one is which?

"Very nice," I comment. *Lucky fucker.*

"What about you?" Taylor asks. "Anyone worth inviting at yours?"

"Not that I noticed, but it was hard to tell over the chattering of teeth. I guess we'll have better luck tonight anyway," I reply.

"Shit," Emmerson blurts out. "Taylor, we're going to be late." He throws the rest of his drink back, grabs his bags and says a swift goodbye as the two of them race out and to their next class.

"You got anything this afternoon?" Jacob asks, despite knowing my timetable as well as his own.

"Nothing but getting the feeling back in my fingers and toes."

"Let's go back to the house and grab some lunch," he says. "I think Oliver's got a class this afternoon, so my room is free if you want to chill without the rest of the house eavesdropping."

"Whatever." I shrug. "Wyatt wouldn't care if you wanted to hang in ours."

It's not the same. Not what I expected.

But I guess we should have considered this would happen. Unfortunately, the details Francesca Barrett had regarding the all-boys club we'd been requested for were minimal, unsurprisingly.

"Cheer up, man. Those girls yesterday… well, Tamsin seems like she's down for some fun."

"Which one's that?" I ask, finishing the coffee as we grab our bags and head to the car.

"The dark-haired one."

"They both had dark hair, Jake." I sigh. "Short or tall?"

"Oh, did they?" he asks knowingly as I nod. "Shorter one." He shrugs, dropping his bag into the boot before we climb in, chasing the autumn chill away with the climate control on full.

"I wasn't expecting to be this far from the campus," he comments. "Might have to consider getting my car at some point."

"Let's see how we get on for a bit first. It might work out okay between us all," I reply, heading past the administration buildings.

"Maybe. But I'm still going to need to get around on my own at some point. And we have no idea how quickly they're planning on going from nine to three. What if one of us doesn't make it, or all the guys with my classes don't?"

How he manages to voice my concerns so succinctly and without any of the inflexion I might have had, I don't know. He's usually the more emotionally driven of the two of us, and yet, here he is, coming straight out with it.

"We can still split-use this one," I answer, knowing there's no way in hell I'm going to leave him behind, here or anywhere else.

"Yeah," he concedes. "It's just something to keep in mind."

"If you think you're bringing the Porsche and leaving me with this, you're sadly fucking mistaken. My fingers glide over the soft wrapped leather of the steering wheel. As much as I love German engineering, no matter the brand, nothing beats the engine in that Porsche.

"As if." He laughs, the tension that was creeping into the car the closer we get to the house dissipating.

"So, they were interested, huh?" I ask, raising my eyebrows and changing the direction of the conversation to safer ground. He's not stupid, he knows exactly what I like, but he's been surprisingly quiet about the whole thing.

"Yeah, seemed to be." He shrugs non-commitally. "Ivy's nice."

I nod, leaving the floor open for him to continue.

"Quieter than her friend, and she paid proper attention through the lecture too, but those legs…"

*My weakness.*

"Didn't notice," I reply, waiting for the garage to open. It's automatic, linked to the registration or something, I stopped listening after he said it would work by itself.

"Of course you fucking did," Jacob says, calling me out on the blatant lie. "Even I did."

I shrug my shoulders, conceding his point as I pull into the garage, shutting the engine off. We make quick work of going through the house, people cooking in the kitchen and some of the guys loitering in the den. We offer them a wave before heading upstairs, giving up on the idea of lunch when we see how many people are already there.

"So, what do you make of all this then?" Jacob asks, kicking his shoes off and dropping onto my bed.

"Hard to know," I reply, taking the books out of my bag and lining them up on the shelf. "We got settled and now we've moved, separate rooms, separate classes. Feels a little personal. A little intentional."

Silence fills the room, an observation I'm sure he's made himself too.

"Glad we came?" he asks.

"I will be once it's over."

Neither of us were given any indication about what would happen here, about what we'd have to do, and I'm not sure we have any better idea yet. But the people I recognised in that room the other night were important, powerful.

Whatever they're going to want us to do is going to cost us a lot. Maybe not financially, but in other ways. There's an innocence to my brother that not many others see, mostly because I'm always there to deflect it, but to get through this, he's going to lose it. We're alike in many ways, but not all.

"Do you think I'll make it?" he asks, twisting his fingers together.

"Do you think there's any choice?" I clip out, turning to face him and leaning against the desk. "Do you really think I'll let anyone get ahead of you?"

"It's not down to you." He shrugs, grabbing one of the stress balls from my bedside table. "And you saw the shit show the other night, he knocked me the fuck out, Nick."

"It's not all going to be physical. You saw the same

people I did; those guys have bodyguards for a reason."

He nods, scratching an itch on his arm, not at all convincingly.

"It's in your head," I decide, his gaze flicking to mine, confusion plastered over his face. "The biggest fight we're going to have to face is with ourselves. That was your issue the other night, wasn't it? You got all stuck in your own head wondering if I was okay and then forgot to defend yourself properly. Once I was there, you were fine."

"So we need to be more independent, is that what you're saying?" He scoffs.

"Unless you were busy checking him out."

"Sure," he replies, rolling his eyes and throwing the ball at me.

"Look, I'm not going anywhere, I'll always have your back, you know that. But if we're going to make it through, then we've got to prove ourselves individually. Make it so they can't say no to either of us."

"Makes sense," he says, shaking off that uncomfortable unsure feeling he seemed to be having as he catches my throw. "And I'm better than you, anyway. No retreat, and no surrender."

"Exactly," I agree. "We've got this."

"So, what's Wyatt like?" he asks, changing the subject.

"Well, we've known each other for all of twelve hours, so yeah, he's the best," I reply sarcastically. "He snores."

"Earplugs for Christmas," he says, sitting up and throwing the ball back to me. "That I can do."

"What about Oliver?" I ask.

"One older brother who's studying to be a doctor or

something medical, I think. His parents divorced a couple of years ago, it's amicable but it means splitting the holidays between them, it's a balance," he adds, catching the ball. He balances it on the back of his hand before flicking it off and catching it in the other. "He won the first round, like you, and Wyatt won the second round, like me. Maybe we're paired up intentionally on the back of the results."

"So, what? They're going to shuffle the rooms after every challenge?" I ask, catching the ball before throwing it his way. "I don't think so."

"I guess we'll find out at some point," he replies as a knock rings out on the door.

"You're good," I call, appreciating the gesture as Wyatt walks in, an embarrassed smile on his face.

"I just wanted to grab a book," he says, gesturing to the shelves on the other side of the room.

"Stay, talk," Jacob encourages. "Nick is shit at getting to know people, so don't be offended that he doesn't know half your life story already. He's just socially anti-social."

"Is that a thing?" Wyatt asks, getting his book and perching on the edge of the desk. "I think I might be one too if it is."

"Someone did well putting you two together then, huh?" Jacob laughs, breaking the ice.

"Well, I do have a few social skills," Wyatt says light-heartedly. "But shoot. What do you want to know?"

"Now there's a question," Jacob says with interest, sitting up and resting his elbows on his knees, throwing the ball my way. "What are you studying?"

"Philosophy, Politics, and Religion. You?"

"Sociology, History, and Law," he replies.

"I'm doing Law, Politics, Maths, and Psychology," I add, joining in.

"Always the overachiever," Jacob explains with a roll of his eyes. "And what brought you here?"

"I needed to gain a better understanding of the basics before undertaking my degree, or so my father told me, but it turns out there's a little more to it than that."

"Well, it's good to know it wasn't just us that was blind-sided," I grumble. "Fucking parents."

"Isn't that the truth? But at least we're not a million miles from a beach, I can still surf when the weather's better," Wyatt explains.

"You can surf over here?" Jacob asks. "I always just assumed that was something reserved for people who live on the hot side of the world. I can't imagine it's quite the same in the cold, dirty, British sea."

"Don't knock it 'til you've tried it," Watt replies. "Yeah, it's fucking cold a lot of the time, but it's still good fun."

"Rather you than me," I reply.

"Have you met the caterers?" he asks. "Apparently, they'll be cooking dinner for us at six every evening, there are menus and the works. There's a canape list for the party and somewhere for you to add alcohol requests if there's something specific you want."

"You added anything?" I ask, conscious that he doesn't look like a tweed-wearing toff, but it's sometimes hard to tell.

He shakes his head, admitting, "I'm a beer kind of guy. I'm happy to join whoever for a decent Scotch after a round on the golf course, but for a party, beer is just fine.”

I agree with a high-five and a nod, something Jacob seems to approve of if the smile is anything to go by.

“So, have you had the chance to get to know anyone else?” Wyatt asks, following the ball from me to Jacob and back. “In your socially anti-social kind of way.”

“Taylor and Emmerson were in my class this morning,” Jacob replies. “They both seem nice enough.”

“I’m keeping to myself for now,” I admit. “Just waiting to see what happens from here.”

The class was small this morning, lucky considering the temperature, but I know it’s going to be helpful when the real work begins. Being able to get my head down and concentrate is always easier without lots of people.

“A couple of us are making a start on studying downstairs, if you’d like to join us? The plan is to head to the mixer event together too.”

I look at Jacob, who looks at me.

“Sure,” we agree.

I mean, half a dozen guys reading books and making notes. How far wrong can that go?

# FIVE

## Ivy

The glass front of the main academic building is lit up by a million tiny dots of light, dancing like a screen as we hurry our steps towards it. You can see them from halfway across campus, so there's no excuse for not making it, I guess.

Pulling my shawl over my shoulders blocks out some of the brisk autumn breeze, and whilst I'm sure Charlotte is mostly warmed by the drinks we had before setting off, and the huge coat, even she huddles in attempting to avoid the worst of it.

The driveway is long, longer than I remember from this morning, and we seriously should have considered bringing one of the cars. Instead, we huddle together, shuffling down the dark road nervously.

"So, what's this all about?" Tamsin asks, breaking the awkward silence. "Is it just so we can meet the staff and get to know the students?"

"I think so," Penelope replies, her heels clicking along at a pace. "Just an opportunity to show off all the money they've spent on the place mostly, I think."

"Surely that would be better aimed at the parents paying for it than the students using it, but whatever." I shrug as we get closer, the light from the main campus shining brightly as we catch up to another group of students coming in the opposite direction.

"It's free booze and an opportunity to check out the boys on campus without stuffy lecturers and dusty halls getting in the way, so who cares?" Stephanie adds. "Just get me in there and warmed up."

The group ahead of us hold the door as we all squeeze our way in. The large atrium is beautifully decorated with autumnal wreaths and harvest decorations, the hay bales and kitsch drinking jars giving the event a relaxed feel.

"Not quite the champagne reception I was expecting." Penelope pouts, accepting a glass of what turns out to be some kind of bourbon and pear cocktail, full of autumnal fizz.

"I think it's cute." I shrug. All five of them turn to look at me, surprise colouring each of their features as I hand my shawl over and straighten the red silk blouse.

"Cute?" Stephanie scoffs. "We're not eleven years old and going to the Fall Ball at high school. I expected something a little classier, considering the clientele."

"Okay, well, why don't we grab another one of these and go find some fun, eh?" Tamsin intervenes, snatching a couple more glasses from a passing waiter and handing them out quickly. Distraction is her forte. "Who's going to the party on Friday night?" she asks, diverting the conversation.

"What party?" Charlotte asks, sipping her drink as the six of us meander slowly around the room.

Nobody knows anyone yet, and it shows.

We're not the only ones sticking to the people we live with in a vain attempt to keep some semblance of power in this place. It's overwhelming with its opulence, despite the seemingly childish theme of the event. It's tastefully done.

"We got an invitation this morning," Tamsin says, pulling the flyer from class out of her clutch. "Didn't you guys get one?"

I don't know why I didn't mention the one at home this morning, she got busy talking about Taylor and Jacob and it sort of slipped my mind…

"Uh, no," Charlotte replies, peering at the paper and reading it with interest. "Does anyone know where this is? Off-campus, maybe?"

"No, this is the big stone house opposite ours," Stephanie says with interest. "I didn't know they'd be doing that this year."

"What, parties?" I ask, amusement laced through my tone.

"No, the Devils," she says, pointing to a small logo at the top of the poster. It's the Pendleton Prep crest in a black circle with gold and silver rivulets running through it, like it's been stuck in a chunk of black marble, almost.

"Ooh, what does that mean?" Tamsin excitedly asks the question on everyone's lips as she slides the paper safely away in her bag.

"It's like a fraternity thing. They throw big parties and do stupid challenges in silly masks. They make a big show out of picking their *angels* and they always end up being the power couples of the year. It's a whole thing."

Ice runs through my veins at the thought of the invitation we received this morning, that said, '*Angels*'. It's got to be a coincidence, surely?

"Did you see the invitation on the table this morning?" I ask, looking from one girl to the other. "Red rose, white envelope, gold writing. Ringing any bells?" The blank looks that come my way says they clearly have no idea what I'm talking about. But it was there, I'm sure of it.

"You're losing it already." Charlotte giggles, the drugs coursing through her veins clearly taking the edge off.

"Well, if it's such a big thing, how come nobody else has any idea about it and why is it such a tiny logo? Surely that's your selling point right there," I say, pointing to where the tiny hidden mark was on the paper that's now gone.

"My sister told me about it, apparently it doesn't happen every year. She wasn't of any interest to them because it happened in her second year and they're only looking for the hottest girls, so the older ones aren't usually in the running. But I guess that means we are…"

"How does a frat not run all the time?" I ask, my confusion evident. But Stephanie just shrugs her shoulders, clearly no more in the know than we are.

"But I remember she said they all live in a big house down the dirt track at the back of the academic buildings. Like the one by ours. And it's quiet and secluded so there's no one to piss off with loud music and drunk students, hence they have the best parties."

"They were moving out," Tamsin says quietly, her eyes wide. "And now they're having a big party with this logo on the flyer."

"Ooh," Charlotte adds, her interest piquing. "Tell me more about your hot friends and their huge house."

"Do you think they could be some of these Devils Frat guys?" Penelope asks, looking around. "Are they here? Were they hot?"

"Yes, they were," Tamsin agrees with a nod. We both turn and look around, the girls already trying their best to point out every hot guy they pass, and there's plenty to choose from.

"Shit," I hiss, locking eyes with someone I certainly wasn't expecting to see here.

"Is that…" Tamsin asks as I duck behind her, not that it helps. "Is that Spencer?"

"Spencer who?" Penelope asks, leaning around me to get a better view "Ooh, he can come and entertain me any day of the week. And he's coming this way."

She fluffs her hair up, moving around me to be better in view, but as I look left and right, panic gripping my throat, there's nowhere for me to escape to.

"Tamsin, darling, how good to see you again." His voice slides over my skin like sandpaper, and I barely manage to suppress the shudder. How did I ever find this guy attractive? "Did I see Ivy Rose around here somewhere?"

"It's Ivy," I reply with a roll of my eyes, stepping out from behind the wall of girls that helpfully moved in front of me. "It always has been."

He moves towards me, a greeting peck on the cheek no doubt at the forefront of his mind, but I step back out of reach. He purses his lips, irritation flicking across his features for nothing more than a second.

"Well, I didn't realise the two of you were going to be here. What a pleasant surprise," he continues, undeterred, ignoring Tamsin completely.

"Sure," I agree. "Pleasant. Have you met the girls? This is Penelope, Stephanie, Charlotte and Aimee."

The four of them smile, offering him a hand, or cheek, or whatever, as Tamsin loiters awkwardly at the side, completely ignored by the man himself.

"Well, you landed on your feet," she comments, gesturing to the group of guys he left. They're all different versions of him; haughty and condescending, if the nasal laughter is anything to go by.

"Oh yes. You'll remember Jackson from the country club," he says, pointing him out. I nod, rolling my eyes. As if I could forget the sleazy ass that spent way too much time staring at my tits over lunch.

"Oh, yeah. I remember him," I reply dryly, more than ready to get rid of him. "Well, nice to see you again. How about we repeat this like... never?" I offer, attempting to get away.

"Don't be like that," he says, the whiny sound of his voice nothing but irritating. He probably wants to continue the conversation, but deep laughter rings out, drawing all our attention to the group of guys that walk in, Jacob front and centre.

"That's got to be them," Charlotte says breathily, her attention rapt, and it's easy to see why.

Dark hair, tanned skin, ink peeks over a collar on one and down the sleeve of another, charcoal shirts and black dress pants that fit perfectly, expensive watches and wafts of cologne as they walk past.

They're like the rest of the guys here, but so much more, and they're heading straight for us.

"Hey, girl." Taylor smiles, his perfect white teeth sparkling in the dim light, his jawline cut sharp enough to pierce. I was way too distracted by Jacob and the feeling from the elevator to notice how good-looking the other guys around him are.

"Hey." I smile as they near. "Oh, Taylor, do you have a minute? Would it be okay for the girls to come on Friday night? These are our roommates." More than one perfect smile goes his way as the girls move as one, pushing Spencer out of the way to get closer to the true prize.

"Of course." He smiles, his hand landing on my arm lightly. "Come and find us in a bit, when you're finished talking with whoever this guy is." He looks Spencer over for the longest three seconds of my life before dismissing him with nothing more than a chin lift and turning his intense blue gaze back to me.

Taylor winks, squeezing my arm before walking away. Penelope's head pops over my shoulder with a sigh as she watches his fine ass strut across the room. Spencer is nothing more than ancient history as the questions tumble from them one after another.

"Nice to see you again." Tamsin smirks as we walk away, Spencer and his history already forgotten.

We don't go far, just a few steps, but it's enough to let Spencer know he's no longer needed or wanted, not that he ever was. The girls huddle around us, attempting to seek out where Taylor and the rest of his group went as an awareness prickles over the back of my neck.

The feeling that someone's watching me is very real, and yet, as I turn, there's no one there. I try to ignore it, but the niggling persists. I flick my gaze over my shoulder again, completely missing whatever question is asked of me, and my gaze locks with Jacob, a look that I can't unpick on his face.

I smile his way, hoping he'll return it as he heads our way. The edge of his lip turns up in a smile as he slides into the middle of the group, an easy, "Good evening, ladies," falling from him, whatever irritation he had disappearing in nothing more than a turn of his head. *Maybe I imagined it?*

"Jacob, I wondered where you'd gone." I smile. "We just saw Taylor, and I assume the rest of the guys you live with, I thought you'd passed, but I must have been wrong."

His smile drops, for just a second, and I can't work out the emotion that flickers there before he plasters that fake smile back on. It was a retreat, for sure, but from what, I'm not sure.

"Yeah? Did he invite you all on Friday night?" he asks, attempting to inject something like excitement into his tone. "Because we need the most gorgeous girls there, and you are all absolutely stunning." He makes a show of complimenting everyone, making sure they're feeling good about themselves, yet missing me out. *Weird.*

He stands close, but not too close, his proximity a confusing addition. I'm sure we saw him walk past just a few minutes ago, and yet here he stands. Taylor somehow managed to get rid of Spencer with nothing more than a dismissive look, and Jacob is now charming the pants off our entire house.

I have no claim over him, and he was more than happy chatting up Tamsin this morning, but there's something about the fake excitement he's wearing that rubs me the wrong way, and I can't place it.

"Well, it was lovely to meet you all, and I'm more than excited to see you at our place on Friday night—don't forget your swimwear! But I'm going to see if I can find a non-alcoholic drink in this place, it's not so much fun being the designated driver." He feigns irritation, but I can tell it doesn't really bother him. "It was nice to see you again, Ivy."

His hand rests against my shoulder briefly, that awareness from earlier on turning electric as his skin caresses mine. It's nothing, barely a second, and the tense smile on his face is as fake as I've ever seen in my life. He doesn't even flinch, and yet I feel like my entire body just jolted to life.

"Yeah, you too," I reply automatically, still reeling from the confusing encounter and the joke this night has turned into.

Not just because Spencer is here and I cowered away like a terrified little girl; not the grown adult I am. *I guess old habits die hard.* But more so because of the weird encounter, and seeming blowoff from Jacob. *What the hell is that all about?*

I know we weren't exactly falling over each other earlier on, but at least he was friendly. Tonight, he's like a completely different person.

# SIX

## Leo

Grabbing an apple from the island in the kitchen, I follow the voices, sauntering through to the den and falling onto one of the empty sofas.

"I don't think you realise how long that driveway is," Emmerson comments before clicking his fingers, an idea sprouting. "We should have a couple of designated drivers, that way everyone else can have a drink."

"What's this?" I ask, conscious I've come in part way through a conversation.

"For the mixer tonight," Jacob says, his gaze flicking to mine. "I said we should just walk there and back, then we can all enjoy ourselves, but someone's too worried about getting his hair wet."

His attention flicks briefly to one of the other guys before coming back to me. He takes his time leaning back in the chair, his interested gaze sliding down the length of me and back, his tongue tracing along the edge of his bottom lip with interest.

Part of me wants to push him, to test the boundaries and find out if the rumours about the twins that play together are true, but one brief glance at the murderous look his brother sends my way and it's clear that's not on the table.

"I'll drive," I say, my phone vibrating in my pocket. "But I can only fit three in my car." Grabbing it out, I check the name before answering. "Be right back."

I don't know if anyone registers my comment about driving, or about me leaving the room, my focus solely on the ticking time bomb in my hand.

"You good?" my father asks as I answer, the words clipped out.

"Yeah, gimme two," I reply, stepping out of the room. I check the movie room is empty before slipping in and closing the door behind me, my heart rate picking up. "I'm clear. What's up?"

There's no reason for him to be calling me now.

I'm here and doing exactly what I'm supposed to be.

So why is he on the other end of the phone?

"Just checking in." He says it as if he calls me every day for a chat and a catch-up, like this is standard practice. "How was your first day?"

"Oh, just marvellous. One of the guys braided my hair and we're about to head out for cocktails," I reply dryly with a roll of my eyes. "Inductions started, I passed the first challenge. They even used me to make an example of someone, which I think has rubbed one or more of these guys the wrong way, but who cares?"

"Well, it sounds like you're settling in nicely then." He chuckles, the throaty sound gruff over the phone line, not that it's ever been much better in person. "Are you coping without Tweedle-dee and Tweedle-dum?"

"Yes," I grit out. His conscious decision to keep my two best friends with him rather than letting them come with me was more than a bone of contention between us—one of many, I suppose.

"Don't fuck this up. I'll be in touch soon."

The line goes dead in my hand.

"Thanks for the pep talk," I mumble before checking my messages, hoping to hear from one of them. But there's nothing.

He only wanted to check I'd been picked up and made it through. As if there was any other option. Unlike the rest of these fools, I know exactly what I'm walking into, and what I'm going to need to do.

I could take bets on which guys will be left at the end, but I'm afraid I'm starting to like more than one of them, and I'm not sure I'm ready to admit they're not going to last. *Frustrating.*

Quietly, I make my way back to the den, falling back into the seat, apple in hand. Everyone else is picking straws from Taylor's closed fist, his smile triumphant as he opens his hand to a full one.

Everyone else lines them up, an irritated growl tumbling from Nick when he realises he's going to drive. Don't get me wrong, I like a drink as much as the next guy, but my life has always been way too unpredictable to allow myself too much. Got to be able to defend yourself at the drop of a hat, and you can't do that half-cut.

"Unless you can get six in Nick's car, you'd better pick someone else too," I comment, finally taking a bite of the apple and sitting back in the chair.

"You can take mine," Taylor comments. "The Discovery is battered anyway, what's another dint or two between friends."

We're not friends. I only know his surname because it was written on the door over from mine when I got here. And whilst he's happy to make friends and play the game, I'm here to win. *There's no other choice.*

"Sure." I shrug.

"Great," Nick growls, glowering in my direction like I cut the straws and suggested playing their dumb-ass game.

I don't know if it's just because I was the one to do it, or because someone kicked his pretty brother's ass, but the guy has a chip on his shoulder big enough to build a house on. Well, lucky for him, taking him down a peg or two will be my pleasure.

"Everyone ready?" Jasper asks, looking around the room.

"Shall we start the party early?" George asks, pulling the baggie from his pocket. Excitedly, a couple of people join him, the line being cut thin with probably as much additive as you can manage, if the slow dilation and the sated shake of his head is anything to go by.

Just because you have money doesn't mean you're getting the good shit, and I've seen first-hand what a clean hit looks like. That isn't it.

Taylor throws the keys in my direction before I bin the apple core, heading to the garage along with everyone else.

Old school Dre pumps through the speakers as I start the engine, Taylor, George, Emmerson and Wyatt climbing in. Someone must have pushed the door button as we wait impatiently for it to slide out of the way and for Nick to reverse, his BMW blocking us in.

The night is dark as we pull out, the tree coverage making navigating the dirt track driveway even trickier as the guys laugh and joke in the back, jostling from left to right.

It's a matter of minutes to get to the main campus , drop the guys outside the lit-up atrium and find a space in the closest car park. It's surprising how many vehicles are out here as I shut off the engine and climb out.

Nick is already parked up and stalking off, his irritation a palpable force that surrounds him. Pushing my collar up, I lock the car and follow him, sliding through the doorway unnoticed. The guys are nowhere to be seen, but Nick loiters just in the entrance, not that I'm interested in getting into it with him right now.

No, this is the perfect opportunity to watch the competition, to get a feel for who they are and what they might bring to the table. The Sect are looking for something specific, they always are, and whilst I know I'm strong in lots of areas, it would be foolish to think some things couldn't be improved on.

"Drink, sir?" one of the waiters offers. "It's alcohol-free," he adds as I hold up the car keys.

"Thank you." I nod, plucking a glass from his tray and making my way further into the room, hesitating by the display cabinets as I people watch.

Mostly, people meander in groups, sticking to those they've gotten to know over the last week or so, in their apartments, I imagine, but there are the odd larger groups and a few pairs and singletons wandering around. Our house is most noticeable as the largest group, a whole bunch of girls already there as Nick heads to them, another excited gaggle following him with interest.

One of the tutors, I assume by the peppered hair, waves an awkward hand in my direction, taking the nod of my head as an opening and coming to join me.

"Mr. Windsor, good to see you here." He beams. "Checking out your father's old trophies?" He gestures to the largest accolade in the cabinet, the one I wasn't even paying attention to.

"Oh, yes. Quite the shoes to fill," I lie.

He adjusts his glasses, running a hand through his greying hair nervously before continuing to fill the void of conversation. "Have you thought about any extra-curricular activities yet?"

"Can't say I've given it much thought." I mean, it is the *first* day.

"Well, debate is always a skill worth practising," he comments, rocking back on his heels. "And, as you know, your father was the best. We could be in for another win with you on the team."

Oh, yes, my father knows how to argue all right. He knows how to get his fucking way too. It's not something I've ever bothered with; debating with him. Although, I imagine I'm one of very few people who could probably get away with doing it in the first place. *Not worth the risk.*

"Sure, I'll think about it," I reply, catching someone's eye across the room. "Sorry, do excuse me. Thank you for the introduction." Not that he introduced himself.

"Of course, yes. Enjoy your evening."

He waits by the glass cabinets, turning to look at the items enclosed like they've not been there for my entire lifetime or more. Taylor's laughter carries across the room, the tittering of the girls following as whatever he said sinks in.

It takes them a minute.

Not that they're stupid. Nobody who makes it here is devoid of brain function, I'm sure. And yet, as I peer around, there's more than one vacant look coming our way.

Now, the women that my father parades around to keep that happy smile front and centre, no matter what is going on around them. You wouldn't see them huddling in corners and whispering or gossiping, not that they'd dare do that in public anyway.

"Did you get lost?" Wyatt asks, nudging my shoulder. "I couldn't find you."

"Took a wander," I comment, noting he was looking for me. "Met one of the tutors, made a decent impression for a change."

"Good idea," he agrees. "Look willing. That's a good plan."

"Sure is." I nod. Not that it had been intentional. "How are you finding sharing a room with Nick?" I ask quietly, pushing to see how much he'll give away in such a public space.

His gaze flicks to Nick, and mine to Jacob as the two of them loiter at separate ends of the group. You'd think, that for someone so protective, Nick would be at his brother's side, but Jacob barely spares him a glance as he regales some blonde with a tale about God knows what, her interested eyes sparkling in the light.

"Oh, he's a barrel of laughs," Wyatt replies, breaking my stalking and diverting my attention back to the conversation at hand. "He's quiet and keeps to himself mostly, his brother seems nice enough though."

"Cool."

"I note you managed to get away without a roommate. That's some luck," he says with an arch of an eyebrow. His beach waves are tied back in some kind of man-bun tonight, his light eyes and square jaw giving his surfer dude look a harder edge.

"Sure is," I reply, knowing it was likely intentional, nothing during this initiation period isn't. And that's how the evening goes; the guys drink and hot girls trip over themselves vying for their attention until it's pushing midnight and Nick is suggesting getting everyone back to the house, girls included.

George and Taylor aren't finished, more than happy for an extra line of that cheap-ass snow as they grab another couple of drinks from a passing waiter.

"You do what you want," Nick clips. "But I'm out."

"You going be okay getting everyone in your cute little BMW?" I ask.

"I'll manage."

He stalks off, the rest of the guys following after deciding taking girls back on the first night was potentially not the best idea they've ever had. *Finally, a brain cell has been located between them.*

No rules have been set... yet. But I'm reasonably sure

inviting girls back to the house is going to be frowned upon.

"So, pool?" Taylor asks, draping his arms over the shoulders of two brunettes loitering nearby.

"I've not got any swimwear with me," one of them replies, a cute blush on her cheeks.

"Me neither." Taylor winks.

The other girl grabs his hand, setting off in the direction of the pool at speed, her heels clicking against the parquet floor as her friend trails behind. George manhandles three or four other girls in the same direction, all of them with more alcohol than needed in their system. Good job one of us is still sober, I guess.

Trailing along behind them, I follow the girly giggling before hearing the splash and making my way to the poolside, dragging a table to where a couple of the girls are sitting, George holding their attention rapt.

"You look interesting enough," one of the brunettes declares, locking her arm through mine and leading me away to a quieter spot at the other end of the pool.

Taylor turns some music on his phone, resting it on the table, before shucking his pants with the rest of his clothes and jumping into the water, his boxers covering whatever modesty he's supposed to have. But with a body like that, I get why he's not shy of joining in.

Although, after what I saw of everyone at the fights the other night, there isn't anyone struggling on that front. It's a surprise there isn't a gym at the house for everyone to keep up with it, or maybe that's intentional too.

"So, one of Taylor's housemates," the brunette says, giving me her attention and slumping into a chair. "Tell me about yourself."

"Well…" I smile. "That could take us a while."

"Tamsin is enjoying herself, so I guess that means we've got time," she decides with a wobbly nod of her head.

"Yeah, I'm sure you do. Are you having a good night?" I ask, changing the subject and dropping into the chair next to her, whilst attempting to keep half an eye on what's happening in the water. The last thing I need is for one of their drunk asses to drown.

"I'm just along for the ride." She hiccups. "Apparently, I wouldn't know a good time if it slapped me in the face and I need to let my hair down."

"Metaphorically, of course."

"Of course."

Her dark hair cascades in smooth lines over her shoulder as she turns to check on her friend, her green eyes muted by all the alcohol in her system. Her features are delicate and petite, her cheekbones high, and the column of her neck long. She kicks off her heels, flexing her toes in the dimmed light as she stretches out.

Feet have never been my thing, although I know more than one person who'd willingly offer her four figures or more for one lick of that smooth, pale skin. But as she rests back in the chair, it's clear she's not preparing to join her friend.

"Not joining in?" I ask, my interest piqued.

"Absolutely not. I have classes in the morning and I'm not getting up early to sort my hair once it's full of chlorine."

Okay, so she's not that drunk after all then.

"Fair enough." I shrug, happy to just sit in the quiet and

watch from a distance.

"You're not joining in either," she comments with a yawn.

"Sober," I reply. "It'd take more than a couple of lines and a handful of drinks to get me in there, underwear or not," I add as a wet bra slaps onto the tiles not ten feet from us.

"Come on, Ivy," her friend calls. "You're supposed to be enjoying yourself."

"I am enjoying myself," she replies, but not loud enough for her friend to hear. She's already turned back around to Taylor, waving her off. "Over here in the quiet."

"Not your scene?" I ask

"Oh, Tamsin has dragged me from one party to another for as long as I can remember." She smiles. "But I usually get to go home to my nice silent empty house at the end of it, not some sorority full of giggling girls."

"Ahh."

"And you can't say anything," she refutes almost indignantly. "You're enjoying sitting here just as much as I am."

"Very true."

"A man of few words, I can appreciate that. Especially when the women I'm staying with have nothing but words." She laughs, the sound bursting forth from her like she didn't expect to say those things out loud, her surprise refreshing. "Sorry, ignore me. I'm drunk and rambling."

"Well, Drunk and Rambling, I'm Leo Windsor," I say, finally deciding to give her the life story she was looking for, or some of it, anyway. "I'm staying at the house at the back of campus with Taylor and George, as you already deduced. And I'm the designated driver for the evening, not that I tend to drink as much as these guys seem to."

"And why's that?" she asks, tearing her fascinated gaze from where Taylor gropes her friend in the pool, hoisting her up to rub his face between her ample tits.

"Long story," I reply, my gaze snapping to hers, an undercurrent of sexual tension fizzling in the air around us.

I don't know if it's just seeing her friend so free, or that she actually wants some of that for herself, but the conversation takes an almost imperceptible change, her attention slightly more focused, her flirting more intentional.

"I've got time," she replies coyly.

Yeah, and I've not got a death wish.

"Another time," I reply with a wink.

"So, The Devil's Fraternity... or something, isn't it?" she asks.

"I'm sorry, what?" I ask with a smirk.

"The logo, the house, the parties. Someone said something about The Devil's Fraternity being behind it all. That's you guys, right?"

"Right," I reply, elongating the word as I attempt to work out a response that doesn't give too much away but amply answers the question. *Should have been better prepared.* "I'm still figuring it all out myself," I hedge.

Taylor is practically fucking the girl when another splash echoes around the room, two more girls joining in the fun as the heat between them drops down a notch.

"I'm Ivy, by the way, and that's Tamsin. She's not normally this... spontaneous. It's been a long few days," she attempts to explain, even though it's not needed.

"They're two adults, leave them to it." I chuckle as she flicks her hair over her shoulder, the heat creeping over her skin.

It's been a long time since I sat with a girl and just… talked. No awkward pauses and no strained silences. The conversation between us just seems to flow easily. The girls at my previous school thought they knew way too much about who I am, or more importantly, who my father is, to want to sit and talk.

They either thought they could fuck me and tame me, bless them, or they wanted nothing to do with me at all. Either of those worked for me, but there was no chance they were going to domesticate me. Not in this lifetime. So, to just chill out with someone not attempting to do either of those things is novel, and I like it.

She doesn't know me, doesn't want to fix me. She's only here to be around for her friend at the end of the night, and maybe have a little fun and flirt with some guy—me.

My gaze flicks over her again. Long legs and a tiny waist, tall, slim and delicate. I could only imagine breaking someone so seemingly perfect. And she doesn't deserve that.

The party continues around us, an air of electricity building as her fingers brush mine over the table.

"I thought you didn't want to partake?" I ask with a smirk. Maybe there's more to the girl than I first thought.

"I'm not getting in the pool," she corrects. "But we could still have fun."

A mischievous twinkle appears in her eyes as she

undoes the top button of her blouse, her silk scarf fluttering onto the table between us as she stands.

Shuffling in the chair, I widen my legs, making space as I lay my arms on the rests, waiting to see where she goes with this. She wants to play, let the girl play. She's still a little drunk, but less so than on arrival. The party is dying down behind us, and more than one of the girls is comatose at the side of the pool.

She perches her petite ass on my leg, doing her best to not look awkward. Sitting up, I slide my ass into the chair as I pull her closer, the heat from her leg pressing against me as my arm goes to her side to hold her in place.

The poor girl has no idea what she wants or how to get it. She's used to the paltry effort of stuck-up toffs attempting to make her feel good, if they even bothered, and she certainly won't have ever had to make the first move, not like this.

"What did you have in mind?" I ask, the words raspy as I hold back the desire to let my darkness break the delicate woman in my lap.

Her lips part, words on the tip of her tongue as her intense gaze flicks from my lips to my eyes and back again. I slide a hand up her arm, grazing the column of her neck before tugging on the lobe of her ear. A shiver ripples over her body, a desire matched by the peak of her nipples through the thin fabric and her short panted breaths.

I lean in closer, my lips brushing the shell of her ear as I whisper, "You only have to ask."

What I really want to do is bite down on the soft flesh, grazing my teeth along her jaw before devouring her plump lips and any moans that might fall from them, but before she can gather enough sense to reply, or for me to snap and take what I want, Taylor calls from the other side, declaring our time's up and we need to get back.

The spell is broken as she jumps back, suddenly realising she's pressed against me, her body moulding to the mere suggestion of my whim.

"Saved by the bell, I guess," I comment, noticing the aroused flush that creeps over her collarbone.

She smiles, climbing from my lap and plucking her scarf from the table, using the light fabric to distract from the sight of her nipples peeking through her shirt.

"Until next time." She smiles, picking her bag up and joining her friend and Taylor as they saunter out the door.

"George, are you ready?" I call, watching her ass swing in fitted black pants.

They'd have been a bugger to get off discreetly, but it would have been worth a try.

He nods from the chairs, giving the blonde girl one last scathing kiss as he fastens his jeans back up. *Lucky fucker.*

"You're driving," Ivy says, narrowing her eyes in my direction as we get outside, the early morning air frigid.

"I am…"

"I know I'm not supposed to get in a car with strangers, but I reckon we probably know you enough by now. What's the chance you're willing to drop three very tired, reasonably drunk women off before heading home?" she asks.

"Weren't there five of you earlier on?" I ask, looking around.

"There were… but two of them don't live with us and one of them is still asleep poolside." Tamsin laughs from

Taylor's side, her dark gaze flicking to his. "Won't you rest easier knowing we're safe and sound tucked up in our beds?"

"I'd sleep better with you tucked up in mine." He chuckles darkly. "But lucky for you, we brought mine, and I've got a big one."

"I bet you do," Ivy replies with a smile. No doubt she's sure to hear all about what he's packing when they get back—girls talk.

"That's his car, not his... anything else," I intervene before the conversation goes even further off topic. "Come on then, ladies. Where am I taking you?" I ask with a surprisingly alert smile. Ivy looks like she's ready to curl up in bed and not reappear for another three days, but I'm still feeling fresh and ready to take the day on, even though it's not started yet.

"Just down the driveway," she replies. "Past the stone house and round the far side of the pool."

My eyebrows raise as I look from Taylor to George and back again, nodding before gesturing to Taylor's black SUV, the one we're standing beside. "Hop in."

The music pours out as I start the engine up, laughter following as everyone does their best to find a space in the car. I'm sure someone ends up on someone else's lap, and there's more than one giggle coming from the back row as I carefully make my way down the winding driveway, following the path past the garage and further around the house.

They're not wrong though, tucked away on the other side of the pools I've not yet investigated is a glass-fronted pool house.

"Thanks for the lift," Ivy says as the girls climb out, steadying their feet before making their way to the front door and sliding in.

"This year is going to be so much fun," Taylor comments, most of the drink seemingly out of his system until he wobbles. "It's fine, I'm good," he adds, righting himself and climbing back in the car.

"I feel sorry for whoever has to sort that mess out," George comments, as we make our way back to the silence of the house just around the corner. *So close and yet so far.*

"Well, thanks for a fun night, gentlemen," I comment, pulling into the garage. "I guess I'll see you both somewhere around lunchtime." I might manage a couple of hours sleep, after I've dealt with the raging need now coursing through my veins, but I don't imagine I'll be seeing them before then.

# SEVEN

## Nick

The air horn blasts just inches from my head, or that's how it feels as I fly up from the pillow, my mind taking a second to orientate itself from sleep to awake as the shouting finally registers through the ringing in my ears and the thundering of my heartbeat.

"Two minutes, people. Go. Go. Go," is yelled out by the police officer in the doorway. Wyatt's confusion is as clear as mine as the two of us jump up, me reaching for a shirt and him grabbing some jeans from the floor, attempting to get them on whilst walking.

"What the fuck's going on?" I ask myself as much as anyone else as the two of us stumble from the bedroom, the rest of the guys being similarly collected as the lot of us wander down the corridors and main stairs, no more answers being provided as we're lined up against the big screen in the cinema room.

Four people sit on the double recliners, black masks covering their faces as they wait for us all to get there. Emmerson is the last one through the door, the officer closing it with a nod as one of the men stands, pulling off his mask.

The chief of police drops his mask to the sofa, clasping his hands in front of him silently as he waits.

The seconds tick on as we all wait, us for him, him for us, and a dozen officers line the room for God knows what. Nothing good, probably.

"Good morning, gentlemen," he eventually begins. "I know it's a little earlier than some of you are used to, and after last night's event, I'm sure more than one of you is feeling a little worse for wear."

For once, not drinking has gone in my favour, not so much for anyone else though. He looks up and down the line, taking in the sleep mussed, still drunk, and those with the start of a hangover as we wait to find out what the fuck this is about. The lighting is dim, giving it a comforting feeling that I'm reasonably sure is about to disappear completely.

"The Sect will ensure you're kept safe, warm, and fed, but if you think that wining, dining, and entertaining pretty young girls is all you are in for, you might as well leave now."

He pauses, giving everyone the chance to leave, but no one moves. No one dares breathe too heavily if the tension that ripples through the air is anything to go by.

"There are six more official challenges, they won't be easy and you won't have any warning, but they're not the only thing coming your way. The Devils of Pendleton Prep have a reputation, something you're going to uphold."

He picks up the mask, turning it over in his hands before descending the steps and passing it to Oliver, who does the same before passing it down the line. The fabric at the back is soft, a contrast to the hard plastic of the face.

"Masks are used to conceal your identity, they're individual and custom, so only those with power will know who you are. Yours are on your beds. You will be available at any time, day or night, when requested. You will undertake whatever you're asked without question. Do you understand?"

"Yes, sir," we all acknowledge.

"Power only comes with sacrifice, something some of you know nothing about, yet." He chuckles, dread swirling in my stomach. There's no way in hell they woke us up in the middle of the night for a little chat and a warning. Whatever this is, it's going to get ugly.

"Now, you've got roughly two and a half hours until sunrise, and that mixer seems to have gotten a little out of hand. I want every student back in their apartments, every plastic cup, gum wrapper, and piece of straw collected, recycled, and removed from the entire campus. Masks on, complaints silent, work as a team. You want this task to be completed before your time runs out."

We look at each other, my gaze connecting with Jacob's as we all loiter awkwardly, no one sure what to do first.

"Don't just stand there," the chief clips. "Masks, shoes, make a start. Supplies are at the administration building, and this campus is much bigger than you realise. I wouldn't waste time right now."

Like a fire's been lit under my ass, I hustle out, everyone else making their way to their rooms too, throwing clothes on and grabbing the masks whilst we're there. I don't recognise anyone once we're ready to go, but I guess that's the point as we gather by the main doors.

"Right, let's separate this. Half on the administration buildings and half on the residential buildings," someone decides from the doorway.

The masks all look the same, pretty much, and telling one person from another is almost impossible in our sleep-deprived state, but I could never mistake my own brother. Grabbing his arm, I call, "We'll take admin." A few others join us as the rest follow the other guy to the residential area.

We might end up sorting through discarded cups and decorations that have been trashed, but I have no desire to pick drunken students up and take them anywhere. The nine of us file out into the darkness, completely sober and focused, any remnants of sleep long gone as all our phones ping, one after another.

**Unknown:** *Two hours twenty. The clock is ticking.*

We all look at each other before putting one foot in front of the other and marching down the driveway. It's a hell of a lot longer on foot than I expect, and as we round the end of the dirt track and get our first glimpse of the devastation left behind, suddenly the urgency makes sense.

"Fucking hell," I grumble, knowing this is going to be a lot trickier than we anticipated. "He said supplies are in the administration building, let's get started."

With a renewed sense of resolve, we head for the office, grabbing what we need and heading out to make a start. Irritation twirls in my gut the longer I walk, filling bag after bag with the shit we so casually left for someone else to pick up. Discarded, ignored, and it irks, my thoughts going back to last night.

Half the bonus of this place being so small was not having to worry about stumbling home half-cut, looks like that's out the window now, though. Well, someone had to drive, and it turns out Leo and I were the ones to draw the short straws, shocker.

Already irritated by Leo's fucking face, the last thing I needed was to walk in and find her straight away. Her perfect ass was right in front of me but next to some sleazy-looking guy, and worse yet, was the way she and everyone else fawned over Taylor.

I don't know why it bothered me so much.

No, wait, I do.

The cold shoulder in the elevator, the way she refused to turn and look at me, despite being more than aware of my presence, if the way she fidgeted with her fingers was anything to go by, and then she stood there with some other guy and drooled over one of my supposed friends, along with everyone else, but still...

To add insult to injury, she called me Jacob.

You'd think I'd be used to people getting us mixed up, we're identical twins for fuck's sake. But it annoyed me more than I thought possible that she didn't know the difference. Well, why would she? We've spent barely three minutes in an elevator together and she had the best part of two hours in a lecture with him today. But she must feel this connection is different, surely?

Maybe not. Maybe it's just me who's got her under my skin. Her brushing me off was like waving a red rag at a bull. No is not something anyone ever says to me, and hell if that didn't grab my attention. But seriously? Jacob?

And then, I couldn't even grab a drink and make light of it. Oh no, someone had to be on babysitting duty, although that seems to have worked in my favour. Unfortunately, it also worked in Leo's. *I don't know why he pisses me off so much.*

Is it just because he knocked my brother out, or because they were paired together exactly for that? The whole match was engineered to knock me off my game, not that it did. Or perhaps it was the interested look on Jacob's face and the tender way Leo reached for him as he stumbled?

He's always been a little wayward, more free with his affection than me, but there's something about this guy that grates, and I can't work it out.

My phone pings again, a thirty-minute warning being received loud and clear as I look around. I opted to work inside the building, and it was a fucking mess, but at least it didn't have that freezing fog. Jacob somehow managed to think straight enough to grab a jacket, so he ended up outside somewhere. Hopefully, he's not got frostbite.

Dragging the full bag over to the bins, I stack it up with the other ones and give the main room a once-over. It's still a mess. The two of us worked meticulously from the back of the building to the front, clearing every room as we went. What the hell was going on in the library, I have no idea, but there's a whole stack of books for the librarian to return. Seemed like a better idea than shoving them on any old shelf and hoping for the best.

The librarian at our last school was a crotchety old witch, and heaven fucking help you if you put a book back in the wrong place. I swear to God she fucking knew, every time.

"How are you doing in here?" someone calls from the doorway.

"Just this and we're done," I reply, looking around. "Fifteen minutes and we'll be good. Twenty tops."

"Good. There's a nightmare in building two, so head there when you're done. It's going to need all the help it can get."

I nod as he disappears, running off to check in with one of the other teams, no doubt. The other guy in here, George, appears from a side room, dragging a bag behind him.

"Everything okay?" he asks. "I thought I heard something."

"They need help in building two and were just checking in to see how we're getting on."

"I'm fucking dead," he grumbles as I grab the bag, hoist it up and place it with the other ones. He lands heavily in the reception chair as I straighten up the decorations, grabbing a wipe and running it along the surface.

"Good time last night?" I ask, looking at the sweat that covers his brow, the alcohol practically leaking from his pores.

"Hell yes. Some of the girls here are really up for a good time." He chuckles, clearly thinking back to something salacious.

I chuckle, nodding along like I have any idea what he's talking about. But I don't. George, Leo and Taylor stayed late, whilst I did two trips up and down the driveway to get everyone else back. I mean, it wasn't ten o'clock or anything pathetic, and they'd all had more than a couple, but I have a feeling the three of them had barely got back before we were all pulled out of bed.

The gold thread through his mask reflects in the fluorescent lights overhead as he stands, grabbing another bag and making a start at the other end of the room. We're finished and cleared through in fifteen minutes, after all, closing up the office behind us and making our way to building two.

A quick look around outside shows the guys have done a great job, you'd never have a clue the state it was in before we started. And as a fifteen-minute warning ping appears on our phones, we both do our best to hustle our steps, but the lack of sleep is catching up, and each step is harder than the last.

The atrium is still glowing as we get there, the lights continuing to flicker through their pre-set show, but there's shit everywhere and nobody to be seen. "Hello," I call out, but there's no reply. "Fuck," we say at the same time, the panic clear as we look at the mess waiting for us.

George rushes for the lights, and I head to the hay bales, starting to stack them together. He throws me a bag, pulling one out for himself as we start throwing cups and discarded trays of food in whole. We separated ours in the other buildings, but there's no time for that now.

"Are you guys... Holy fuck," someone says from the doorway, clearly not expecting this here either.

"We've just got here," George replies. "Give us a hand, will you?"

Whoever it is calls outside, and another two people join

him and make a start. The room is huge, the open space littered with bits of food and discarded glasses as someone calls out, "Help," from nearby.

Dropping the bag, I rush over, having no idea what the hell they could need help with in here. Anyone can lift the hay bales, but when I get there, I see the issue. There's some drunk guy passed out behind them, and as I check my phone, we've got less than ten minutes to get him out of here and back to his apartment, with no idea where the hell that is.

"He just said to get them back to a residential building," I say, grabbing the guy by the collar and hoisting him up and over my shoulder. "He never said it had to be their apartment, or even the right building. How far is the closest one?" I ask, crossing the room.

Whoever found him hustles his steps alongside me, opening the door and gesturing across the car park and to the right as our phones go again. Neither of us checks them, looking at each other before we set off running. "Don't let him throw up all over me," I comment, doing my best to keep him still, and failing.

The adrenaline kicks in almost instantly, giving me the boost to get there, but as he holds the door and moves some cushions on the entranceway chairs, it lags. Hauling him down and into them without dropping him is a herculean task, but I manage it.

I've got barely fumes left as I drag my ass back out, dropping to the edge of the curb as police cars pour from the driveway, swarming through the campus as they march from building to building.

"Thanks, man," the guy says, joining me as we watch

the officers sweep from one place to another. "We got everyone in the residential buildings."

"Good news. We took buildings one and four. I don't know what the fuck happened with building two, but I hope to God they managed to get it sorted out in time."

"It wasn't looking too bad when we left," he reassures. "And I've swept from the far end of campus to here. Everywhere else is good."

"What about building three?" I panic.

"Pristine."

"Awesome." I sigh, my relief clear as one of the police cars pulls up alongside the two of us.

"Time to head back, boys," the older officer says, holding the door open. He gives no indication as to what we're heading back to, just waiting quietly for us to climb in and then heading down the driveway.

The lift is greatly appreciated, I have no idea how we would have managed to get down here without it. Both of us are absolutely exhausted as the doors unlock and we wearily haul ourselves up and out, thanking him as we go.

Grabbed from our sleep, battered, and made to fight, then pack up and move twenty-four hours later whilst attempting to get to know our new housemates, who are also incidentally the competition. The first day of lectures, broken heating, and a social event I didn't want to be at, not to mention another night of broken sleep and nearly three hours of manual labour before the sun is even up. I'm ready to sleep for a week.

But it appears we're not done.

We're ushered back into the movie room, the rest of our

rag-tag band already there, the door closing behind us with an ominous click.

"Not quite the level of teamwork I was expecting," the deputy mayor comments idly from the recliner. "But I've seen worse."

"It wasn't up to standard," the chief of police adds. "Despite some impressive last-ditch efforts." He tips his head to where the other guy and I stand, almost looking pleased.

"You're limited to two drinks each on Friday night," the deputy mayor decides. "And you're on clean-up duty."

"You are having a laugh," someone comments, a scoff falling from him. "I think you're forgetting who the hell we are. More than your fucking clean-up crew, that's for sure." He grabs the mask, rips it off and shoves it into his hoody pocket.

"I think you're the one forgetting your place," the chief of police says, stalking his way to the front. "And who the fuck you're talking to." He closes the distance, and time itself seems to slow down. His hand flies out, a baton landing in his open palm as it flicks open, swinging back and landing the blow with disconcerting accuracy.

It takes half a second, surprise registering first as the entire room holds its collective breath, his face crumples, the pain finally registering as the bone snaps and George collapses, his pain ripping through the room. But no one reaches out to catch him.

He drank too much, didn't sleep enough, and now he's giving shit to the chief of police, who incidentally is also a senior member of a secret society. I might be tired and pissed off, but even I'm not that stupid. Seems like he is though, and that was an example the chief did not hesitate to make.

The officer collects his baton before hauling George up, someone coming to help him before they march the howling, whimpering and blubbering mess from the room, the silence pregnant.

"Two drinks allow you to look sociable whilst still keeping your head clear enough to deal with any issues as they arise," the deputy mayor continues, like the incident in-between never even happened. And I'm not sure if that's more distressing than the clearly broken bones. "Had your work this morning been sufficient, you would have been afforded a cleaning team. It wasn't."

Nobody argues with him. Nobody moves, breathes, or even fidgets. Accepting anything and everything without question.

"Keep your phones available at all times, masks are to be kept secure. And there is something else." There's an awkward shuffle somewhere down the line as we wait for the explanation that's sure to come, whatever it is not good. "Now, I'm not about to tell a room of hormone-driven eighteen-year-olds not to have sex, I'm not that ridiculous, but…"

"The Devils of Pendleton Prep have a reputation, and the three of you that make it through to The Sect will have a big job on your shoulders. You can't do that alone," the chief of police continues, the other two guys still seated, silent and wearing their masks. "They're called The Angels, and they're your end game. They're closer than you think.

Enjoy the freedom whilst you've got it, boys, because your days are numbered."

He makes a point of looking each one of us in the eye before nodding. "Now go get cleaned up, or grab an hour's sleep if you can. Classes will begin soon."

We all file out silently, heading for our rooms. Jacob offers me a small smile as he passes, weariness seeping from his very being.

Oh, it's going to cost us all right, one way or another.

# EIGHT

*Ivy*

"Have fun, see you tonight," Tamsin calls as I slide the door closed, the rest of the girls repeating the sentiment as I attempt to shut them all out.

Leaning back against the wood, I close my eyes and breathe out slowly, counting to ten. I knew sharing my space with other people was going to take a minute to figure out, to adjust, and it is. It'll be fine, soon, hopefully.

A light flickers on in the building opposite, a reminder that we're not out here alone as I hurry my steps to the car.

It's just so constant. The people. The noise. And it's not bad, there's no fighting and arguing, no things being thrown at each other yet, they're just around. All. The. Time. I might end up in the gym just to get some peace and quiet. Maybe.

At least I get this one class on my own. Apparently, nobody else was interested in advanced biology, but that works out well for me. Drizzle permeates the fog that rolls between the buildings as I head down the driveway, the thick trees blocking out the worst of it as I keep to the middle of the road, hoping there's no one coming the other way.

Parking is straightforward as I jump out, pulling my coat hood up before climbing out, attempting to keep out the worst of the wet weather as I make my way to the right building, coffee in hand.

The dry air hits me with force as I come through the glass doors, closing them quickly behind me before making my way to the labs. This building is gorgeous. It was special enough last night with it's kitsch charm, but I take the time to appreciate the fresh flowers scattered around as I manoeuvre my way through the winding hallway, locating the right room and letting myself in.

"Good afternoon." The tutor smiles from behind his desk. "Grab a seat, we've got ten minutes before I start."

"Good afternoon," I reply easily, the shackles of other people's expectations falling away as he turns back to his book and I look around the room.

"I'll be back shortly," he says, addressing the rest of the class before turning back to me. "I'd better top up the caffeine before we get started, thanks for the reminder."

He gestures to my travel mug before slipping out of the doorway behind me. I find a seat over the far side of the room by the expansive windows. One of these days, warm sunlight will stream through here and make this one of the best seats in the house. Today, it's grey and miserable, but one day it'll be better.

Dropping the books on the desk, I pull out my pens and notebook, slide onto the stool and look around. Unsurprisingly, there's only one other girl in here, and she's got her nose well and truly in her phone, completely avoiding everyone else in the room. Just as I'm considering whether I should move closer to her, solidarity and all that, movement to my left catches my eye.

"Ivy Rose, you realise this is an *advanced* class, right?" Spencer's condescending smirk irritates me more than usual as he pulls out the stool beside me. "Maybe I should join you… give you a hand."

"I'm sure I'll be fine," I reply, plastering a saccharine-sweet smile on my face.

I've no idea why this would be a surprise to him, he's more than aware of what I want to do and where I want to be. It was one of the reasons we split up, after all, me refusing to be the docile stay at home barbie-doll he was looking for. I'm sure he'll have his pick of those one day, and I hope to heaven she has a good doctor willing to prescribe her all the drugs she'll need to get through it.

"We should catch up. It's been too long." He continues the conversation like I didn't just rebuff him. I'm reasonably sure it was clear last night I have no desire to be anywhere near him, and I certainly don't want to spend hours together every week in class. But having a one-sided conversation isn't unusual as he ignores everything I think.

"Honestly, I'm fine. Thank you. Go join your friends, I'm sure they're missing you already." Being direct never works with him, but I can't help but attempt to assert some kind of authority here. It's like he has selective hearing and tunes out anything that isn't what he wants to hear.

"I'll grab my books," he declares, placing his hands flat on the desk.

"I think the lady said no." The words rumble on the back of a growl, and as I follow the direction they came from, I come face-to-face with none other than Leo, an awareness twirling around my stomach. He places his bag heavily on the desk, just inches from Spencer's fingers. "You're in my seat." His dark gaze moves, pinning Spencer with an irritated look.

"Leopold," Spencer squeaks out, visibly paling as he pulls his fingers back quickly. "I didn't realise you were in this class."

Turning in my seat, I can't help the amusement that covers my features. Never in my life have I seen the self-satisfied look fall off Spencer's smug face so fast, fear replacing it, as a smile creeps over my own.

"You okay there?" I ask as Spencer stands, taking a step back before knocking into the bench behind him in his bid to escape.

"Of course. Fine. Everything's just great." He over-corrects himself, knocking a book off the edge of the desk and fumbling to catch it, but it tumbles through his hands, spinning and landing at Leo's feet.

The smile that breaks free is resplendent as his panicked gaze flicks from the book to Leo's face and back again. The two of them stand there, looking at the book. Leo with agitation, and Spencer with fear. It's hilarious.

Spencer goes to pick it up, his hand reaching out before Leo moves and Spencer darts back again, bumping into the table.

"Move," Leo growls again, glaring at him.

I watch Spencer scurry across the room and back to the safety of his friends as Leo picks up the book, dropping it back on the table behind me.

"You're going to have to teach me how to do that," I comment idly as he takes his books from his bag, grabbing a tablet out too.

"Sorry, am I okay to join you?" he asks, pointing to the seat beside mine, tablet in hand. Like he just realised he barged in here and declared 'MINE' all over me.

I nod, my smile smaller as I think about the way I climbed over him last night. *Oops*. "Of course." I shrug, pushing it down. "You're my hero."

The smile that graces his face is priceless, his dark eyes seeming to lighten as they twinkle with mischief the way they did in the dim lighting of the pool.

"I'm no hero," he says, dropping into the seat and swivelling my way. "But I'll take it." He grins, his straight white teeth on full display. "So, advanced biology is an interesting choice."

He leaves the sentence open-ended, waiting with interest for me to fill in the blanks.

"Psychology." I shrug. "Got to know how the physical attributes work alongside the mental ones."

"Makes sense. How do you know him?" he asks, any further explanation not required.

"Spencer?" He nods. "Oh, we go way back." I sigh. "He plays golf with my father." And the rest. "And, we, uh… Well, we used to… date?" It's not something I particularly want to admit to, especially with someone I'm maybe, kinda, a little bit interested in, and it comes out as more of a question than I anticipated. "Hang on, did he call you *Leopold?*"

"It's just Leo, usually."

"So, how do *you* know him?" I ask, hoping it's less embarrassing than mine and attempting to divert the attention away from my admission.

"That's a long story for another day. You, however, need to fill me in on this 'sort-of dating' you did with him."

"Well, you know how it is." I sigh, realising he's not going to let this go. "Our parents shoved us together for years. They nudged, suggested, and recommended until I finally gave in and agreed to go out with him."

"And…"

"And… he was as much of a self-important tool as I always expected he would be." I nod.

"Shocker." He smiles. "Leave it with me. He won't bother you again."

My eyebrows raise, surprise covering my face, but anything I might have said or asked about it is cut off as the tutor comes back in, a steaming mug of coffee in hand. "Now then everyone, let's start at page twenty-four. I hope you came prepared."

Luckily, I have, and anything I was unsure of, Leo was able to help me with. Hopefully, he doesn't end up saving me all year long. That could get a little tiresome. I've not quite been the damsel in distress, but he was certainly there to help me out, more than once.

The class comes to an end, the quickest hour and a half of the week, and my brain is full, so full.

"I think I'm going to need some extra resources for this," Leo says, sliding a receipt back into the text on the table. "It could be a trip to the library for me. Do you fancy it?"

"I've got another class in twenty minutes," I explain, quickly checking the time on my watch before hustling to get my things together. "But I'm totally up for a study session another time."

The words come out much flirtier than I intended, the breathy tone a surprise to even me, but he smiles easily, accepting the *not-for-now* rather than an outright *no*.

"Sounds good." He nods, rotating his neck left and right before shaking out his shoulders. "I take it you guys were okay when you got back last night?"

"Yes. Charlotte was more than a little worse for wear when I left this morning." Well, she looked like death warmed up on the sofa—she'd clearly spent way too long throwing up, or maybe that's just how she looks without makeup on. "But I'm all good. You?"

"Yeah, I'm good," he replies with a weary smile, standing and gesturing for me to go first.

A blush raises over my cheeks at the simple gesture, something so lost on other guys, not that I'm thinking of anyone specifically. I risk a furtive glance at Spencer, who's watching us with narrowed eyes and keen interest. The two of us head through the building together, the tension that's been building over the last hours sizzling away.

I was going to kiss him, he was going to kiss me. All of a sudden, my mind's back in his lap, sweat beading at the back of my neck as he growls in my ear, his breath fanning down my neck. Heat blossoms deep in my belly, pooling between my legs.

"I, uh, I'm just going to head to the ladies' room before finding class," I say, darting in that direction. "See you around."

"Sure thing," he replies, confusion and amusement laced through his tone.

I don't turn around and look, but I can feel the heat of his stare as he watches me run away, probably thinking that I'm some kind of crazy person. *I guess I am.*

He made no indication that's where he wanted to pick up today, and everything has been purely platonic until my head got involved.

The bathroom door closes behind me, the stalls empty as I run my hands under the cold tap, dabbing them against the back of my neck. Closing my eyes, I attempt to tamp down the insane part of my brain that wanted to be back in his lap, the part that was waiting for him to kiss me before heading off to the library and me to my class. Until the door opens and closes.

Because of course it does. You can't even have a moment of peace in a bathroom here, let alone the house you share with five other women.

"You need to watch yourself with him."

Irritation rolls over my body at nothing more than the tone of the man I know is stood behind me.

"Excuse me?" My eyes fly open, connecting with his in the mirror. "This is the *ladies' room.* What the hell do you think you're doing?" Aside from attempting to tell me who the hell to be friends with, because that didn't work out well last time either.

Spencer stands there, blocking the doorway with his arms folded across his chest, his usual pissed-off look nowhere to be seen. It should give me pause, the vulnerability he's finally showing, but all I can think of is the last time he told me he didn't like my friends. *Fuck him.*

"Seriously, Ivy Rose, you need to listen to me," he attempts to placate. "You have no idea who he is and what he does. He's dangerous."

"I'm quite capable of looking after myself, thank you," I reply with a sigh and a roll of my eyes.

Drying my hands off, I turn, breaking his eye contact and throwing the discarded paper towel in the bin, pulling my bag further up my shoulder as he attempts to get closer, reaching his hands out for me.

"Not with this you can't," he says. "Just trust me, okay?"

"Not a fucking chance," I clip out, slipping past him and his outstretched hands and heading for the door. "I've got a class to be at. Thanks for the chat, but next time keep your opinion to yourself."

"Ivy Rose…" I hear the plea in his voice even as the door closes, and I quicken my steps, more than ready to leave the warmth of the building and head out into the cold to find my next class.

I don't know who he thinks he is, telling me who I can and can't talk to. That didn't work for him when we were together, and it sure as hell isn't going to work now.

I'm not some silly little girl falling over herself at the first boy to ever show her attention, not that Leo is the first guy… and he's aware of that too. No, I'm not like the blonde that was fawning all over him the last time I saw him.

And Leo's not like that. There's something magnetic about him, something different and interesting, and it's nothing to do with Spencer. Absolutely nothing at all.

# NINE

## Nick

"**D**o you think George is coming back?" Emmerson asks, pushing open the main building door. "Or do you reckon he's out for the count?"

"I guess we'll just have to wait and see," I reply with a shrug. I honestly couldn't care less one way or another. He's just someone else in my way.

"Yeah, but what do *you* think?"

"Dunno," I brush off, more than ready to be away from him and in my class. Jacob wasn't lying when he said I'm anti-social. "I'll meet you back here, yeah?"

"Sure." He nods, heading to his class whilst I head to mine. "Catch you in a bit," he calls.

He seems nice enough, most of them do, and yet somehow it still feels like they're all waiting to trip me up. Firstly, someone knocked me out of the line-up, and then there was that shit show over the building being completely missed when I was the one that said I'd take inside the buildings. It's like I'm being singled out, and targeted, and I can't work out why or by who. *It's frustrating.*

My brain is anywhere but where it's supposed to be as I make my way through the building, searching out my class just as Ivy gets to the doorway, a harried look on her face, and I can't help the protective streak that rears its head.

"Is everything okay?" I ask, rushing to catch up with her.

"Huh?" She turns, her mind a million miles away as she finally notices me standing there. "Oh, Jacob, hey." She smiles.

"Ah, actually, about that…" I start, more than ready to clear up this miscommunication. I can't blame her for not knowing the differences between us, no matter how irritating it is that she doesn't realise we're two different people.

"Wow," she says, cutting me off as we stand in the doorway looking over the busy class. "Ooh, look, there's a couple of seats over there, if you're happy to join me?"

She doesn't wait for an answer, making quick moves to get the last pair of seats before anyone else does, seemingly quite happy to spend the afternoon with my brother, despite my brush-off last night.

I was pissed off. I can admit it.

It's not just that she doesn't seem to know the difference between the two of us, lots of people don't, but that this undercurrent I can feel sizzling between us doesn't seem to register with her.

"Man, what a day." She sighs, the weight of the world seemingly on her shoulders. She grabs her stuff out as I join her, any conversation being hushed as the tutor appears, making a start on the lecture.

I grab my notebook quickly, dropping everything else under the table without thought as the tutor begins her introduction. *So much for clearing up who I am and finding out who or what is bothering her.*

The lecture crawls on at a snail's pace.

Maybe it's just because there's someone else I'd rather be talking to, or maybe it's because after our late night and my early class this morning, I've had next to nothing of a break, but all I want is for this class to be over, and it won't fucking end.

The finish time comes and goes, a couple of people making a show of packing up their things or repeatedly looking at their watches. Eventually, the tutor realises she's been rambling on for an extra fifteen minutes when someone gently apologises before leaving because they've got another class to go to.

"Well, that could be awkward if it happens every week." Ivy chuckles, whatever had been ailing her earlier on seemingly forgotten or pushed to the side.

"Hopefully it was a one-off," I comment, packing up. "You seem happier, was everything okay earlier on?"

I got most of what the tutor was talking about, but I couldn't seem to stop my mind from wandering to the multitude of things that could have upset her. What if some guy was coming on to her, or someone giving her shit? It could have been the barista making her coffee wrong, or her tripping over something on the way in.

My brain conjures everything from the inane and mundane to the outright ridiculous. At one point, I'd managed to convince myself it was an issue with a guy and

I was going to need to find someone and hurt them. Not that I'd be averse to that.

"Yeah, all good," she replies, snapping me back into the conversation at hand. "I just had a run-in with my ex. He's decided to try and run my life again." She rolls her eyes. "It didn't work when we were together and it sure as hell isn't going to work now. Don't worry though, Leo's on it."

"Of course he is," I mutter under my breath.

"What's that?" she asks, popping her head back up over the edge of the desk, bag in hand.

"Nothing. I'm just glad you managed to get it sorted. Let me know if he bothers you again."

"Sure thing. Are you finished after this?"

"Yeah, just meeting Jake and Emmerson before we head back to the house," I say without thought, grabbing my stuff as we make our way out.

"Jake? That must get confusing." She laughs, the tinkling sound being swallowed up as people filter from various classes, the corridor getting busier by the minute.

"Well, that's what I was trying to say when I saw you. I'm not actually—"

"Nick, wait up," Jake calls from behind us somewhere, and Ivy turns, her confusion clear.

"Jacob's my brother. I'm Nick."

I'm not sure if she catches my words in the hustle of the corridor, but he joins us quickly as she stands there looking from me to Jake and back again, gobsmacked.

"Ha." Her amusement is clear as she looks between us once more. "Well, I'm glad you turned up, I'd have been calling him a liar otherwise and cursing you out for trying to ditch me."

"Ditch you?" Jacob says with a chuckle. "I would never."

"Yeah, well, twins aren't exactly common," she adds with a small smile. "Identical twins even less so."

"Less than half a per cent."

"So, wait, why has it taken you so long to tell me?" she asks.

"I figured you knew?" I shrug as people push past, the three of us an island in the middle of the corridor before we start moving with the rest of the students towards the exit.

"How?"

"We were both in the elevator the other day," Jacob explains.

"Oh." She swallows nervously.

She didn't even see him.

Didn't notice.

She only saw me.

The smile that stretches my face is unintentional but victorious.

Of course she recognised Jacob the next morning, he looks just like me, slightly different dress sense, and personality wise we're quite different, but she wouldn't know that. Not yet.

"Well, I guess that makes sense. No wonder you were pissed off last night." She barks out a laugh, her surprise showing.

Suddenly, all the pieces are falling into place for her, and my confusion and hesitation make sense. I'm not as outgoing as he is, so him chatting with her that next day wouldn't have been awkward, but being called your brother's name is obviously a complete turnoff.

"It's fine, don't worry about it," I say, just glad we managed to get it sorted out and confirm the interest is there. Not that I had any concerns, not really.

"The split lip didn't give it away?" Jacob asks, pointing to the offending article, the shadow of bruising still on his face.

She obviously doesn't know anything about the fights at the weekend, and whilst he did better in the second round, he still has the bruises and marks to show for it. I'm not sure how I'd have handled it had that gone differently, I was already pretty strung out after Leo knocked him out.

"Apparently not." She shrugs, an incredulous laugh falling from her like she can't believe she missed the differences, looking from me to Jacob and back again, her look far more flirtatious than I think she means to be.

"Well, now you know there's two of us and you don't have anywhere else to be, does that mean you've got time to grab a coffee?" I ask. "To make it up to me, of course."

She quiets, one eyebrow raising.

"Hey, you were the one that thought I was someone else," I counter.

Her dark eyes connect with mine, a smile starting to peek at the corner of her lips. "Fine," she agrees, looking up at me through thick dark lashes. "But we're not going to that godawful tea shop."

"I would never," I counter with a triumphant grin.

"And what about us getting back? You're driving," Jacob comments as Emmerson rounds the corner.

"You'll be fine. It's not that far," I say, conscious this might be a now-or-never kind of opportunity.

"Really?" He smiles, shaking his head. "Better haul ass then."

He pushes the two of us towards the car, heading towards Emmerson to cut him off before he has the chance to interrupt.

"We can just take mine, leave yours for your brother," Ivy offers.

"There's no way on God's green earth I'm going to let you drive me anywhere, sugar." The lights flash as I unlock the car. "Jump in."

Opening the door for her, she giggles, dropping her bag into the footwell whilst looking over her shoulder. Emmerson's glower can be felt from over here as he marches in our direction as I run around, jumping in and starting the engine before peeling out of the car park. He's barely a dozen steps behind us when he gives up, his irritated glare following us long after it should.

"I'm gonna pay for that when I get back, I can tell."

"Probably." She smiles. "So, where are you taking me?"

"You'll find out when we get there, it's a surprise."

"A surprise, huh?" she ponders thoughtfully. "You guys must have been here a while already if you know places to take me for a surprise." She smiles, looking out of the window as we pass through the quiet country streets.

"About two weeks, yeah," I agree. "One of our flatmates has lived locally his whole life and he was kind enough to share some of his favourite spots with us. And, to be fair, there aren't that many places around here, it's kind of hard to miss. See…"

We pull off the main road into the one-and-only industrial area nearby. It's not fancy, there are no branded coffee and takeout joints here, but it's worth the short trip. Ivy fires off a quick photograph to her friend, "For safety, obviously," she confirms with a smile as we jump from the car and cross the car park. *Smart girl.*

Dark roast permeates the air as I push open the door, holding it as she slides through the gap. Distracted, I practically walk into the counter, the sway of her hips far more interesting as she meanders the room, taking everything in.

"I'll have a double shot Americano. Ivy, what's your poison?" I call, getting her attention.

"Oh, can I get a Caramel Latte Macchiato, please?"

"Anything to eat?" I ask, gesturing to the rows of fresh cakes and desserts. "Or there's sandwiches and stuff if you want something else?"

"I'm good, but thank you."

"I'll bring those over for you," the barista says as I flash my card.

Ivy picks a table, carefully putting her phone in her coat pocket before placing it over the back of the chair, shaking off the frigid drizzle that's done its best to soak us between the car and here.

"So, psychology is an interesting choice," I start, attempting to break the ice.

"Not when you want to be a psychologist," she replies with a small shrug of her shoulders.

"Hence the sociology with Jacob." I nod, the barista

banging the coffee in the background. "And what is it you were in before our class?"

"Advanced Biology."

"Wow. Quite a mix. Makes sense though, considering the psychology stuff."

"I would have just done psychology and advanced bio if it was up to me, but my father insisted I needed to do something with broader applications."

"You're close then, huh?" I ask, the stab of pain in my chest unusual.

My relationship with my father was… complicated.

He loved us, of course he did. And he was around, some of the time. At least when he was around, he was present, unlike my mother. No, you could sit with Francesca Barrett and be one hundred per cent sure her mind was anywhere but in that room. But my father, when he was there, he was really there, you know?

"We used to be," she dodges. "Anyway, let's not talk about that. You need to tell me more about this Devil's Prep thing. The info Stephanie had was minimal, and Leo was tight-lipped about it last night."

"The Devils of Pendleton Prep? I'm surprised Leo didn't tell you everything you wanted to know and more," I grumble.

"Nope. But I'm hoping you will."

Her expectation is unfounded and I have no idea what I'm supposed to tell her.

"I'm not sure I have much more information about it than you do at this point." I scoff out a laugh. "They have a lot of history here, or so I'm told, a reputation to uphold."

The drinks arrive and she wraps her hands around the mug, her attention rapt as she leans over the table.

"Go on…"

"They go on to do amazing things," I hedge. "They have big money and big lives, power beyond your wildest dreams."

The interest tumbles out of her like a balloon that's been popped, her face dropping, the sparkle that was there just seconds ago draining out of her, much like the interest in the conversation. "The reputation I've heard about isn't the same… they sound like dicks."

"I could take offence to that, if I knew anything about it," I comment.

She narrows her eyes at me, waiting patiently to see if I'll give her anything else.

And I could… I guess.

Yes, darling, The Sect. A group of men that do the kind of things that delicate eyes like yours should never have to see. They're politicians, heads of huge corporations, and more, if the faces I recognised the other night are anything to go by.

These are not men to cross, and not ones to gossip about either.

"I hear they're not the only ones with a reputation though. The Angels of Pendleton Prep are as notorious as the Devils. They're the hottest, smartest, and most attractive in just about every way." I attempt a lighter tone, something to break the irritated edge from the look she's giving me. It doesn't work.

"Well, I'm not here for that." She crosses her arms over

her chest in defiance, jutting her chin out.

"No?" I smile, desperately trying to ease us back into the banter we had just moments ago. Where the easy conversation flowed effortlessly.

But it doesn't come as she shuts me down with nothing more than one word.

"No."

"Well, you could have fooled me." The words are clipped out, my own irritation beginning to show through as she continues to push back. It's no joke that Jacob is the easier going one of us, my temper gets me into trouble more often than not, and I have no idea how to pull it back once it starts. "Well, you looked friendly enough with Taylor when I walked in last night, and it sounds like you're cosying up with Leo just fine too."

She slams her lips shut, her fury ricocheting between us as she gets up and storms across the room, making a bee-line for the bathrooms.

Shit. *What the fuck is coming out of my mouth right now?*

With a sigh, I take a huge gulp of the burning coffee, attempting to calm myself and work out how the hell to get this back on track.

It was going so well.

She was happy, we were chatting, and then she didn't get the details she was hoping for and the whole thing goes to shit. *Fuck.*

I take three deep breaths, closing my eyes and pulling it all back in. There's something there, something I want to investigate, and I'm not going to let her hard-on for information run me out of something I want. Standing, I stalk to the bathrooms, not one to be deterred by something as straightforward as a woman with a bee in her bonnet.

"Look, we seem to have gotten off on the wrong foot here," I say, barging open the ladies' bathroom door and finding her at the sink, running a stick of ruby red along her lips.

The thought of that red smeared across the base of my cock, her lips wrapped tightly around the thick of me as she sucks me deep causes me to hesitate, sucking in a breath.

"Really?" she asks, as if she can read the thoughts straight out of my mind.

"I'm not sure what details you were looking for, but I really don't know anything else I can tell you," I admit, attempting to explain.

"You're a dick." She clips the words out as she pockets the lipstick in her tiny purse, the one I didn't even realise she had with her, breaking eye contact in the mirror.

"I've heard that before," I placate gently with a cocky smirk, closing the distance between us.

She feels this, I know she does.

"That doesn't make it any better," she argues, turning around to face me, one hand going to her hip. But she doesn't realise how close I've become until she turns, backing up against the counter as her other hand comes to my chest, a gasp breaking free as her eyes darken, lust twirling in the air between us.

"I think you like it," I goad. "You like it when I'm a bit of a dick, when I don't give you what you want." The flush of her cheeks could be annoyance, but it could also be arousal, and if the way her breath see-saws in and out is anything to go by, my money is on the latter.

"I…"

"You're so used to men dropping to the ground you walk on to worship at your feet that you have no idea what it's like when someone wants you and isn't willing to bend." My gaze flicks to those cherry-red lips, the ones parted and almost panting as her gaze holds mine once again.

"You don't know anything about it," she argues, but there's no power to the words, they come out breathy and wanting, giving away way more than she was hoping, I'm sure.

Her breath collides with mine, the next-to-nothing distance that was between us being eaten up as I push her back and she pulls me forward, the hand that was trapped between us twisting in my shirt to get purchase. A vein attempt at a control that she'll never have, never own, as my lips come to hers.

We're a tangle of tongues and teeth, and she gives just as good as she takes, wrapping her legs around my waist as I lift her onto the vanity in one smooth motion. Her nails dig into my arm as I slide one hand through the thick of her hair, guiding her where I want her to be.

"And you'll never believe what he said," someone says from behind me as the bathroom door slams open and they continue. "He said if I didn't believe him that I should just fucking go."

The owner of the conversation doesn't stop or blink an eyelid at the two of us in here pressed together against the counter, my semi doing nothing to negate the sexual tension crackling through the air that they clearly didn't notice as they close the bathroom stall, locking it and continuing to discuss their relationship, loudly.

"I guess we should…" I whisper, my lips brushing the shell of her ear before pulling back, adjusting myself and making my way out of the bathroom, leaving her to do whatever the hell it was she needed to do. Take stock. Have a minute. I *could do with one of those myself right now.*

# TEN

## Ivy

"It's about time you made it back," Tamsin calls, her head peeking up above the back of the sofa long enough to acknowledge my arrival. "We've been waiting for you."

"Looks like you've been sat around nursing a glass of wine to me, but whatever." I brush her off as I come around the corner and swiftly exit to our bedroom. Whatever they've been waiting on me for will hang on for just two more minutes, I'm sure.

My head is still reeling from the altercation with Nick, his musky cologne swirling around my brain and making everything else fuzzy. *That infuriating dickhead.* Not only does he make me madder than I could even possibly consider myself to get, but then he goes and soothes it with that tone, that growl, the offer of a pleasure you know is going to be oh-so-good.

We took our coffee to go, the attendant already making preparations by the time I'd finally pulled myself together enough to get back out there and face him. *The presumptuous little shit.* Not that I'm complaining. The drive back was electrified, stuck somewhere between overwhelming annoyance and pure lust, and neither of us could seem to manage the right words to bridge the gap.

He dropped me at the car. I thanked him for the coffee. And he left. Then I climbed in my own and swore profusely.

I'm such a joke.

I wanted details, details he didn't have, and then I gave him shit about it. I wanted them. Needed them.

I'm here for a reason, I can see it, feel it, but not understand it. And it's infuriating.

The answers are just a taste away, practically on his tongue.

The tongue that was in my mouth.

And it was good. So fucking good.

"Oh, girl, you've got it bad," Tamsin sing-songs as she comes in, placing a glass of wine on the bedside table.

"Uh, no I don't," I argue, already worrying how much she saw on my face just seconds ago.

"Of course not." She smiles, not believing a single word out of my mouth. "So, come on, spill. Who was it?"

"Who was what?"

"Who did you go for coffee with?" she asks, sipping her wine and dropping onto one of the chairs by the window. "Because I know for a fact it wasn't Jacob."

"And how do you know that?" I ask on an exhale, grabbing the glass and taking a healthy swig.

"There's this new technology, you've probably heard of it, they're called *mobile phones*. You can literally get in touch with anyone anywhere, providing you have their number." She laughs at her own joke, waving her phone at me.

"Taylor," I deduce, not aware they'd swapped numbers as well as bodily fluids last night.

"And Leo was with him, so don't hold out on me. Who's the new mystery guy?"

"No mystery guy, you've met him." *You just didn't realise it at the time. None of us did.*

"Please, for the love of all that is holy, do *not* tell me you let Spencer take you out." She groans, rolling her eyes back in disgust.

"That's a hard pass," I reply. "But it turns out that particular dick is in my advanced bio class, which means I'm gonna be stuck with him the entire time we're here. On the plus side, so is Leo." I grin, thinking about Spencer falling over himself to get away from him. It falls away just as quickly when I remember the very real plea in his voice as he asked me to stay away from him.

"You knew he would be though..."

"Really?"

"After all the time and effort your mother went to, to get the two of you together, and then your father demanding you come here... If you think there was any chance he wasn't going to appear at some point, you're delusional."

"Yeah, maybe."

"No maybe about it, chick. So, come on, mystery guy..."

"Oh, I went with Nick," I brush off. "Apparently, Nick and Jacob are twins and I've been managing to mix them up... that didn't go down so well."

"Really?" she asks, her interest showing. "Twins. Now

that could make for a fun time. How did neither of us notice that last night? Surely having both of them in the room should have been easy to see… no?"

"You'd think." I laugh, thinking about how much it makes sense and how completely oblivious I've been. "Anyway, I think Jacob's forgiven me for the mishap, Nick maybe not."

"No?" she asks, settling in for the details.

"It doesn't matter. What were you waiting on me for?" I ask, diverting the attention. She raises her eyebrows, noting the change of conversation. "And what have you been texting Taylor about anyway?"

"Nice try." She chuckles. "Don't think I'll forget you didn't spill the tea, but I'm way too interested in what's inside these boxes. Come on."

"Boxes?"

With a roll of her eyes, she hands me the glass of wine and drags me back out into the main room.

Calls of, "Finally," and, "I can't believe we actually waited this whole time," ring out as the girls all gather around the dining table excitedly. There's a large dress box placed at six of the place settings, a single red rose and inlaid card abandoned in the middle of the table.

"It says we have to open them together," Penelope explains as I reach for the card. "Otherwise we'd have just opened them."

They all stand in front of the ones with their names on, mine left for me as they look from me to each other before tearing the lids off and ripping the black paper apart. I'm still peeling the paper back as they pull masquerade masks out, each one slightly different than the last. As I part the papers, dark blue lace comes into view, feathers curling at the edges of the mask as a corset-style lace crosses over the bridge of the nose.

I'm still taking in all the tiny details as cocktail dresses glitter and glimmer, the girls lifting them from the boxes with a gasp. Emerald green, ruby red, black as the night, black lace cascading over a nude base, black with silver detailing, and then mine, a deep blue plush velvet. The off-the-shoulder dress has a small cut out at the bust and is a mermaid fit, crystals scattered across the collar line and down the front, so it looks like a night sky. The silver clutch and matching heels show the attention to detail that's been taken, the consideration for all the little things.

Not just a covering, not only a dress, these have been chosen with each of us in mind. The darker green twirled through the length of the skirt matches Charlotte's skin tone much better than the ones in any of the other dresses. And yet, I can't help the unease that swirls in my gut.

Someone picked these out for us, individually. My shoe size is correct, no doubt the dress will fit like a second skin, and these have been delivered to the house, much like the invitation that came the other day, without us noticing.

Someone is coming and going in a locked space, somewhere that's supposed to be a haven, our home away from home, unannounced and unnoticed. But to what end? To bring pretty stationary and expensive gowns? No, there's more to this, there has to be.

"Aren't these a little dressy?" I ask, looking at Tamsin. "Didn't that flyer suggest an informal gathering of the masses to you?"

Obviously, the dresses are gorgeous and I don't need much of an excuse to throw on a pair of heels and a beautiful gown, but not if it's a casual event. There is such a thing as being overdressed and it is *not* a good moment to find yourself in.

"Who cares?" Penelope scoffs. "The card says these are for Friday, that the cars will be here to collect us at seven sharp and we're to be ready. If everyone else turns up in jeans and trainers, let them."

The rest of the girls agree with her, comparing gowns and heels as they disappear excitedly to try them on. Without any further thought, Tamsin grabs my box and hers, disappearing into our room as I trail behind, a gnawing in my stomach and the card in my hand. "Grab the wine," she calls.

Sliding the card under my arm, I top up both glasses before following her into our room, the animated sounds of the rest of the girls in their rooms an uneasy background that I close out with the click of the door.

Her dress is halfway up her body by the time I've got the wine on the desk and she pulls her hair to the side for me to draw the zip up. Yes, it fits her perfectly. The midnight dress isn't as dark as I originally imagined, silver rivulets cascading delicately through the brocade, a thigh-high slit giving it all the sass you could imagine the eldest daughter of an international diplomat might have.

The red bottom heels, black clutch and mask finish the outfit impeccably. The attention to detail is as impressive as it is concerning, that same embossed logo running beneath my fingers on the card as I take in all her glory. She's radiant, my best friend, and despite my reservations, I can't help the smile that covers my face.

"There's something wrong with you if you don't put that dress on right now," she comments, turning in the mirror to check out her ass. "It's going to look fantastic."

Throwing the card down, I cross the room, peeking through the black paper to the dress in the box. It's a matter of minutes to discard the concerns of the day, along with my trousers and blouse, leaving it all laid on the back of the chair as I step into how our weekend is going to begin.

I allow myself just a minute of hesitation before falling headfirst into the enthusiasm that courses through the house. There's only so much you can second guess everything before you have to give in and just enjoy the moment. Yes, there might be an ulterior motive for this, but that's not the dress' fault, and it certainly isn't hiding any answers.

"I'll have my manicurist come on Thursday," Aimee says, the sound carrying from the living room.

"My makeup artist is only an hour away and I don't trust anyone else to do that," Tamsin adds, opening the door and joining everyone else as I follow. "Except for maybe Ivy…"

"Call Mads," I reply. "See if her assistant can come, and between them, they could do everyone."

"Ooh, good plan," Stephanie says. "I'll find out if my stylist can bring her assistants for our hair too. What a totally fun girlie afternoon we could have!"

There are better things I could think to be doing with my time, but just for the minute, why not lean into it? Let the worry and the concern go and stop seeing things that might not be there.

That conversation with my father jaded my outlook, it made me start to question everything, things I would have accepted and not thought twice about I'm now second-guessing and falling over myself to figure out.

There doesn't have to be a reason for everything. Sometimes, things just… are.

"Right, get those gowns hung or boxed, ladies, I think it's about time we got to know each other a little better." Charlotte smiles, grabbing another bottle of Prosecco from the fridge. "Loungewear on, film to choose, it's truth or dare time."

And that's how the next few evenings go.

We spend time together. We laugh. We joke. We find out the good things about each other, and some of the not so spoken about things. We learn to start to trust each other a little more than we did before. So, when the engines rumble outside and the bell goes at exactly seven o'clock on Friday night, the anticipation that tumbles around the room is electrified.

Two black SUVs are waiting for us, engines idling as we're directed to the back. I climb in with Tamsin and Penelope, Aimee, Charlotte and Stephanie getting into the lead car as we lock up and pull away.

"Erm, isn't the party at the house?" I ask as we drive straight past it and head down the driveway. "Come to think of it, weren't people supposed to arrive from half seven… so, where the hell are we going?"

"Maybe you misread it?" Penelope offers as she looks

out the window nervously.

The door locks engage with an ominous click as the driver calmly explains, "There's a meeting before the event, ladies. Nothing to be worried about."

Yeah, because isn't that what all serial killers say? *Nothing to worry about…*

Tamsin and I share a look, this is not what either of us had in mind. This is supposed to be a fun night out, not an awkward drive to God knows where in the dark. But we don't have time to contemplate the upcoming change of direction as we're swiftly pulling down a dark lane not ten minutes later, following the tail lights of the other car. *Well, at least we're going out together.*

We pull into the car park of some old huge building, a church of some kind. It would look ancient and dilapidated if it weren't for the lights on inside and the group of people standing at the side of the building. As we climb out and the car doors close, they stand to attention, one on either side of the door and one coming to meet us.

Charlotte's giddy giggle echoes around the empty space, and for the briefest second, I wish I'd dropped a pin in the location on my phone whilst we were in the car, it would be way too obvious to do it now.

The six of us huddle together against the chilly evening air, lifting our skirts to keep the trains from landing in the dirt.

"Good evening, Angels," a man calls to us from the middle of the car park, gesturing for us to join him. He's shrouded in darkness, tall and wearing a black mask, something glittering down one side. My steps falter and

Stephanie titters, clearly amused by the interesting turn of the evening. "Thank you for joining us, you all look beautiful. They're almost ready for you."

Masks.

Us.

They.

The excited anticipation of the afternoon twists in my stomach, unease creeping back in, morphing through anxiety and into fear. *We shouldn't have come here.*

This isn't a party venue.

No music blasts through the building, and as he leads us to the doorway, the heavy wood being pushed open worryingly quietly, I hesitate. But there's nowhere to go. A graveyard archway stands to one side of the building, nothing but trees on the other, and as I take a peek over my shoulder, the two drivers are following us, now wearing simple black masks matching the two beside the door.

There's nowhere to go, except onwards.

Attempting to push down the panic does nothing to quell the unease that seeps through every pore. Tamsin takes my hand in hers as we enter the building, the sound of voices not far ahead of us as we make our way down a cold damp corridor and through a vestibule before entering the main church building.

Our guide pauses in the doorway, holding us in the darkness with the security behind us for just a few breaths before announcing us and entering. The light is blinding as we step into the main church. Almost sightlessly, we follow him to a patch of carpet covering the engraved stones on the floor, attempting to give my eyes chance to adjust to the light.

I want to look around, to put off the inevitable, I want to absorb every nook and cranny of this place before I can finally take in whatever we've found ourselves in the middle of. Something with men in robes and masks. Nothing good.

But all too soon, someone is clearing their voice in front of us. A man. Another man in a mask and a robe. "Well, ladies, that is perfect timing. Thank you so much for joining us." I'd like to think he smiles, the voice familiar but I can't seem to place it. "The Angels of Pendleton Prep, let me introduce you to The Devils."

He steps back, waving his arms open as my gaze lands on almost a dozen men suited and booted, black masks covering their faces with red, silver or gold veins threaded through them. The hair on the back of my neck raises as I turn my head, a crowd of robed people loitering where the congregation would once have been.

Some are disinterested, gathered in small groups paying little to no attention to what transpires on the stage, but there are plenty front and centre. Here for the show. Whatever that might be.

Stephanie shivers with excitement beside me, her excited anticipation a far cry from where my head's at right now. There's no way we'd make it out of here if we needed to. No, we'd die here if that's what was decided.

"I'll keep this quick," the compare continues, as our guide disappears into the waiting crowd. "I don't want to make you late for your own event." *Yeah, because this sure as hell isn't it.* "The Angels and The Devils of Pendleton prep are the elite, the cream of the crop, so to speak. But then, that's no surprise really, is it? You, ladies and gentlemen, are going to make history."

He pauses, taking a drink from his glass before perching it on the altar and looking our way. "So, now you've officially been introduced, let's get you paired up for the evening, shall we? There's a little disparity between the numbers at the moment, but I'm sure that will be dealt with shortly."

The words fall ominously from behind the blank mask, the robes he wears not helping to ease any of the anxiety rushing through my body. *What the hell have we found ourselves involved in?*

"You get a choice here, ladies. You should take it whilst you can," he says.

There are a million things I want to know before I make any such decision. What is the expectation here? Is this a date, a relationship, a team that we're becoming? Or is this just a night out with a nameless, faceless man in an impeccably tailored suit?

I'm not the only one that looks them over with as much trepidation as interest, but when I notice the ink peeking over his collar, I manage to pick Taylor out pretty easily, all things considered, and some of the concern I had tumbles from me. There might be a whole lot of dramatics involved, but this is just the guys from the house; Taylor, Nick, Jacob, Leo and Emmerson, amongst others.

Before any of us have a chance to do or say anything, one of them steps forward, a gold slash running from left to right across the black-as-night mask covering his face. He holds his hand out in my direction and demands, "Ivy." I recognise the tone and inflexion immediately, his proximity in that coffee shop bathroom flashing hot under my skin. "And Jacob."

My feet are moving towards him without thought, the same way Jacob's are when the compare's words stop us mid-stride. "Let's stick with roommates for now, shall we? So, Nick, if you're requesting Ivy, then, Wyatt, you're up."

Tension ripples across Nick's shoulders as Jacob steps back into their lineup and whoever this other guy is joins Nick. The two of them arrive either side of me and my arms thread through theirs silently as they turn me towards the audience fully.

Any resemblance to a church is merely the building itself, the pews that probably once resided here stripped long ago. Most of the old stained glass is boarded over or covered up, small amounts of the night sky peeking through the odd broken square or triangle.

I'm distracted from the task of categorising the minutiae of the ancient building as Taylor's voice booms from behind me. "Well, if that's how we're playing this, Tamsin."

Her excited squeal echoes down the two small steps and across the room, the bodies parting to allow us passage as we head for the main doors at the far end.

"Jasper," the compare adds. I guess, making sure everyone knows who everyone is as we're paired off and sent away. Where to and what for, who knows?

# ELEVEN

## Nick

Irritation bristles as Wyatt opens the back door of his Guilia, waiting for her to climb in before closing it. "I'll drive," he adds.

I can only imagine the bemused look on his face, because it's hidden by the mask. I got the girl I wanted, though she's likely less than impressed about it, but I don't have Jake. You win one, you lose one.

I thought I'd died and gone to heaven when she strutted through that doorway, the plush fabric hugging her every curve, the jewels at her throat accentuating the gentle slope of her shoulders and the column of her neck.

For the first time, her hair is tied up, pulled and twisted in some intricate thing that probably took hours to do. And yet, all I could think of was pulling it free and running my fingers through it, wrapping my hand around the delicate skin of her throat and reminding her just how hot she gets when she gives up that control.

The engine rumbles beneath us as I loiter with one foot in the car and one on the tarmac, Jasper, Taylor and Tamsin exiting the church laughing. They're already making her more at ease than we are, and it's about to get worse. Sliding the black velvet bag from the seat pocket, I finger the silicone-wrapped steel before pulling it out and dropping it in her lap, climbing in to fasten my seatbelt before Wyatt peels out of the car park and heads back to campus.

"What the hell is this?" she asks, holding the belt up, hung over one finger, a very unimpressed look on her face. She eyes the item warily, and so she should.

"Insurance."

"And what on earth do you expect me to do with it?"

"That is a chastity belt."

She flicks it on the seat between us with disgust, wiping her finger on the leather before looking out the window. *I knew she'd do this.*

Just because we knew what was happening tonight, doesn't mean they did. And if the confusion that crossed her beautiful features after the lights wore off is anything to go by, they had no warning at all.

"We're going to a frat party full of drunken teenagers high on freedom, and anything else they can find. You're an Angel, so that should provide some amount of protection, but I'm not willing to risk it. Put it on."

It's not just the house full of strangers that has me on high alert, she's been getting close with Leo and I don't trust him as far as I can throw him, I imagine the feeling is mutual. There was also nothing said about the Angels being ours, now, forever, or at any other point, so I'm sure as hell going to make sure he gets nowhere near that sweet pussy. *She's mine.*

"No."

She doesn't even turn, crossing her arms over her chest

in defiance, pushing those tits higher than they already were and making my mouth water. What I wouldn't give to wrap a tongue around one of those nipples right now, sliding the belt up her thighs willingly. *Yeah, I knew that wasn't how tonight would go.* Wyatt catches my gaze in the mirror, shrugging his shoulders.

"It wasn't a request." The words tumble out on a growl and the atmosphere in the back of the car changes, a hint of the lust I saw on her face the other day breaking free.

"It's a no-go," she replies, turning to finally give me her full attention. Not that I haven't had it this entire time. "Panty lines." She smirks, thinking she's won this round. *Like I give a fuck.*

The flush that creeps over her exposed collarbone is unexpected but hot as hell, as is the breathy way her argument falls from her.

"And how did you get around that one, Ivy?" The air between us crackles and sparks, the tension a physical living breathing thing. Her only response is a single raised eyebrow, and that almost takes my breath away. "Are you seriously sitting two feet away from me right now with no underwear on?"

Her embarrassed smile is the only answer I get as the seconds tick by. "We're two minutes out, bro," Wyatt adds from the front, only adding to the melting pot we're trapped in.

"You're not going in there naked," I warn.

"I'm fully clothed," she counters.

Although the arch of my eyebrow makes it clear that *fully* in that sentence isn't exactly the case.

"Make me."

She throws the challenge down between us, pressing her thighs together, hopefully in anticipation, if the way her breathing picks up is anything to go by.

"You don't think I will?" I ask, unclipping both seatbelts and picking the discreet but sturdy belt from the seat. Her eyes widen as her breath hitches, her interest clearly piqued. "Come here."

With a thick swallow, she shuffles her ass around slightly, the dress not allowing for a great deal of access. She shivers as I grip her ankle, goosebumps breaking out beneath my touch as I slide one foot and then the other into the thin straps before pushing it roughly up the inside of her dress. The first time I get up close and personal with her it isn't going to be in the back of a car with my roommate driving.

I stop at her knees, gesturing with a nod for her to get it in position. I'll do it, if I have to, but part of me wants her to want this, to hand over the control willingly. Because I know it's got her as hot as I am hard right now.

She sighs and rolls her eyes, but she pulls the belt up, settling the silicone-wrapped steel over her hips, the cool metal covering her pussy making her gasp. "Happy?" she sasses.

That beligerant acquiescence doesn't get her anywhere as I yank on her thighs, pulling her down to me and pushing the dress up to get my first glimpse of her locked up and only available to me. My dick throbs at just the sight of her like this, draped over my lap in the dark.

Pulling the sides together and sliding the lock through, I

make sure it's tight enough for her to feel, the lock glinting in the light of the campus as we turn down the driveway to the house. Her gasp as I close it is almost too much to take.

"What about when I need the bathroom?" she asks huskily, quiet enough for Wyatt not to hear.

"Better stay nearby then, huh?"

It doesn't need unlocking for her to go, but she doesn't need to know that just yet. No, it's better to keep her close.

"Masks stay on, everything else is optional," Wyatt reminds me as we pull into the garage, her legs still splayed over mine, her pussy nothing more than inches away from my already hard cock. "The rest shouldn't be far behind."

Neither of us move, our breaths coming rapidly as my hand wraps around her delicate throat. The two of us are trapped in something else, something a million miles away from the conversation Wyatt is having with us, something that's just ours. She raises her chin as I adjust my fingers, heat flaring in her eyes as I press my weight against her, my hard-on more than obvious.

I'd put money on the fact that she's wet already, the metal warming against her heat.

"Just remember this moment, sugar. You're the one sprawled out half-naked with my hand wrapped around your throat and your wet cunt locked up tightly. I'm the one in control here."

I can feel her swallow, her legs tightening on either side of me as she attempts to close them. Wyatt taps the roof of the car twice, apparently he got out and neither of us noticed, too wrapped up in the way she feels beneath me. "And I like your hair down better than whatever this is."

Peeling myself off her is significantly harder than I imagine it would be as I pocket the keys and open the door behind me. The garage door is less than half closed before it starts to open again, Taylor's Range Rover appearing just seconds later as Ivy climbs from the back of the car.

"Was that really necessary?" Wyatt asks quietly as we watch Jasper help Tamsin from the back of the car.

"O.M.G, what happened to your hair?" Tamsin gasps, looking at the less-than-perfect style Ivy's now rocking. I smirk as Ivy blushes, her hand reaching up self-consciously as she feels the damage done in the back seat. "Let me see what I can do."

Ivy turns, her gaze locking with mine as her friend fusses around, attempting to fix some of the mess we created. I can't help but smirk at the blush that covers her cheeks or the knowing arch of her friend's eyebrow.

"Are we waiting for the others?" Jasper asks, his hand already on the handle.

"No, let's get these ladies a drink," Wyatt decides. "At least one of them has already earned it," he adds quietly, waiting for Tamsin and Ivy to finish up before guiding them through to the main entrance, the music already spilling through from the house.

The guests have littered themselves comfortably throughout the house already, more than one confused and intrigued look being sent our way as the six of us make our way to the kitchen. The island is covered in trays of canapes, with more than one person pottering around and making drinks as someone hands Tamsin and Ivy champagne.

Wyatt grabs a fistful of beers from a fridge, pops the

tops and hands them out. "Well then, ladies. Welcome to our house," he declares, opening his arms wide and turning in a circle.

"It's bigger than ours," Tamsin comments as she plucks some tiny food morsel from a tray. "But then, I guess there are more of you living here, so that makes sense."

I try to take it in as they're seeing it, tile floors and marble counters, shaker cupboards and brass handles. It's like a farmhouse kitchen with a very expensive makeover. It's not somewhere I've spent a lot of time this week, but then cooking isn't really my thing.

"So, what's the expectation here?" Ivy asks, ignoring the small talk and cutting right to it.

"You're just our date for the evening," Wyatt explains gently. "Despite how that came across on the journey over here. Our resident caveman isn't great with explanations, apparently."

"On the contrary, I think I explained myself more than clearly," I grumble, the rest of the group starting to pick up on the tension as Tamsin looks between the three of us. "So, now that you've got a drink, how about we give you the grand tour?" I ask, attempting to divert the attention to something else.

"Yeah, do you want to come and see my bedroom?" Taylor asks with a wiggle of his eyebrows. "There's *plenty* I can show you up there."

"Unless Jasper is joining you, I think that's off the cards, my friend," Wyatt says with a chuckle, tipping his beer back.

"I mean, I'm not—" Taylor starts, but Ivy cuts him off

before he even has the chance to finish the thought. "Not happening, Taylor."

Tamsin is decidedly quiet between them, and for half a second, it looks like she's considering it, her gaze flicking up and down Jasper with interest. "Not tonight," she decides with the tiniest hint of a blush.

The entire conversation is forgotten as everyone else arrives, the expansive kitchen being swallowed up with the other nine people in our party.

"I'm never going to remember who's who," one of the girls says with a giggle, looking from one black mask to another.

We're all in black suits, and aside from the markings being in slightly altered places and different colours, the masks are almost identical too. I guess it would be tricky to tell who is who. I'm the only person with the keys, so at the very least, Ivy needs to be able to tell me from everyone else.

"Okay, how about this? Jasper, roll up your sleeves. Taylor and Jasper are easy to tell, they've both got visible ink, so that's Tamsin sorted out," I explain.

"Olly, if you go grab a red pocket square for me, that could be our tell for Stephanie," Jacob adds with a nod.

"And you can take one of these," Wyatt says, offering me one of the thousand shell bracelets that line his wrist. "That way Ivy will be able to pick us out."

"Leo has those gorgeous blue eyes," the girl in the red dress declares. "And George is in a cast, so that's easy enough." She sniggers.

Emmerson grabs a bandage from the closest first aid kit,

wrapping it around his thigh in solidarity with George.

"Does that work for everyone?" I ask. Not that Ivy will be leaving my line of sight, but better safe than sorry. Various agreements ring out from the group as Oliver reappears, tucking a red handkerchief into my brother's top pocket. "Right then, let's introduce this rabble to The Devils and The Angels of Pendleton Prep."

Leo links his arm with one of the girls and heads out into the hallway, clapping his hands together loudly. For some reason, that's enough to get people's attention, and as more of them filter from the other rooms, the rest of us join him, with the main doors at our backs. The music cuts off, the DJ informing those who missed Leo's subtle call to gather where they're supposed to be.

"Good evening, everyone." He starts this off like he's some kind of leader, the gathered rabble hanging off his every word as they look at the fifteen of us dressed to impress. "Thank you for joining us tonight. Let me take this opportunity to officially introduce you to The Angels of Pendleton Prep."

Whoever the girl is with him gives a little twirl, the black lace spinning out around her feet as the rest of the girls shuffle together and awkwardly follow suit.

"We are the Devils of Pendleton Prep, and anyone who wants to get to these girls does it through us," Taylor declares, pulling Tamsin into his side roughly. Not just marking her off-limits, but all of them. I can't argue with the sentiment, but the interested looks that flicker around irk.

"Let's get to know each other a little better," Emmerson continues. "The Devils hid some tokens around the house earlier today." He flicks one to a random guy loitering nearby. "Find them and meet us out at the pool."

"They're only on the ground floor," Taylor adds. "Upstairs is off-limits too." Like he wasn't just offering to take Tamsin up there.

The token is passed from one person to another, people gathering around excitedly for a peek before they disappear, scurrying to find the rest. Wyatt slides up behind Ivy, his hand landing on her lower back as he points out the different rooms, guiding her through the house and out to the back deck.

Despite the shitty weather earlier this week, it's finally eased, the late summer warmth taking the edge off the most recent autumnal chill. My jaw clenches unintentionally as I watch his proximity to her. He's more than aware she's mine, he was in the car after all, and yet he whispers in her ear before she turns my way with a smile. *Why can't I get her to do that?*

"Smile, brother," Jacob intervenes, blocking my line of sight. "This is supposed to be a party and you look kike you're about to rip his arm off and beat him to death with it." I imagine the words tumbling from him with a smile, something the two of us have become adept at doing. He nods politely at someone as they pass us, a far cry from the tone of the conversation we're having.

"Interesting thought, I might just run with it."

"I think the idea of pairing us with our roommates was to avoid the death and destruction that comes alongside jealous tantrums, don't you?"

"Sure," I reply with a roll of my eyes, dropping it.

"See you out there." Stalking away earns me nothing but a chuckle that follows me out into the evening air. Jasper is already topping up the girl's glasses as Leo gets them comfortable on their viewing platform.

"So, what are the tokens for?" one of the girls asks, a creamy thigh sliding between the split layers of her midnight black dress as she sits.

"The tokens earn them the opportunity to take part in a game," Oliver says as he passes the doorway I quietly loiter beside. "Truth or dare."

"Really?" she replies with a scoff. "What are we, thirteen?"

"It's actually a truth and a dare," Jasper corrects. "Angel's choice. One for your Devil and one for the person bringing the token."

Ivy adjusts her legs as she sits, crossing one over the other and then swapping. I smirk as her gaze flicks to mine, pressing her thighs together before she tucks her feet to one side.

"Ooh," Tamsin says, rubbing her hands together with glee. "There are plenty of things I could think to have *my* devil do."

Yeah, I bet there are.

I flick the radiant heat panels on, the gentle glow enough to keep the edge off as the six of them settle in together, whispering ideas whilst everyone else searches the house.

People-watching isn't my usual forte, I tend to be in the thick of it, being and doing, but pressing myself back into the darkness, the rough bark of a tree makes a welcome change of pace. The party continues, excited squeals breaking free over the now slightly muted music as the boys laugh and joke by the side of the pool.

*The spiky bristles pinch into the back of my arm, but I don't move. If I do, he'll find me. And I can't be found first, that'd make me a loser. The first loser. The biggest loser. And I might be small, but I'm not a loser, and I can't care what he says.* Brothers are stupid anyway.

*A couple pass, their hands wrapped together as they laugh and whisper, looking over their shoulders before making a run for it and heading further into the gardens. They're big, the gardens, with two different play areas and a lake we get to canoe in during the warmer months. Andrew practices water polo and rowing in there, but he hates it and says I will too one day. It looks fun though.*

*The longer I stay pressed in the bush, the less convinced I become that anyone's coming to find me. A spider creeps along the back of my knee, making it jerk as I flick it away with a shiver.* Creepy creatures. *It's not exactly hide and seek if no one comes to find you, is it? But if I go and find them, then I don't win either.*

*Indecision swirls in my gut.*

*I'm close enough to the party to hear the grown-ups laughing, their chatter mingling into an altogether too loud mass of indeterminable noise, but far enough away to not be picked out. It seemed like the perfect spot. Maybe too perfect if nobody can find me.*

*It's the giggling that first catches my attention, her raven hair swinging as she rushes past, her pink dress blowing in the light breeze. Much like the couple, she checks over her shoulder before venturing further, and something about her garners my interest.*

*I don't know who she is, this raven-haired girl. Not that that's unusual at one of these things, there are lots of people here I don't know, but as she presses away from the house, I follow. She's small, smaller than me, and alone. She doesn't know this garden, what if she finds that other couple and gets in trouble? It would be her word against theirs, and nobody ever believes a child, do they?*

*Although, there's something about the confident way she carries herself, her head held high as she looks from flower bush to hedgerow, through the rose garden and into the corridor of cherry blossom that makes me think the adults would listen to her, they'd believe her.*

*No, nobody would call this girl a loser. First, last, or any other kind. She doesn't see me as I sneak along behind her, creeping from one tree to another as I keep just enough of an eye on her to be sure she is well and truly lost.*

*She circles the rose garden twice, coming at it from a different direction as her frustrations grow by the second. The game of hide and seek is completely forgotten as she stamps her feet before dropping onto an old wooden bench, tucking her feet up and crying.*

*She doesn't bawl and sob like any other eight-year-old I know. She doesn't scream and cry and shout for someone to come and find her, to help her. No, she sits quietly, tears tracking down her cute little face when delicately she says, "Are you going to help me, or what?"*

*So much for being stealthy, I guess.*

*"I thought you were doing just fine by yourself." I shrug, stepping out from behind the tree, scratching at an*

*itch from the ivy I jumped in not five minutes ago.*

*"You'll want to get some cream on that," she comments, her gaze flicking to the raised angry rash covering my arm and spreading. "I can just follow you back."*

*"I don't, it'll be fine," I argue, not really sure why I'm arguing. She's right, it burns, but it's been fun, following her through the gardens in the quiet. Her getting lost, and me being found.*

*I'm not ready to go back to the party. To the rooms full of people, the noise, and everyone in my space. I can do it, usually, put on a face, smile and be happy. Be the twins that nobody can tell apart. It's just a thing we do.*

*And sometimes there are benefits to that. Letting Jacob take the maths test I didn't want to do and me getting to do his drum lessons for those couple of weeks whilst he got four levels on his latest game. Nobody notices, nobody cares. But she did.*

*Just for half an hour walking around an unfamiliar garden, she saw me. She saw me and she let me. Only waiting until the moment she thought she needed me before calling me out on it.*

*"Maybe I don't know the way back either," I offer. "Maybe I'm just a guest here too."*

*She narrows her eyes in my direction, weighing my words for their truth as I cross the path to her, sitting down on the bench beside her with a sigh.*

*"Who are you hiding from?" she asks.*

*And isn't that the question of the year.*

# TWELVE

*Ivy*

"**H**ow do you want to play this?" Charlotte asks. "Because I'm totally up for seeing what stupid things we can get them to do."

"Anything that gets that suit off Taylor's body is a win in my book," Tamsin agrees with a nod.

"Come on, ladies, think bigger than that. This is an opportunity to get some serious dirt on them," I whisper, attempting to lean in closer, the metal pressing against me as another reminder that, once again, I'm not my own woman.

It's not uncomfortable, per say. It doesn't dig in or chafe, yet. But just the thought of being locked up and held at someone else's whim is demeaning and disgusting, and unfortunately turning me on just a little. The heat in his stare as he closed that lock, and the way he licked along his bottom lip had me thinking about his tongue in other places, places his hands were very fucking close to.

"What on earth do we want dirt for?" Penelope asks, jolting me out of my lust-induced haze. "When we can get them naked and wet and covered in all sorts of disgusting things."

"Exactly," Charlotte agrees. "We can get them drunk on dirty pints and do whatever we want."

Does nobody else see this for the game it really is?

They marched us in here like the prized ponies we are. All dressed up and paraded around the ring, shown off to the commoners who were warned well away from us. Tamsin might think it's cute, from the man she wants to fuck right now, but in two weeks when she's bored or he's done, she's not going to feel the same.

Then she's going to be pissed the hell off, just like I am.

*"Anyone who wants to get to these girls does it through us."*

They've got to be having a fucking laugh.

But the more that happens tonight, the more we get to see behind the curtains, metaphorically speaking, and the more I'm one hundred per cent sure us being here is intentional.

Tamsin and I being in that house rather than standard accommodation was not a lucky accident, not an *upgrade* that my father has paid for. Not in the traditional sense anyway. This might be an upgrade that *we* pay for, in one way or another.

The Angels of Pendleton Prep. The Elite.

There's something more going on here and I'm determined to find out what it is and why we've found ourselves in the middle of it. It's by design, I'm sure.

And they know, they must do.

These men parade around in expensive suits and hide their identities. Not that we don't know who they are, but still… it's all just a game to them. One they know the rules to and we don't.

"Well then, Angels, I hope you've had the chance to think up your first few ideas, because Jessica, here, has a token." The red pocket square means it's Oliver, the voice clearly not Jacob, as he places his hands on the girl's shoulders, making her jump in anticipation.

Stephanie smiles as we all look at her expectantly, waiting for more people to filter from the house, no doubt. She likes an audience, and it appears she finally has one. Captive too. "So, Angel's choice, a truth and a dare, right?"

"That's right," Jacob confirms, pressing through the throng of bodies to join Oliver and Jessica.

"Okay," she ponders, rubbing her hands together. "Let's start the guys off with something easy, a truth. And because it's easy, you should totally both answer." They shrug their agreement as she stalls, drumming her fingers together. "A truth, a truth, a truth. Okay, I've got it. If you could only hear one song for the rest of your life, what would it be?"

With a sigh, I lean back in the chair. Not where I was hoping we'd be going with this. But as I look around, everyone is entranced, egging the boys on and calling out all sorts of ridiculous options.

"That's a hard one," Jacob says. "Like maybe I could pick one genre, or artist, but one song... Wow. That's harsh. Now, you're not going to hold me to this after, right? I'm still going to be able to listen to other music after tonight is over, aren't I?"

I can almost picture the cheeky smile on his face, the dimple popping on one side of his cheek as his eyes twinkle mischievously. A couple of people laugh as Stephanie smiles and nods. "Of course."

"Then I think it would have to be *"Keep on Moving" by S Club 7.*" The group around him erupts into laughter, and I can't help the smile that breaks free as he calls everyone back to silence. "Hear me out now. Hear me out. It's got a good steady beat, you can dance to it if you want, and it's got a totally uplifting motto behind it. You're never getting depressed listening to that one."

He crosses his arms over his chest with a nod, clearly impressed with his answer, despite the amused jeering that comes his way. When Oliver announces *"Spice Up Your Life" by The Spice Girls*, I think everyone has clicked on just how serious these guys are taking their little game.

I can't imagine that joviality would stick if someone decided to try their luck with one of us though.

"That just leaves Jessica to do the dare then, I guess," Penelope adds with excitement, looking at Stephanie. "What did you have in mind?"

"Well, this could be a good moment for us to get to know Jessica a little better too," Stephanie says, taking a sip of her champagne as she looks down her nose at the petrified girl who looks like she's seriously reconsidering whether she should have handed this token in. *I don't blame her.* "Let's have a little show and tell… with the contents of your purse. Get it emptied and tell us all about it."

A shadow falls over me as someone leans down and whispers, "Fancy a walk?" in my ear. If I didn't know the voice already, the tattoo on the back of his hand as it rests against my arm would give him away; Leo.

With a shrug, I make my excuses to Tamsin and link

my arm through Leo's as he guides me down a couple of wooden stairs and around the edge of the pool. If Nick is anywhere to be seen, I can't find him, my gaze flicking over the groups of people gathered around the pedestal we were seated on. Because of course we were.

"I can't believe your house is just the other side of here," he comments. "You've been right under my nose the entire time."

"Yep," I agree with a small smile.

"You look a little stressed out. I just want you to know that I've spoken with Spencer, you won't have any more problems with him, and he won't be showing his face here tonight either, so you can relax and enjoy yourself."

"Know me that well, do you?"

"I don't need to," he replies, adjusting the back on one of the sun loungers before pressing me down onto it and taking my shoulders in hand. "I can see it all over your body language."

His skilful hands work along my shoulders, massaging into the sides of my neck in a blissful way that has my head rolling forwards whilst I do my best to not let a moan tumble from me. *Yeah, it feels that fucking good.*

"You're confused and scared, you can't sit still for all that fidgeting you're doing. You've barely looked at Nick since we arrived, and you're completely on edge," he rattles off, smoothing the words with the artful way he plies my body. "You just need to relax a little and enjoy the party. It's for you after all."

"It is?"

"Yes, your introduction to the world of the elite. Nobody

steps foot in Pendleton Prep without a huge chunk of money behind them, but money only gets you so far in life, Ivy. Some things have to be given, others taken."

The rough tenor of his voice elicits a response I wasn't expecting, heat pooling low in my belly as goosebumps break out down my arms. We're once again beside a pool, alone but not alone, a party going on around us as we slip into another world together. His breath caresses my neck, his lips must be barely inches from the shell of my ear as anticipation twirls around us, his hands continuing to work along my shoulders, building me up whilst simultaneously calming me down.

Nick was quick to lock me up, to think so little of his brother and housemates that they might take something that isn't theirs, or that I might offer something that isn't his to keep. There's power in his belt, not just for the man that holds the keys, but for the woman he's so afraid of slipping through his fingers.

It's the cough from behind us that breaks the spell, Leo's tongue swiping along the outside of my ear before he stands to his full height, turning to give whoever it is his full attention. "They need you for Truth and Dare," Nick says, the words innocuous enough, if it wasn't for the tone with which they're delivered.

"Remember what I said, Angel. You can relax now," Leo says before his hands disappear and his steps retreat across the pool and back to the cacophony of the party.

"That's two other men that have touched you tonight. That have whispered words in your ear and turned you on."

I could have guessed who it was just from Leo's reaction,

but the vague threat in his words annoys me almost as much as it turns me on.

"You're being ridiculous."

"I bet you're fucking soaked, again." His rough chuckle holds almost as much menace as it does amusement, but he's not wrong. With no fabric to soak up the evidence, my sticky arousal is obvious, to me anyway.

"I need the bathroom," I declare, not willing to give him anything. Least of all admit that he's right.

"Be my guest."

"The keys?" I ask, turning to look at him as I place my hand out.

It's hard to admit how good he looks in that suit as I press my lips together, standing from the lounger to take him in. I never understood waistcoats on people like Spencer—tall, angular, slender—but that taper against the offset of his broad shoulders is enough to make any woman think twice about walking past and sliding her hands across the hard expanse of his chest.

His dark chuckle caresses my skin before he shakes his head and turns, making his way back to the house. People part like the Red Sea as he approaches, one hand thrust in his pocket, the other still nursing the beer I haven't seen him drink as I wave at Tamsin, letting her know where I'm headed.

The music in the house is muted, background noise for the people in there laughing and getting to know each other, the copious amounts of free booze clearly doing their job. Just when I think there must be toilets by the entrance, Nick turns and heads upstairs, the plush carpet eating any sound as he goes.

It's not quite what I had in mind, but I'm here now, committed, and a bathroom break whilst it's an option really wouldn't be a bad idea. Who knows when and where he might disappear again? I follow him up the stairs silently, down a corridor and through a heavy wood door as he holds it open for me.

But it's not the bathroom I expected, it's their bedroom. His oaky cologne fills the space, except it's mingled with the fresh salty smell of Wyatt's. *What an interesting combination*. The rough and the smooth, the demanding and the easy-going, the one who offers and the one who takes.

"The bathroom is through there," he states, gesturing to the door opposite as he pulls out a chair, popping the button on his dress shirt as he drops into it.

"Keys?" I ask again, holding my hand out impatiently and reminding myself not to leave this to the last minute. If he's going to drag out every last second of control that he can, I better not leave this until I'm doing a little dance.

"Not required." My mouth pops open to speak, but before I can argue the point, he continues. "If you'd taken the time to look at the belt I bought for you before discarding it like trash, you'd have noticed there's access for waste to flow through. You don't need to take it off to relieve yourself in that manner."

"That's disgusting. What about being clean? And dry. Surely that can't be done through this damned contraption," I bluster.

It's been on for a while now, but it feels tighter and more restricting than it did. The way he pulled it all together before locking it flashes in front of me. It was hot. It did turn me on. But spending the rest of the night walking around in the remnants of my own pee does not sound like fun.

His hand flicks and I catch the keys carefully in my outstretched hand. Without another word, I storm into the bathroom, flicking the flimsy lock before pulling up my skirt and unclipping the confounded thing, dropping it onto the counter.

Relieving myself and washing my hands takes just a few moments, but as I warily eye the belt beside me, I can't help but take notice. He bought this for me, like some kind of gift, and spent an amount of time considering my needs before ordering or buying or whatever.

I turn the straps over in my hands, hard but smooth, cooled from the counter, but I know first-hand how quickly they warm to the touch. It's solid and yet delicate, the sieve-like structure that sits between my legs clearly intended for its obvious purpose now I'm actually looking at it.

I'm still not sure it's hygienic, but the fact that he even considered it warms me more than it should as I slide it up my legs, pulling it together snugly before clicking the lock back in place.

I'm not sure why I choose to do it. Maybe only because I know there's no way I'm getting out of that room without it and I'd rather it was my choice than by force, but there is some kind of warmth that ripples over me as I move, intimately aware that it's there.

His stare hits me like a wall as I unlock the door and step out, his gaze travelling up and down the length of me with interest. He holds one hand out, his thick thighs spread apart as I step between them, dropping the keys to his outstretched palm. But as I pull my hand back, his other snatches my wrist, dragging my hand to his mouth and wrapping his lips around my first two fingers.

His tongue travels up and down each digit, his gaze holding mine as I'm wrapped by his heat, my pussy pulsing with need. My thighs clench and his eyes flare, releasing my fingers with a pop. "Good girl."

Yeah, that hits in a whole bunch of places I wish it didn't. My hand drops to my side as his hips rise to slide the keys into his pocket, and I swallow thickly.

"Hmm." I hum my agreement through a haze of lust, considering whether I should be lifting the dress and making myself comfortable over his lap. How much worse would it be for him to have me close enough to feel but not touch?

"Just had to check you weren't taking care of yourself in there, sugar."

He might as well have thrown an entire bucket of cold water over my head, his words dousing any arousal I might have felt his way in irritation.

"You... I... Wow," I bluster, once again, attempting to form coherent words and failing. "First off, I'd wash my hands afterwards, stop being gross. And secondly, you'd sure as shit know if I'd been in there getting myself off."

He shrugs, his smirk front and centre as I stamp my heel and storm out, making my way back down the stairs and outside, snatching a glass from a passing waiter as I go.

"What's the system here?" I ask nobody imparticular. "It must be my turn by now."

"You can be next, babe," Tamsin placates. "Blake here

is just letting Wyatt update his socials, then it's truth time for Taylor and Jasper."

I drink half the glass of champagne in one go, Wyatt narrowing his eyes as he hands the guy's phone over and steps back. I have no idea how long I've been away and who noticed what, but my pissy mood isn't missed as Tamsin asks her guys when they were last caught checking someone out.

Of course Jasper has some contrite answer about how anyone he fancied a look at would know about it, and Taylor just winks her way, more than overtly checking her over, much to the amusement of the rest of the guys around.

Some cocky little shit of a man stalks up, flicking his token in my direction, and just for a second, I reconsider giving him the truth and instead making him do something truly awful, then Nick steps beside him and all my irritation settles on his broad shoulders.

"So, we've done all the basic shit, right? Asking him the truth about his tiny dick isn't going to get us anywhere." Whoever the hell this guy is smirks, shrugging his shoulders as everyone behind him laughs. "So, it also wouldn't do any good to know the weirdest thing you've done on a dare, or the kinkiest thing inside the bedroom, or out of it."

Nick's fist clenches at his side, the other slung in his pocket as the guy shuffles awkwardly between him and Wyatt.

"So, I guess the truth I need from you is…" I ponder, reaching for the first thing that comes to mind. "What's the most awkward thing you've ever been caught doing?"

"Ooh," he says, running his hand along his jaw,

pondering his answer. "Probably that time I was checking a loose thread on my jacket in a store window." *Checking yourself out more like.* "You know the ones with the partly mirrored glass? Well, anyway, it turns out the mannequin was a store assistant and I didn't realise until she moved. It scared the shit out of me." He shakes his head with a chuckle at the memory.

"I don't know if she thought I was weirder for checking myself out in the mirrored glass, or for screeching like a girl at a moving fucking doll." The embarrassed chuckle that falls from him is almost endearing enough to let him off the hook, until he wishes Nick and Wyatt good luck and makes his escape.

"So, a dare… something for both of you." That rules out the ice down the pants I was going to suggest; not fair on Wyatt. "Let's have a striptease. Nick can do it for Wyatt and Wyatt for Nick!" Embarrassing? Yes. Actually going to hurt either of them? No. Going to hit Nick's ego more than Wyatt's? Absolutely.

"Ooh, I have the perfect song for this," Aimee squeals, grabbing her phone and turning up the volume.

"You have got to be kidding me," Nick grumbles as someone places a dining chair behind him and presses against his shoulders to get him to sit down.

The first bars of *Def Leppard "Pour Some Sugar On Me"* ring out, and the smile that splits my face finally feels good. Wyatt's jacket is gone, his shirt untucked, and as he pops each button to the beat, more than one person gets behind him, Nick even manages to crack a smile as he straddles one thigh much more naturally than I expected.

By the time the music cuts out, he's unfastening the zip to his pants, the groan of frustration as the song ends echoing around the pool. Until *Kellis' "Milkshake"* begins, and Aimee giggles, looking at Nick with amusement while Wyatt takes his place on the aptly placed dining chair.

He's awkward at first, but as his gaze comes to mine, he starts to melt, to sink into the music. The jacket, the waistcoat, the shirt, and the ink that I wasn't expecting to find running across his chest and over his shoulders. He grinds his ass against Wyatt's chest, who swats it playfully.

Nick is well and truly in the moment as he gasps, his hand covering his mouth in playful surprise. All too soon, the music cuts out, not nearly as many clothes on the floor as I was hoping for, but the happiness that courses through me feels good. A genuine and honest feeling of positivity that I have felt since… well, since I can remember.

Wyatt plucks a glass from a waiter, making his way to me and placing it in my hand, a kiss coming to my cheek despite the plastic mask between us. It's a sweet gesture that I appreciate more than he realises as he disappears into the throng of people. All too soon, someone else is handing over a token, and the evening continues, but it seems I've set a theme.

Instead of show and tell and random song requests, we have ice bucket challenges and the sharing of guilty pleasures. Wyatt and Nick never bother to slide back on their clothes, and before too long there is a whole lot of abs, ink and skin on display. *This is definitely not where I planned this going.*

The tokens slow, that initial slew finally over as we settle in for the rest of the evening. More than one person ends up in the pool, but considering the gowns and masks, and the lengths that have been taken to assert our prominence, we don't join in.

Two or more of the Devils are with us at all times, their attention confusing. Are they here to guard us? To ensure we stay where we're supposed to be? Or are they here because they want to spend time with us? I'm not sure it matters, or why I even care as the champagne twirls its way through my system.

We make our way into the house at some point, the den becoming our space as everyone else filters out. The music is quieter in here, nothing more than background noise that manages to cover the sound of Taylor and Tamsin getting up close and personal, and they're not the only ones.

Leo and Oliver, or Jacob, are whispering over the other side of the room, Charlotte continuing from the other night with George as she does a line off the back of his hand. I'm vaguely aware he probably shouldn't be doing that with the drugs from a broken leg, but who I am to stand in the way of his fun?

Penelope and Aimee dance, and I find myself joining them, the freedom of our intimate group exhilarating. I'm aware of Leo's attention, but he's one of a few watching us, and it doesn't have the same kind of sizzle as when Nick is in the vicinity. *Sad but true.* He joins us intermittently, dropping the keys discreetly in my hand and explaining where his and Wyatt's room is.

He's always there when I come out of the bathroom, but there are no more altercations between us, something I'm both grateful for and surprisingly disappointed by. I kind of enjoy getting a rise out of him.

The hours roll on, the guests leaving in dribs and drabs, their smiles placating, mildly amused by the seeming change in hierarchy, but no one comments. When I attempt to hand the keys back to Nick at some early hour of the morning, he wraps his hands around mine, telling me to keep hold of them, for now.

There's a delicious promise in the words, his touch and proximity making me feel alive, my body ablaze with this secret between us. He steps back, giving me space as he disappears down the corridor to the rest of the house. Stephanie, Aimee and Charlotte are prepping to head back to what we now know as the pool house, our place, when I make it downstairs, some of the Devils in tow.

"Hold up and I'll join you," I comment, heading into the den to collect my clutch.

"Do you mind if I walk you back?" Wyatt asks, holding it out for me.

"Of course not." I smile, secretly glad for the company. I'm openly grateful for the jacket he drapes over my shoulders as we get outside in the early morning air, his comforting warmth surprsing.

As a group, we meander down the driveway by the light from our phones. Charlotte stumbles on a stone and limps back with Oliver's help, the two of them disappearing quickly in the house. Aimee and Stephanie say goodnight before going to check on Charlotte, but for some reason, I hover, not quite ready to let Wyatt go.

"So, it's been an interesting evening."

"Yeah," he agrees. "That's definitely one word for it. Have you had a good time though?"

"I have," I agree. It's not been sunshine and roses all the way through, but overall it's been fun, and even Nick managed to make it good in the end.

The light above us goes out, the motion sensor flicking itself off as we've been standing here. He moves in closer, and the heat from his body brushes against mine, awareness zapping over me as the light flicks back on. It's hard to read him with the mask covering his face, but as one hand slides to the back of my neck, his gaze goes to my lips and back, and I know what's coming.

Nick might be interested in locking up my pussy, but he's made no further suggestion of kissing me. My hand brushes against the cool plane of Wyatt's chest, his shirt still nowhere to be found. When he lifts the edge of the mask, sliding it up his face and drawing my lips to his, I go willingly, excitedly.

His tongue caresses mine, gently, teasingly, pressing against me before pulling back. There's barely a taste of him on my tongue before he's gone, a longing tangling around my limbs. Wyatt has none of the jealous control that comes with Nick, or the tempting darkness of Leo. He's light, bright, and comfortable. It would be so easy to fall into his soft words and gentle arms. *So easy.*

"Good night, Ivy," he promises, the words spoken against my lips before he draws back, sliding the mask back into place. "Keep hold of the jacket, I'll get it from you soon."

With nothing more than a wink, he turns and heads

back down the driveway, the light flicking back off again and plunging me back into darkness. I quickly let myself in the house, locking it behind me before grabbing a couple of bottles of water from the fridge and a pack of painkillers from the cupboard. If I don't need them, Tamsin will.

Taking the belt off is both a joy and a disappointment, the freedom surprisingly confusing. It's only been one night, but it felt good. The control I held, and that I gave away.

I'm changed and in my pyjamas, the belt and keys locked safely away when Tamsin finally arrives back, rolling on a post-sex high I can only imagine, but not too closely. Because the more I imagine how amazing she feels right now, the more I want it too. The problem is, three men are working their way under my skin.

# THIRTEEN

## *Jacob*

"That's the last of the rubbish from outside," Leo says, dropping the bag inside the glass doors and closing them behind him. "The speaker system needs removing but the DJ is coming back to do that tomorrow. Well, today, actually, I guess."

"I knew what you meant," I reply with a weary smile, rinsing the champagne flute and placing it on the draining board.

It's been one hell of a long day, night, whatever, and I'm more than ready to be done with this cleaning up shit and curled up in my bed. Doing that with someone would obviously be the preference, but the chances of that are looking exceedingly slim right now.

"It helped that Nick and Emmerson have kept on top of it for most of the evening," he admits. "They've done a really good job."

"It's good that you two are finally managing to work together," I comment. I never held anything against him over the fight, we were all there to win and he was better than me, that's all it boils down to. But Nick was seriously pissed off about it, and he doesn't forgive easily.

"Sure." He shrugs. "I'll do a quick run around down here and see if there are any more glasses or whatever. Anything else can go in the dishwasher."

I nod, finishing another glass as he disappears. Taylor rolls through the door, the last of the Devils to make it back, and the satisfied grin on his face tells me he got what I won't be getting on the way back to her house. *Release.*

"All back safely?" I ask.

"Yes, sir," he replies. "Now, where do you need me?"

"The rubbish needs collecting from the den, I think. Everywhere else is covered."

He slaps my shoulder with a nod, grabbing a bag from the side as he pitches in to help. George and Emmerson turned in early, and all things considered, I'm not surprised, but I can't see either lasting for very long in this competition.

The more that I think about the things we've done this week and the way they're pushing us together as a team, the more I can see those not here and getting on with everyone being the ones that leave early. It's going to take more than the effort of an individual to show your true worth in this strange situation we find ourselves in.

Whilst I'm tired, and a lot of us are, Leo still seems to be firing on all cylinders, placing a  couple of glasses on the side with a wink. The muscles in his back ripple as he loads the stray plates into the dishwasher, and I'm not complaining about the amount of time he and the rest of us have spent shirtless.

Both Jasper and Leo have abs worth getting to your knees for, I'd more than willingly lick every dip and curve, but getting myself tangled up with one of my housemates is a bad idea. So I've done my best not to ogle too much—it's hard, and I'm reasonably sure they're straight anyway. *Shame.*

"Right, I think that we're good," Leo says as he closes the dishwasher. "Outside is cleared, each of the rooms has had the rubbish collected and the plates and glasses removed."

"I've straightened up the sofas in the movie room and swept up all the bits of popcorn," Nick adds from the doorway. "FYI, people are disgusting, and the den is back to its pre-dancing state."

"The changing room was a mess," Jasper comments as Taylor passes him with a partially full bag of rubbish, dropping it by the doorway with Leo's. "But it looks like someone has at least given the bathroom a once over. Whoever that was, much appreciated, my friend."

I dry my hands on a towel, checking over the now-clean surfaces one last time.

"Food is covered in the dining room," Wyatt checks off.

"And all the loungers are back in place outside," Leo covers. "I think that's our jobs done, boys."

"Did the girls get back okay?" Nick asks as Wyatt slides through, a couple of plates in hand. He nods, loading them in the dishwasher as Taylor explains he got the last of them back without issue. "Well then, boys. It's been nice spending time with you, but I'm ready to hit the hay." The words are no sooner out of his mouth before someone knocks at the front door twice. "What the…"

The six of us head to the door, Nick pulling it back

to find the compare from our meeting earlier on waiting patiently on the other side, two security with him.

"Good morning, gentlemen. Nice to see you're all still up. Well, most of you," he says, looking at the group gathered. "Shall we?" he asks, gesturing to the den as he strides past us and into the house, making himself at home.

It strikes me that we have no idea how long this has been going on, or how many sets of young men have lived and loved in this place. Has he lived here before? Slept in the beds upstairs, fucked on the sofas in here, eaten at the table in there? Recently? A long time ago? How could we know?

The two security guards with him disappear around the ground floor as we follow him into the den, making ourselves as comfortable as possible, all things considered. He sits silently, unnervingly, and I'm unable to read him because of the mask that covers his face as we wait.

The security reappears, whispering in his ear before taking up residence behind him as we all wait anxiously. Or, at least, I'm anxious. Nick looks like he couldn't care less, but I know it's not the case—maybe that's just a twin thing.

"Nice work, gentlemen." He nods. "How do you feel the introductions went? It seems like some of you have met our chosen Angels ahead of this evening."

"Yeah, we met some of them at the mixer," Taylor replies. "And I'm pretty sure I share at least one class with Charlotte, maybe Aimee too, it's hard to say. My mind's been a little preoccupied with one inparticular."

"Indeed," he muses. "But overall, the choices are good. Yes?"

General calls of agreement ring out, heads nodding as I wonder how to break this to him.

"There's just one thing," Leo interrupts, holding his hand up. "For those of us that have interests in *other things*, what's the process there?"

"Elaborate."

"Let's break this down to something very basic. I like women, yeah?" The compare nods. "I also like men." *Wait, what?* "And I'm not the only one that's more interested in the person inside than the package they come in. Does that make sense?"

He nods again, his gaze seeming far away before it zones back in on Leo. "The moment will come when you have to decide who is going to stand by you. Every move is purposeful and deliberate, and this moment will come sooner than you expect it to."

He holds our attention rapt in the palm of his hand. This is important information, and some of our group skipped out early and are missing it. I want to feel bad for them, but the hottest guy in here just admitted he likes men and I'm totally here for it.

"Ten men and six women were chosen at The Pendleton Prep elite candidates. No, you won't all make it through to the end, but the six of you that do will become a unit, a team, a support network, even when you're at differing ends of the country, or further. The candidate pool is where you will find that partner."

Leo looks my way, the expression on his face hidden behind the cold hard plastic mask we still wear, but I'd like to think I see interest in his eyes. There's certainly interest in mine.

"What about the girls? Surely, they're not going to be asked to do the same things we are?" Wyatt asks, concern laced through his tone.

"Don't worry about the Angels, their director will be liaising with them in due course."

"And what if the person has already been eliminated from the running?" Nick asks.

"Then they're no longer in the candidate pool," he replies. "There will be three Devils remaining, and there's not an automatic pass for those interlinked with them, Angels or not. Everyone earns their place, one way or another."

His answer is ambiguous enough to leave further questions on the tip of my tongue. I know Nick is adamant we're going to make this through together, but I'm not so sure. Maybe being on the arm of a Devil is enough. If I were to pass that test. Whatever that might end up being.

"Treat them well, they're as important as each of you are. Now, I'm going to bid you all good night, you've done a wonderful job this evening."

Whether he's just talking about the clean-up, looking after the Angels, or the evening as a whole, I have no idea. But I'm not sure anyone else does either as Nick follows him and his security out, thanking them for their time and locking up behind them.

"I don't know about you guys, but I'm going to fucking bed," he rumbles from the doorway. "See you tomorrow." He waves a hand in the air, raising his chin my way before disappearing up the stairs.

He's not the only one ready to leave, and quickly it ends

up being just me and Leo sitting in the quiet of the sleeping house, the sound of our housemates settling in for the night a strange but comfortable background noise.

"Thank you for the clarification," I blurt out, peeling the mask off now the event is over and the inspection complete. No one is coming for us now.

"It wasn't just for you," he admits. "But you're welcome." His mask lands on the sofa beside him with a thump. "Looks like your brother is staking his claim."

"Yeah, he can be like that. I remember this one time, we went with our father to collect a new mare for Sophie, at least that was the plan." I chuckle, thinking of the argument they had and the stilted conversation that went on for weeks afterwards. "Well, Nick saw a beautiful grey stallion, and to be fair, it was a nice-looking horse, and of course, he wanted it."

"Does he ride?" Leo asks, his surprise warranted.

"Not at all. And he didn't even attempt to learn after managing to talk him into buying the thing either, but he used to go with Sophie to the stables and help out with the upkeep and whatever. Eventually, Nick agreed to let the riding school work with him, the horse, and they said he's one of the most laid-back stallions they've ever worked with, he's a dream. Perfect for the nervous children, despite his size."

"So, he's got a good eye then, huh?"

"Oh, he knows something good when he sees it," I reply with a weary smile. "And there's hell to pay when he doesn't get it."

"I know how that goes," he replies.

"Siblings?"

"Only child," he corrects with a shake of his head. "But my father is not a man accustomed to not getting his way."

"Family, eh?" I chuckle. "You can't live with them and you can't bury them in the garden."

"Well, no. That's true enough." He smiles, rubbing his hand across his forehead. "Come on, you look shattered, let's get you to bed."

"How very forward of you," I comment with a yawn, the long day catching up with me. I know he doesn't mean it that way, but it's fun to imagine all the same.

"I meant your bed, but I like where your mind went."

I blush as we both get up, turning the lights off and checking the doors are locked before grabbing our masks and heading up.

"I know I'm ready to sleep, but you don't even look tired," I comment idly as we head up the stairs.

"I don't sleep well," he whispers. "I'll probably just work out until I pass out or something."

"Now that's an image that is not going to help me sleep," I reply with my hand on the door knob, ready to go in, but not quite ready to leave.

"Sleep well." He winks, passing and heading down the corridor to his room at the end.

My gaze lingers long after it should, and I hurry into the darkened bedroom, quietly closing the door behind me. Olly is soundly asleep as I place the mask carefully on the bedside table and strip what's left of my suit off, throwing it in the basket before washing up and climbing under the sheets.

Not putting some kind of proper sleepwear on is probably a mistake, considering how often these people like to drag us out of bed, but I'm hoping since we've already had the inspection, our morning will come easily.

But as I lay in the darkness with nothing but the sound of my roommate's heavy slumber to keep me company, my mind wanders. Not far, just down the corridor, to thoughts of the man now hot, sweaty and working out. *Fuck.*

# FOURTEEN

## Ivy

It's the smell of smoky bacon that rouses me, mingled with the heavy dark-roasted coffee I bought and the sound of laughter coming from the next room. The ground-floor bedroom would not have been my choice, but we were the last ones here, so you've got to take what's left, I guess.

Tamsin closes the door behind her, blocking out both the noise and the smell before she drops a bottle of water on the pillow beside my head, cracking her own open and popping a couple of the painkillers out. She's already dressed, sweating slightly as she drops to her bed and removes her trainers, pulling the buds from her ears.

"You've been out running?" I groan, the words coming out like I've been eating sandpaper as I push up, opening the bottle and taking a healthy swig as she preps for her imminent shower. "And here I was thinking that's what you were getting up to last night, blowing the cobwebs off."

"Oh, haha." She throws her buds in my direction, the wires getting tangled as they land on the floor somewhere between my bed and the bathroom doorway. "Aimee is making breakfast. You might want to get up."

The bathroom door closes quietly, the sound of running water following swiftly as I lay there, still, attempting to cobble the pieces together from the night before. I'm no closer when she swans out, towel wrapped around her head, a fresh pair of leggings and a loose tee hanging from her perfect frame as well as the dress from last night.

"You're not seriously going to waste the day away lounging in there, are you?"

Two knocks ring out at the door before I have a chance to reply, "Breakfast is ready," being called out.

"Time to haul ass." She smiles as I flip her off, already done with her overly chirpy morning self, before heading out and leaving me to my overactive brain.

Quickly, I throw on some lounge pants and a vest, tying my tangled mess of hair in a high pony and running a brush over my teeth in double quick time. *That coffee did smell good.*

Charlotte hands me a rack of toast as I appear from our bedroom, muttering something about perfect timing before heading back to grab something else from the kitchen.

The rest of the girls are sitting around the table as we join them, the sunshine streaming in the full-height living room window behind me as I sit.

"I wasn't sure what everyone's favourite hangover breakfast would be so I've done a little bit of everything," Aimee explains, gesturing to the table full of food. "Of course, as we get to know each other better, I'll get this refined down. Perks of being a morning person."

I smile, but it doesn't meet my eyes as I pluck a couple of pancakes, some bacon, and a bunch of fruit out and set them on my plate. Everyone else picks their poison and there's easily enough food left for at least four other people when the front door slams closed.

"Didn't you lock that when you came in?" I ask Tamsin.

She nods around a mouthful of food, concern creeping over her features as a red-head rounds the corner, two of those black-masked robe-wearing security guards with her. The mask she wears is not dissimilar to the ones we wore last night, a combination of black and white lace, delicately edged with feathers.

"No need to get up, ladies. Please continue your breakfast," she says with a smile, pulling a chair out at the head of the table and joining us. "That coffee smells fabulous, do you mind if I join you?"

"Ah, sure?" Charlotte replies, the statement definitely sounding like a question.

One of the black-clas men grabs her one. He doesn't struggle to find it, there's no looking through them all to find the right one. No, he goes straight to the right one, grabs a mug out, and hands it over. *It's disconcerting.* One loiters by the corridor to the entrance, arms folded as he leans his shoulder against the wall, and the other one stands behind her silently as she fills the mug and sits down with a smile.

"I'm sorry, who are you?" Penelope asks from the other end of the table, continuing her breakfast without so much as looking her way.

"You don't know... You weren't told I was coming. Why am I not surprised?" The interloper sighs, dramatically rolling her eyes. "I'm Liselle, current wife to… well, I don't suppose it matters, and former Angel."

The table is silent as she pauses, looking from one of us to the next before continuing undeterred. "I'm sorry I'm late, I would have liked to be here last week to meet you but the schedules didn't marry up."

Well, I guess that answers the question of who she is... why she's here is still anyone's guess.

"So tell me, how did the introduction go? I swear, when we met our Devils, the entire night was a complete sham. Kitty hated the entire lot of them on sight, and I'm sure she never got over it," she rambles.

"We met some of them at the mixer," Penelope comments. "That was a fun night."

"Uh-hmm," Tamsin agrees with a nod, finishing her food. "And just in case he wasn't clear enough last night, Taylor is mine for the time being, and I don't share."

"Ooh, you're coupling up already. These boys work quickly," she says with interest. "Anyone else?"

"Ivy—" Aimee starts.

"No," I cut her off.

He might have called me out in front of everyone else, and he might have done his damned best to manipulate me into submission, and I have to give it to him, it certainly gave me pause for thought, but if for one second he or anyone else thinks that means I'm his, they're mistaken.

I'm not some pretty girl to be lined up and demanded, controlled and manipulated. I still have choices here, I still have power. And nobody is going to take those from me.

"Ooh, go on. Ivy what?" Liselle asks, her interest piqued.

"Ivy nothing," I clip, glowering at Aimee.

"Ivy was chosen by one of them, first, actually." Aimee grins, pleased as punch with herself.

"Well, that's great. Two of you have secured yourself some Devils. The rest of you really need to work on that." Liselle grimaces, and I can't help but chuckle, because clearly securing yourself a man is the only thing gorgeous and intelligent women are good for.

There's no point being a prude about it, these girls are beautiful, but they're also sweet and kind. I mean, they had personalised travel mugs made, and cooked enough food to feed twelve people. They're also taking some seriously impressive classes, and not even Tamsin is cruising through her time here.

We are not trophy girlfriends, and I won't be treated like we are.

"So, you probably have questions. I have answers. Limited though they might be. What do you want to know?"

***

"Are you sure about this?" I ask, hustling my steps closer, the depth of the gardens around us disconcerting.

"The pool is heated," Penelope says, waving off my concerns and drawing me back into the moment. "We just have to get from here to there."

"It's freezing."

"It's fine," Tamsin says, dismissing me, much like Penelope did. "Get out of your own head and live a little."

"I'm living," I argue, dropping the towel on the closest lounger and quickening my pace to the water. *Yeah, it's fucking freezing out here.* "I even made it through an entire week."

The warm water sloshes around my ankles as I test the top step, making light work of the rest and submerging my frozen body in the heat of the pool. *It's bliss.*

"She says this like we're assholes," Stephanie comments as she ties up her hair. "Like living in a beautiful house with a pool and a whole host of hot guys over the road is some kind of hardship."

"It's not you," I start, awareness prickling over my spine.

"I swear, if you finish that sentence with *it's me*, we're seriously going to fall out," Charlotte interrupts, climbing into the water with me.

"I'm just not used to being around so many people all the time," I finish, sticking my tongue out in her direction.

"Because you're the only one here that's an only child," Stephanie says as she joins Tamsin at the deep end, dangling their toes in the water. "We all had lives before we ended up here, you know?"

"No, I know that. I just..." Don't care? Too harsh.

They've been nothing but nice all week. And it's not that I don't care about *them*, I'm finding myself more and more inclined to keep an eye out for them, especially after our discussion with Liselle yesterday.

I don't know her deal, but she sure as hell isn't someone who's here to help, support, guide or advocate for us. No, she's gone through this damn brainwashing and come out the other side. Clearly, that's what we could end up like; those of us that make it through.

And I'm not sure I want that for them, or me either. She smiled in all the right places, nodded too, gave vague answers to specific questions and generally left us more confused than we were to begin with. *Surprise surprise.*

"It's fine," Stephanie says, not needing me to finish the rest of the sentence. "I'm surprised Aimee and Penelope didn't want to come though."

"Same," Tamsin agrees. "But I get prepping for the week ahead too. These schedules aren't likely to ease up any time soon."

"And what do we have here?" Taylor says, pushing off a tree and stepping out of the shadows as he sits on a chair at the side of the pool. How long has he been there, and how much has he heard? "Enjoying an afternoon swim, huh?" Mischief twinkles in his eyes as he looks at Tamsin, and I'm reasonably sure she gave the game away.

"We said no boys," I complain, looking her way.

"I never said anything," she argues, splashing water my way.

"So, your boyfriend just happens to be the one to find us out here and you had nothing to do with it?" I ask, narrowing my eyes in her direction.

"I would never! Pinkie promise," she swears.

"Hey, I've just been out running. Not my fault that sounds carry out here, and you're not exactly being quiet," Taylor intervenes. "But the swimwear pic was hot, babe."

He jumps up, running around to the edge of the pool where she sits and placing a quick kiss on the top of her head before running off, his laughter echoing around the pool.

"You totally gave us up," Stephanie agrees. "But I can see why."

"Can't we just have one day without the local penises getting involved?" I grumble.

"What about yesterday?" Charlotte asks, turning to do another lap around the pool.

"Yesterday doesn't count, we were still over there in the early hours of the morning," Tamsin says with a roll of her eyes. "And there's absolutely nothing wrong with the local penises, I'm quite fond of one, actually."

A chill creeps over the back of my neck again, but I can't see anything as I turn around, just the thick bushes that line the pool.

"So, are you ladies ready for some company?" Taylor asks, Jasper helping George down the stairs from their back porch with his crutches.

He doesn't wait for an answer before jumping in the pool, water flying everywhere, but for some reason, he doesn't re-emerge. I'm not the only one looking around, but our view is limited by the water. That is, until Tamsin screeches and she's pulled off the side and dragged into the water, the two of them laughing hysterically.

I lean up against the side, resting my elbows in the channel and doing my best to keep as much of me as I can in the heated water, but the longer we're here, the less the autumn chill bothers me. Wyatt winks my way as he comes out, board shorts slung low on his trim hips as he glides into the water.

Stephanie joins me in the water, Charlotte and George whispering at a table before she dives back in. Before too long, Emmerson joins George, and Leo and Jacob find their way into the pool.

I don't know exactly how, but I'm starting to notice the little differences. Not just the missing charge in the air, but the way his eyes don't wander to a single one of the half-naked girls loitering around, instead fixing on Leo's ass and staying there. The mannerisms are similar, but not the same.

And I don't even need to turn around to know the heat at my back is his brother, his cologne surrounding me as his thighs land on either side of my shoulders, his feet touching the water and swishing it around absentmindedly as he gets comfortable. Just about everyone else plays some kind of tag in the water, Tamsin doing surprisingly well as she carves through the underwater gracefully.

"You'll get cold up there," I comment, his hands coming to my shoulders and massaging gently. "You could come and warm up in the water."

"You want to warm me up, sugar?" he asks. The words tumble, whispered and raspy, some kind of tone that makes even the most innocuous statement sound like a proposition, and I can't help the way my body reacts to it.

"Nope, sit there and get cold." I shrug.

He might elicit some kind of a response from my body, but I'm still pissed he managed to demand me the other night, and I went. I think it's safe to say that I can't be trusted around him. I'm also more than aware of the way Leo looks over periodically, and Wyatt didn't miss his arrival. The atmosphere is charged, but I'm not sure anyone else feels it.

At the end of the day, it was Wyatt that made the move, he's the one I went to bed thinking about. It just wasn't *only* him for very long. Now, with Nick's hands on my skin and Wyatt and Leo just steps away, I can only imagine the carnage that would be in real life.

I'm not convinced anyone else notices the shift in the air as Nick shuffles me forward, sliding into the water behind me.

"You can still rest, just wrap your legs around me."

"I'm good," I reply, shuffling over and leaning back against the wall of the pool. He joins me with a chuckle, clearly not expecting that to work as he winks and smirks my way.

"There's more than one way to do this," he whispers before calling loudly, "Who's up for wrestling?"

"Ooh. Me, me, me," Charlotte replies excitedly, swimming over to Jacob and grabbing his arm. "We'll be a team!"

He shrugs, going with her as Tamsin jumps up on Taylor's shoulders. "Come on, baby. We've got this." Her laughter echoes around the pool, steam billowing from her skin as the cool evening air swims around her.

Charlotte hops up on the side, lowering her legs over Jacob's shoulders before steadying herself as he moves away. The two girls laugh as the guys do their best to steady them, Tamsin reaching in for Charlotte's hip to tip her over but not managing it.

I barely manage to follow what's happening before both girls are falling off and landing in the water, the guys following them as everyone tumbles together.

"Winner stays on," Nick calls from beside me. But I have no idea who won.

"No problem," Jacob replies. "But you're up next, brother."

"You're on," he replies, grabbing my hip. "Come on, sugar. Looks like we're up."

"You think… yeah, no. That's not happening," I argue, pressing my back into the side.

"Don't worry, I won't let you fall," he baits. "I've got good balance."

"Stephanie will do it," I deflect, calling her name loudly.

"You're on your own, girl. He's hot, but I'm quite happy here." She goes back to her quiet conversation with Jasper, completely ignoring us.

"Don't tell me you're a little chicken," he goads, that mischievous twinkle in his eye so like Jacob's. "My girl is not afraid of a little water, surely?"

"Fuck off," I argue with a smile.

"Come on," Charlotte calls. "I'm getting cold up here."

Jacob drops back down in the water, warming her up before standing up again, an amused look on his face. "I think she's a little scared, bro. You'd better give the lady a hand."

Nick's gaze catches mine as he turns my way and I prepare to swim, because I know for certain he's going to get me. We wait there for the longest half-second known to man whilst I contemplate where the hell Leo and Wyatt are and why on earth they aren't saving me from this. Surely that's what the boys that kind of like you do, no? They rush to your rescue. Oh, but not these two.

He lunges for me and I splash water his way, hoping to escape before he gets to me. And I manage it for a second. But all too quickly, his hands are on my hips and I'm being hauled out of the water and hoisted up. I grab on to something, anything I can hold on to, mostly his head, as he places me on his shoulders like I weigh nothing.

I try to wiggle off and jump back in the water, but his hands hold my legs steady as he heads towards Jacob and Charlotte, Tamsin and Taylor taking the defeat better than I expected as she high-fives me as we pass. The whole thing is a blur as Charlotte comes for me, the two of us grappling for the top spot above the brothers who are just as competitive as you'd expect them to be.

Movement in the bushes behind Charlotte catches my eye, and I'm almost certain there's a flash of light, a phone or a camera or something. But that distraction is enough for Charlotte to get the upper hand, tumbling me into the water. I'm laughing as Nick hauls me up, checking me over with interest, Leo and Wyatt not far behind.

I'm only half paying attention as I look back to the bushes.

"You okay?" Leo asks, following my line of sight.

"Yeah, I just thought I saw something…"

It's probably nothing, just the masked men and hidden threats playing tricks on me.

"Where?" he asks. But he doesn't sound like the fun and easy-going version of himself that I've got used to, he sounds cold, detached, and taking this way more seriously than I anticipated.

"Just over there." I point as he jumps out, water cascading down his back and leaving a trail. "It was probably nothing, just a cat or something. Don't worry about it."

I feel foolish even mentioning it, especially as Nick jumps out too, handing me over to Wyatt like some doll that needs protecting. "Always trust your instincts," he disagrees.

The two of them nose around the general area I pointed out, not saying a lot to us as they whisper between themselves. Leo bends down, looking at the base of the tree as Nick shrugs his shoulders, coming back to the pool.

"Might have just been a cat or something," Nick says with a smile.

"Or just an excuse because you lost," Charlotte adds, breaking the creeping tension. "I didn't have you down as a poor loser, Ivy. But I'll give you another go if you think you can take us."

"Oh, it's like that, is it?" I ask, more than up for giving it another go, even if it is only to shake this feeling off. There was someone there or something. I'm sure of it. "Come on, Nick. Let's show them how it's done."

Wyatt backs up as Nick drops down, allowing me space to climb on his shoulders, by choice this time, before he stands up, the night-time chill wrapping its embrace around me.

"Fuck, it's cold." I shiver.

"Better make this quick then," Nick comments from between my legs. "Then I can warm you back up."

# FIFTEEN

*Leo*

Ivy banters with her friend in the pool just a few feet away, except it feels like a million miles as the sound of them splashing around breaks through the brain fog. My gaze finally focuses on something, instead of the blur of nothing that was registering just seconds ago, it just happens to be the perfect section of skin that stretches across her lower back, dipping in at her tight waist before flaring over her hips, Nick's manicured hands holding her legs tightly.

But any thought I might have had for joining her and everyone else back in that water is gone. Much like the men that were here just moments ago, not that I let that on. No, my appetite for entertainment has all but disappeared, soured by disappointment.

I find myself heading away from the water where everyone laughs, sliding the glass doors open and dropping onto one of the benches to dry my wet feet with a towel. Pans clatter in the kitchen, the two male cooks organising dinner with barely a word passed between them, well, at least from here.

I dry off quickly, throwing the towel and wet shorts

in the basket before slinging on a pair of sweatpants and a tee. To be honest, I thought a changing room was a little superfluous, somewhere for guests or whoever was partying to get changed. A complete waste of space that could have housed a rack or two of free weights at the very least, but as I shuck the chill of the cold air and water off, and slide on some dry warm clothes, without having to drip water all over the house, it suddenly makes sense.

The cooks are now chatting as I head into the middle of the house. A quick look at the clock and I notice everyone will be coming in for food shortly anyway.

"Fucking wanker," Oliver calls from the games room, and rather than heading upstairs, I find myself going to investigate.

I loiter in the doorway, his attention firmly on the screen in front of him as he manoeuvres through a building, shooting the guy who appears on his left before continuing through.

"I know you're in here, you little bastard. Now, where the hell are you hiding?" He turns into a room, an opponent backed in the corner opposite practically waiting for him as he shoots and ends his turn instantly. "Fucking hell," he grumbles, waiting for the re-load and dropping back in his chair.

"You need a hand?" I ask.

"Shit." He jumps, turning around. "Sorry, man. I thought you were outside with Jake."

"Was. Change of plan."

There's no point getting into the details with him, not that I would if I could. They left that mark there for me to find because nobody else would have thought twice about it, just assumed it was a small animal or something, but we have a system. We've had to.

"This motherfucker must have got me a dozen times," he rants, gesturing at the TV. "You fancy showing him what teamwork looks like?"

"Why not?" I grab a control, getting comfortable as my system loads up. It's been too long since I sat with my boys and had a gaming afternoon, way too long. "I'm probably a little rusty."

"Just a distraction would be enough at this point," he comments, his request flashing up as I load in.

"That I can manage," I agree with a nod.

"Had enough out there?" he asks, waiting for me to join.

"Something like that. You didn't fancy a dip?"

"Not in the pool," he mutters.

"Something else you fancy dipping in?" I ask with a chuckle, peeking at him in my periphery.

"Uh, no," he corrects. "It's just a whole lot of tits and ass."

"Not your thing?"

I didn't think he was gay, and I'm usually pretty good at spotting that, but maybe I'm wrong.

"Totally my thing." *Good to know.* "But Taylor and Nick have been more than vocal about who they want and what they want from them. I'm in no way interested in getting into an argument with them over a stray glance or a sideways comment with so much skin on show."

"Fair enough. Although they were both doing okay whilst I was out there, I get it. Cavemen can be assholes."

The conversation falls to the wayside as we both concentrate, me following his lead as we make our way through the same building, his hidden opponent seemingly elsewhere.

"He's got to be in here somewhere," he grumbles as we case from one room to the next, turning a corner to a shotgun that takes us both out "That motherfucker!"

I barely had time to register it before we were out, only one kill each under our belts. "Well, that could have gone better."

I used to be good at this, once upon a time.

Dex, Blaise and I spent way too many hours hiding from my father, tucked into the cubby in my bedroom playing games. It was barely big enough to squeeze two in, so how all three of us managed it, I have no idea, but we did. Often.

The nights when it was throwing it down and we didn't want to shimmy down the trellis on the back wall to get out, or the brunch meetings that meant we had nothing more than half an hour to kill, those were the moments we legged it upstairs and shoved ourselves in that cubby out of the way.

He never bothered us whilst we were in there. A firm thump on the door and a barked order were more than enough to ensure compliance. If he was feeling particularly magnanimous, he'd send one of the girls to coax us out instead.

But that didn't happen often.

No, nineteen times out of twenty it'd be a hard word and a snarled order that got our asses moving. But it is what it is.

I knew the second I left he'd have the two of them on some other assignment far far away from wherever the hell I was going to be. There was never any question about it. And yet, that mark.

*What are they warning me of, and why?*

If they'd been the ones watching, and no doubt reporting back, they'd have let me know by now. And if he believed anything they reported back, I'd be surprised, really surprised. If he was going to get them to observe, he'd have just paid the damn tuition and saved all the damn cloak-and-dagger action.

So, they aren't the ones tailing me, not normally anyway. They've found a reason to get here, to issue a warning that only I would understand. And yet, it still doesn't get me any closer.

Oliver and I die, a lot. That same wanker kills us at least twenty times and we make very little headway. Oliver does significantly better than I do, but then, considering how distracted I am, it's hardly a surprise.

Dex and Blaise have been the devils on my shoulders for as long as I can remember. One would come up with some stupid idea, and the other would up the ante, then I'd come up with something even worse and we'd all end up in trouble. But that's how it's supposed to be with your blood brothers, isn't it?

Ride or die and all that bullshit.

My father knew exactly what he was doing by separating us. He's finally free to manipulate them into the mindless assassins he's always wanted them to be, whilst I'm here making sure to follow in his footsteps. *Just not in the debate club.*

"Gentlemen, dinner will be served shortly in the dining room," one of the cooks explains from the doorway.

"I'll let the guys know," I reply, dying again.

"That's already been done, sir. The ladies will be joining you also." He nods once before disappearing.

"Hopefully they'll be wearing more than wet bathing suits," Oliver comments with a groan.

"Yes," I agree. "That would chafe like a bitch."

The two of us burst into laughter as I die on the screen, again, choosing to wait out the rest of the round watching the kill cam.

"Well, I'd say thank you for the help—"

"Except I'm not sure I was any help at all," I interrupt.

"The company was useful regardless," he finishes, the sound of everyone coming in finally registering as the consoles wind down.

"It's this way, isn't it?" one of the girls asks, the sound of them all ambling through the house a cacophony of noise I can't believe we drowned out with the game.

"Better go show our faces," I say, plugging the controller in to charge.

Oliver agrees with a nod, wandering out, only to be replaced by Nick, his broad shoulders blocking the doorway. "So, what did you find?"

"What? You were right there, you saw exactly the same as I did," I bluff.

"Yeah, but your poker face needs some work, and I wasn't about to let that spook the girls. They were having a good time, and whoever or whatever it was isn't anywhere to be seen now."

"You were making progress and you didn't want to put her off is more like it." I scoff.

"You're hiding something." He crosses his arms over his chest, like there's any way his puffed-up ego intimidates me.

"Good chat. Let's do it again sometime." I smile, it's as fake as the excitement I have for this conversation as I make to push past him, but he grips my arm. "You don't want to do that," I growl.

The tension in the doorway crackles as his fingers twitch against my skin, the unimpressed look on his face mirroring mine. His brother might be cute, and interested, but I have no problem with making a statement, should it be needed.

"I know you don't know me very well, and we certainly started this thing off on rocky territory, but you don't want to make an enemy out of me." The words come out in a much calmer tone than I feel, each coldly calculated word held back.

My blood rushes through my body, a steady thrum in my ears as I wait and harness the rage that I know can come. I could peel each digit from my body and snap them as I go. He has no idea who the fuck he's dealing with, and it shows. But his ego is too big to back down.

"Tell me what you saw that I missed." He grits the words out under a furrowed brow.

He'll miss it again and again if he goes back to look because the system is supposed to work that way. Dex, Blaise and I are the only ones that would know those marks from something innocuous.

"You're keeping something from us," he dismisses, refusing to meet my gaze, his hand still wrapped firmly around my arm.

His jaw is like stone, and I don't miss the irritated twitch as he clenches his teeth. So much like Jacob, and yet not like him at all.

A door closes down the hallway as Ivy steps out. "Oh, good. I seem to have lost everyone. You can show me where I'm supposed to be."

The soft black leggings hug each curve, her top half covered by a loose oversize jumper that drapes off one shoulder. Tying her hair in a loose chignon, she closes the distance between us, completely unaware of the tension rippling through the air.

"Well, you ladies came prepared," I comment, plastering a smile on my face and shaking Nick off my arm. "You look lovely."

"Oh, not at all." She smiles. "But sitting down to dinner in towels didn't seem appropriate. Luckily, your assistant guy said there were clothes available. Now, I'm really trying my best to not read into the how and why of the womens clothes in your house, but they're super comfortable."

"I couldn't possibly comment," I say, threading her arm through mine and leading her into the dining room, avoiding any further conflict with Nick. She looks from me to him and back again, a question appearing on her features. "But I definitely didn't bring any with me."

"Are you sure? If you actually go by Louisa at the weekend, that's totally cool." She smiles and winks, nudging her hip into mine as I push open the door.

"It's Angelica, not Louisa," I comment quietly as she passes, making her way to the table with a smile and an amused shake of her head.

I step in behind her, noting Nick storming his way in our direction as I let go of the door. I'm not interested in getting into it with him again, I'm already on edge. Ivy slides in next to her friend, and I join Jasper and Oliver nearby, neither of them are The Sect material, but I guess time will confirm that... or not.

# SIXTEEN

_Ivy_

“**Y**ou have got to be kidding me,” I grumble, seeing the thick inlaid card on the table, again. “What now?”

“Time to haul ass, girls. The cars will be here in five minutes,” Penelope says, holding her hand out for our travel mugs.

“We’re barely through the door,” I complain. “What would have happened if we’d gone to the library or something?”

“Don’t know. Don’t care. I’ll get these filled whilst you get changed,” she replies.

“What are we getting changed for?” Tamsin asks, picking up the card from the table as I disappear into our bedroom. “A meeting? Well, that doesn’t sound fun at all. And what the hell is Timeless Inc?”

“Three minutes,” Charlotte calls as Tamsin hustles into the room, dropping her bag on the table.

“Looks like we’re going like this.” She sighs, switching her blazer out for a light jacket and running a brush through her hair. “I guess I’ll do.”

"So, what and where have we been summonsed to now?" I ask, collecting my refilled cup from Penelope as we all head to the entrance, the doorbell ringing. "And I thought Liselle was supposed to be managing this now, anyway?"

"Timeless Inc, one p.m., and I have no idea." Charlotte sighs, joining us as we march down the corridor, heels clicking as we go.

"I guess these guys aren't going to give us any deets either," Tamsin comments as she opens the door to the same two black SUVs from the other night. "Yay."

The six of us file into the cars, much like we did on Friday night, not bothering to ask the drivers for information they're not going to give us. "I swear, if we end up at that spooky place again, I'm moving out," Tamsin comments. "I am not dressed for this cold weather."

Luckily, we don't end up at the old church, but neither do we head to the small village that Nick showed me the other week, instead travelling further away and finding ourselves tucked in an expensive-looking office in the middle of a town God knows where.

"Glad you could all make it." Liselle smiles as she strides through the glass doors, a red and black mask firmly in place, a brunette following behind her. "This is Amy, she's the head of the Big Sister programme here at Timeless, and she's going to talk you through your first training session."

She drops a notepad in front of each of us, gesturing to the pot of pens conveniently placed in the middle of the table as I look from her to Tamsin, and back.

"And what exactly is that?" Stephanie asks.

"If you give her a chance, Amy will answer all your

questions," Liselle replies with a fake smile and a roll of her eyes. *Bitch.*

"Good afternoon, ladies," the brunette starts. "As your mentor explained, I'm Amy, and thank you for taking the time out of your day to begin your Big Sister training." She looks from one to the other of us, clearly picking up the fact that none of us has any idea why the hell we're here or what on earth she's talking about.

"So, it was great of you all to enrol in this programme. Your little sisters have all been picked out and matched perfectly to you. They're excited, I can tell you that." She smiles, again, clearly hoping for some kind of exhilarated reply, but none comes. "This is going to be the first of your twice-weekly training sessions covering mentor training, peer training, guidance and support. Once we're through all this, you'll just have the weekly support and debrief catch-ups, most likely by zoom."

"And when are we supposed to fit this in?" Stephanie asks. "My calendar is already pretty full with the additional classes I chose."

"Spaces have been created, and your online calendars have been updated," Liselle replies.

"I'm sorry, what?" Stephanie attempts to clarify, cocking her head.

"This is non-negotiable, your schedule has been adjusted." She doesn't even look up from her phone to answer before dismissing any further questions with a flick of her hand, gesturing for Amy to continue.

"Yes, so aside from the training sessions, you'll meet with your Little Sister at least twice a month, you're free to organise that at your own convenience." *Great.* "This programme makes a massive contribution to the self-esteem and prospects of our young women, it's also a fantastic opportunity for you ladies to gain some new skills and give back to those that haven't been afforded the same luxuries you have."

"So, we're going to be giving a hand-up to a bunch of degenerates. Great." Penelope sighs with a roll of her eyes, leaning back in her chair. "Just what I had in mind."

"The young women in our programme are the forgotten ones," Amy continues undeterred. "They're not the top of the class, the popular girls, but they're also not the bottom of the social ladder either, those girls get plenty of support from other areas. No, we target those in the middle, the ones with potential that just need the right kind of contacts and support to really make themselves something special."

And so it continues, for the next two hours…

"When she said some new things would be on the agenda, this is not exactly what I was expecting," I comment quietly, climbing into the back of the SUV behind Tamsin and Stephanie.

The driver is silent as a black privacy screen slides up between us, the locks engaging loudly before we pull away.

"I can't believe this. She's just cancelled my nail appointments for the foreseeable future," Stephanie grumbles, flicking through her online calendar.

"To be fair, those can be rescheduled pretty easily. Coordinating time with six people is probably not the easiest," Tamsin attempts to explain. "And mentoring sounds fun. I'll be able to pass my good fashion sense to someone at least, my actual sisters couldn't care less."

I chuckle, flicking through the changes in my calendar. Luckily, it's just additions and there are no class movements or anything. It just means some of the time I'd mentally allocated I no longer have. *Totally fine.*

The car manoeuvres its way through the town with ease, but in nothing more than a few moments we're pulling into an underground car park behind Liselle, everyone filing back out.

"I thought we were going back to the house?" Aimee asks as Liselle marches to an elevator, the seven of us waiting as two of the security guys head up first.

"Not yet. There's someone I'd like you to meet first," Liselle says with a smile.

I have no idea whether the smile is good news for us or not, not knowing her well enough to be able to decipher her moods just yet.

We all wait anxiously for the elevator to return, none the wiser as to where we are or who we're meeting as she types in a code before we start to move. It's clearly a private elevator, with no buttons to push, and no reception to go to as the display shows us flying from floor to floor. The metal doors pull back, Liselle's security waiting with a blonde woman holding a clipboard, and yes, even more security.

They poke through everyone's handbags and cautiously but efficiently pat us all down. *What the hell?* Nobody questions it when the perky blonde with the clipboard thanks us all, asking us to follow her before setting a pace across the marble floor.

The entranceway is cold and efficient, but as we push

through double doors, it's clear this isn't some random office building, this is an apartment. A penthouse. We're ushered through a living room before finding ourselves in what looks like another meeting room, the space feeling odd, considering this looks much more like a hotel than an office.

"She's just on a call," the blonde explains. "She knows you're here."

A private entrance to a penthouse suite. Who on earth have we come to see? A musician, a celebrity, a designer?

Liselle thanks her whilst we wait, completely confused. Nobody says a word as we look at each other and attempt to absorb the surroundings. Nobody bothers to ask Liselle who it is or why we're here, or any of the other million and one questions that are no doubt tumbling around everyone else's minds as well as mine. No point.

"Sorry about that, sometimes it just won't wait," a woman says, closing the door behind her as she comes in, heading straight for Liselle and offering her a hug and air kisses.

"Don't worry, this was totally a last-minute thought. Thank you so much for making time to see us."

"Oh, of course." They smile, turning to look at the six of us as we look from Liselle's red hair and black mask to the slightly older woman's silky grey locks. They're dyed, not aged, and the balayage is done perfectly. "You have no idea who I am, do you?" she asks, her amusement clear.

"Sorry, I'm afraid not," Charlotte replies with a shrug, clearly the bravest of us all.

"Well, I guess that's to be expected. She pours a glass

of water for herself, taking a sip before joining us at the table. "I'm the editor-in-chief for WOMAN magazine, I'm also part of the board of directors for one of the largest publishing houses in the world."

"Wait, what?" Penelope asks. "You're Lauren DeMarco?"

"The one and only."

"The woman behind DeMarco bags?" Stephanie asks, holding her purse up as an example.

"Indeed."

"So, you're a designer, an editor, and you coordinate a huge publishing house?" Aimee confirms. "Talk about girl power!"

"Well, I don't do all of those things alone, but yes," she agrees. "And one day some of you will be able to do these kinds of things too."

"Sure," Aimee replies with an awe-struck yet dismissive wave of her hand. "We can absolutely all do this."

"Well, no, because Lauren here does all that," Liselle intervenes. "But the point is, that this opportunity opens doors for you. You can be more than just the woman behind the powerful husband, if you want to be. Each couple dynamic is different."

And suddenly, it all makes sense.

We can be more than just trophy wives for high-powered men with too much money that are only interested in sticking their dicks into the newest office assistant. This 'step-up' into the world of the elite can be ours too.

For the first time since we moved into the house, a sense of excitement creeps over me. This doesn't have to be a waste of a year, or two, biding my time until I can follow my dreams.

It doesn't have to be a stop-gap. Instead, it could be the start of something. A way to get that practice of my own quicker, to build contacts with people that need my help but don't have the ability to pop into an office for a regular catch-up.

This could be a way to fulfil my dreams, bigger and better than I ever imagined they could be, to go further than I ever dreamed. There's only one catch, I've got to be on the arm of one of the Devils of Pendleton Prep, and more than one of them has already set me in their sights.

"Okay, quickly, Lauren has five minutes for us," Liselle says. "Any questions."

"Why purses?" Stephanie asks, just as Penelope asks, "How did you become editor-in-chief?"

"Purses because I love them, and I started as a writer when I was at Pendleton Prep. Time, perseverance, and some friends in high places got me the rest."

"Now, that's not to say you didn't work for it," Liselle intervenes. "I remember those late nights and early mornings you used to do."

"Oh, absolutely. You've got to be willing and able to put in the time and effort," Lauren continues. "But you'll see… well, some of you will."

She smiles broadly at each of us, clearly excited about the prospects that wait for us at the other end of whatever the hell this is… but not everyone will be afforded these luxuries.

It's a strange place to find yourself, sitting in front of

someone worth millions and contemplating if one day that could be you, if only you could get on board with the right guy. So much of this hangs on what happens with the Devils that it makes me uneasy.

It's all well and good dangling a shiny carrot in front of us, but at the end of the day, we've got to back the right man. And with no idea of the criteria required, how can you be sure to pick the right one?

"Sorry to interrupt," the clipboard lady says from the doorway. "Your next appointment is expecting you shortly." She nods quickly before closing the door again.

"Well, I guess that's time up," Liselle adds with a clap. "Thank you so much for making the time whilst you're here. We'll have to catch up next time you're in Milan."

Who the hell is this woman, and what on earth is she doing in Milan? Another designer perhaps… someone we might recognise, otherwise why wear the mask all the time? It's infuriating.

"Of course," Lauren agrees, standing and giving Liselle another quick embrace. "And it was lovely to meet you all."

She disappears out the door, security waiting to guide us back out and to the cars as we head back to the house. Aimee and Tamsin chatter excitedly as I twist my travel mug in my hands, my mind anywhere but on their conversation.

Charlotte has the kettle boiling by the time we're walking through the door, Stephanie talking about making some salad and grilling some tuna steaks and chicken for an easy dinner, as I nod and disappear into our bedroom, still needing to process.

"When do you want to make a start on the sociology

assignment?" Tamsin asks, closing the bedroom door behind her and dropping onto my bed.

"Tomorrow is jam-packed but I've time on Wednesday morning, if that works for you?"

"Sure. Now, first up, you've got to tell me what's going on with Nick. You've been avoiding me for days. No more."

"Nothing's going on."

"You sure about that?" she asks, throwing a cushion my way and settling against my pillows. "The two of you looked good together yesterday, but you barely gave him the time of day on Friday night. And don't think I missed you sneaking off with Leo, either. The two of you looked cosy on your way to dinner yesterday too. So, come on, spill."

"There's nothing to spill," I argue. "Nick picked me out on Friday night, and then he was a controlling jerk all night, but I guess he was trying to make it up to me yesterday or whatever."

"And… did it work?"

"I'm not sure I'd go that far."

"So, Leo then?"

"Leo's great. He took me away on Friday night to let me know Spencer wasn't coming and that he'd talked to him. Spencer warned me away from him, I'm sorry that I never mentioned it to you, but Leo stepped in like he said he would, he's a nice guy."

"Warned you away from who?" she asks, confusion crossing her face as I join her on the bed. "I can't believe you never told me about this."

"Leo. And you've been in a Taylor bubble all week, so

it didn't seem important. It was just Spencer trying to throw his weight around again, that's all. You know what he gets like."

"Yeah, I suppose… I can't believe he has the balls to try that shit here though. Fucking idiot."

"Exactly."

"So, no double dates yet then?"

"Afraid not."

She sticks her bottom lip out, painting fake sadness on her face as she gives me puppy-dog eyes.

"That look is not going to get me double dating with you. Not now, not tomorrow, not ever." I laugh.

There's friendship with Leo, understanding, we have shared interests and he knows just how to make me feel safe, and cared about. But then there was that kiss with Wyatt… sweet, tender, gentle. He makes me laugh and has broken the tension between me and Nick more than once, and I didn't miss how quickly he moved my way yesterday when I thought I saw something in the bushes.

And yet, Nick is the one that makes me feel like my body is full of anticipation, almost buzzing with it. Not just because he knows exactly the things to say to piss me off beyond words, but because he stokes those flames with a desire that I can't seem to control. I want to hit him, then kiss him, and sometimes, the other way around.

He drives me crazy.

"You're totally thinking about it."

"Huh, what?" I ask, tilting my head to look up at her from where I lay on the bed.

"Your cheeks have gone pink, and I can see your nipples

from here. Who are you thinking about, Leo or Nick?"

"How bad would it be if I said neither?"

"Jeez, girl. Who else has caught your eye?"

"Wyatt may or may not have kissed me when he walked us back the other night." I cover my face with my hands in a vain attempt to hide my embarrassment.

"Like, a peck on the cheek, or like a full-on smacker?" she asks, way too interested in this.

"It was not a peck on the cheek." I can't help but think back to the softness of his lips and the perfect, but way too brief, kiss we shared. "And I want to do it again."

# SEVENTEEN

## Nick

"**S**eriously?"

"What? You need to fuck or fight, bro. And you know it." Jacob laughs as he jabs me in the shoulder again, my pen skittering across the page.

"You're a little shit." I chuckle, ignoring him and attempting to concentrate on the books in front of me.

"Come on, you've been a grumpy ass for days now. You're clearly not getting any, so this is your best bet."

"Say again? You play punching me whilst I try and get ahead of this lot is my best option… I can think of better ways to work out my frustrations."

"You could ask Leo about his weights," he says excitedly.

"Ooh, I could work some of this out on Leo's face. That's not a bad idea."

"Give over."

I don't need to turn to know he's rolling his eyes behind me, attempting to work out how to goad me into starting something. "He's keeping something from us. I can feel it."

"It'll all come out in time, I'm sure," he placates. "Until

then, you need to chill the fuck out. I thought the party would have loosened you up a little, but I guess not."

Throwing the pen down, I slide markers into the books before slamming them closed. *He's right.* The party had me more on edge than I expected, trying to keep an eye on my girl while still giving her space, and then when I got another chance and we were having a good time at the pool, Ivy saw something and Leo's hiding it. *Fucker.*

"We don't have space in here," I decide, turning the chair around.

"Now we're on." He rubs his hands together gleefully, a twinkle of excitement in his eye that I haven't seen in too long.

"What's got into you, anyway?" I ask, narrowing my eyes. He's more than capable of looking after himself when he's not eye fucking the competition, but sparring would never be his go-to.

"Well, you know, the other night was so much fun, getting my ass kicked, that I thought, *hey, let's give it another go.*"

"Sarcastic twat."

"You've not been boxing for at least a month, and whilst I know our brother is a whiny bitch about most things, he's good at that." I nod my agreement, shucking my shirt and throwing it on the bed. "No one is going to want to fuck you whilst you're being such a grumpy pain in the ass."

"And since when did you get so interested in my sex life?" I scoff out a laugh, throwing my hands behind my head and planting my feet on the ground. *Nosy fucker.*

"Since I got trapped in a house full of hot men." He

laughs, his thoughts a million miles away. "I've got to focus on something, haven't I?"

"Keep your fucking nose out of it," I say, pushing up out of the chair and barging past him. The last thing I need is for one of us to fall and break something that isn't ours. Pissing off Wyatt is not on my to-do list right now.

The dining room is full of breakables, the movie room is full of sofas, and the den has more people in it than I'd like, so as we get to the bottom of the stairs, I turn and swing. He knew it was coming, dodging back out of my way with a smirk before parrying with a return of his own.

I swing, he connects, and the two of us go down in a tangle of limbs in the entranceway.

"What the…"

More than one person appears from the other rooms to find out what on earth is going on, dragging the two of us apart whilst we laugh. A bust lip and more than a couple of bruises are about the worst of it as we both stop, Jasper stepping between us as Wyatt comes to my side.

"You good?" he asks, looking me over warily.

"Just blowing off some steam," I reply.

"He's gonna need stitches," he says quietly, gesturing to where Emmerson sits with a cloth against Jacob's face.

"It's fine," Jacob replies with a cough. "I started it."

"What the fuck happened here?" Leo bellows, blowing through the doorway, taking one look at Jacob and getting right up in my face. I tense in Wyatt's grip, ready for whatever he throws my way.

"It's fine, I'm fine," Jacob intervenes, waving his hand.

He doesn't hit me, just presses his forehead against

mine, nostrils flaring as his chest heaves, his rage barely restrained.

"We were sparring," I grit out, itching to hit him.

"In a fucking hallway?" he hisses, pushing his head into mine before snapping back and going to Jake. He peels the cloth back before pressing it again and cradling the back of his head to gain pressure. There's something possessive about the way he got between us, something a little more than friends if the way he checks my brother over is anything to go by. Like recognises like, after all.

"And where the hell do you suggest we do this?" I snap. "This was his idea, by the way. Why the hell am I the one getting shit for it?"

"You're not the one bleeding," Leo growls.

"Uh, actually," Jacob intervenes, again, gesturing to my lip. "He kind of is."

Leo rolls his eyes as I wipe it off with the back of my hand, shaking out my shoulders. I've got to give it to him, though, I do feel better.

"Can't you just use one of the gyms on campus?" Oliver asks. "That's what I've been doing."

"They're all linked into the biometrics for the relevant building," Jasper replies. "You can't get in. I've tried."

"Just get someone to buzz you in." Oliver shrugs. "Easy peasy."

"And do any of them have a sparring ring? Boxing? Martial arts?" I ask, conscious I don't remember there being any in the one we visited before moving in here.

"Ah, maybe not," he replies sheepishly, my tone clearly still holding more irritation than I expected. "But they've got some decent machines.”

“I’ll stick with my free weights,” Leo grumbles. “Does anyone know where there’s a walk-in to get this stitched up?”

“It’s slowing down,” Jacob argues. “It doesn’t need stitching, it’ll be fine.”

“I’m just trying to preserve your pretty face,” he replies, peeling the cloth back for another peek. *Yeah, something is going on there.*

Most of the other guys have sated their curiosity and gone back to whatever they were doing before, just leaving Leo, Oliver, Jacob and I loitering in the hallway as they mostly glower my way like I did this on purpose.

“Great. Well, thanks, guys.” I clip the words out, heading out the door and slamming it behind me.

Not a single one of them says anything, and nobody does a thing to stop me. They just watch me go.

I’m halfway down the driveway before I even realise I’m marching, adrenaline still coursing through my body as headlights come into view, brightening the path ahead. I don’t stop as the black car passes, it’s not my problem, but my steps do slow. *What if it’s The Sect coming back, and actually, it is my problem?*

With a sigh, I turn and head back, just as a voice calls my name, a lone figure running my way in the afternoon sun. But it’s not one of the guys.

“Nick, are you okay?” Ivy calls, her concern clear as her hot hands land on my chest and her gaze flicks over the rest of me. “What happened? You’re bleeding.”

“Oh, this…”I brush against my lip, smudging where it

had stopped bleeding, only for it to start again.

"Yes, this. You're out here in nothing but jeans, bleeding… You don't even have shoes on!"

"I don't…" The two of us both look at my sock-clad feet, as I finally feel the gravel underneath my soles. "Oh."

Her gentle fingers run along the bruise on my jaw, tracing across the black eye that's no doubt starting to show as she categorises each mark and bruise.

"You should see the other guy," I joke, but it falls flat.

"Let's get you to the house and get you cleaned up and sorted out," she suggests.

"That's probably not the best idea, sugar. Jacob decided we needed to let off some steam and the sparring drew a bit of attention. Looks like I caught him a bit harder than he caught me."

"Jesus." She sighs. "So, this is just the two of you fucking about? I thought someone had hurt you." She pounds a tiny fist against my chest, most of the concern that lined her eyes just moments ago vanishing into thin air.

"Wait, how did you even know I was out here?"

"We just drove past you," she says, gesturing back towards the houses. "I jumped out as soon as I could and came to find you because you're barefoot and bleeding, you fucking idiot."

"Only you could make something so caring sound like an insult." I huff out a laugh, my back pulling from where we landed on the ground, and I wince.

"You're hurt." The concern creeps back as she looks from me, down the driveway and back again. "Where exactly were you going?"

I shrug.

"But you don't want to be back at the house?"

The raise of my eyebrows is enough to answer that one.

"Well, then, I guess it looks like you're coming back to our place. There's a shortcut just further up ahead, we can skirt around under the trees."

"So we're walking further away to get closer, is that right?" I chuckle, gingerly following her over the hard rock and into the brush. "Are you sure you know where you're taking me?"

We walk along the edge of the road as she looks for something higher in the trees. She points out a reflective purple mark on one of the trees before cutting through and following a sort of cleared path through the dense woods.

"Please tell me you guys don't actually walk through here alone, in the dark?"

"Absolutely not. What do you take us for? Idiots?" She sighs again, brushing a stray hair back. "Honestly, I take you off that awful floor and give you somewhere to hide out until your idiot friends don't want to punch you in the face, and knowing you, that could be a while. I want to punch you and you've barely even pissed me off," she rambles. "And even after all that, you're still giving me shit."

She turns back to look me over again before rolling her eyes and continuing to lead the way.

"We only ever use this in pairs, at least, and only once at night." She shudders. "We agreed it was too scary and we wouldn't do it again. But you can *not* repeat that, do you understand?"

"Cross my heart," I agree with a smile, some of the

tension seeping out in the cool afternoon air.

"If you follow that blue marker, it brings you out by your garage," she says, pointing out the blue mark. "But considering you've somehow managed to piss everyone off, it looks like you're coming with me."

We walk for a while, the sound of water dripping from the leaves and the small birds and animals scurrying away the only noise. The campus is too far away, the houses locked up tight. But just for this moment, it's the two of us. Alone. Finally.

"I think this is the most you have ever said to me," I comment, stopping to quickly yank a small twig from the side of my foot before hurrying to catch her up. For a short girl in heels, she knows how to get some distance.

"Yeah, well, I ramble, sometimes."

"When you're stressed."

"I'm not stressed," she argues. "I'm fine, totally fine."

"Sure."

She huffs out some kind of irritated noise while flipping me the bird.

She's not fine. Seeing me like this has sparked something in her, something she hasn't been willing to admit or let herself feel.

"Then what's with the rambling?" I ask. *Silence.* "Not that I'm complaining at all. It's good to finally get a peek into that gorgeous brain of yours."

"Incredible—"

"Thank you."

She growls and I can't help but smirk.

"If you'd let me finish, I was going to say, even beat up

you still know how to land those lines. That quick wit must get you plenty of women."

I can practically taste the jealousy dripping from her words.

"Absolutely," I agree with a nod, not that she can see it. "But I have a feeling you're not so interested in thinking about me with other women."

"Ha, and why's that?"

She's quick to refute my argument, but she knows just exactly how hot that kiss was, how much she enjoyed wearing that chastity belt and knowing that she was only mine. Even if it was only for the night.

We must be almost back to their house, the distance being eaten up by her frustrated strides, and I can't help but slow slightly, hoping to drag out this alone time with her, to make the most of the opportunity.

"Oh, ouch," I say, stopping and perching on a rock as I pull a stone from my foot.

"Shit, are you okay?" she asks, hurrying back to me and dropping to the ground, any irritation she seemed to be harbouring disappearing in an instant.

My dirty bare feet don't deserve to be in her hands, the socks stuffed in my pocket when we made it onto the soft damp path. And yet, as she gently presses against the indented mark, I can only imagine those hands in other places.

"Sorry, I've just been charging ahead and not thinking about the state of you," she apologises.

"It's fine. Honestly. I'm okay," I admit, catching her gaze and holding it. She swallows thickly, her heat radiating out from my foot as the seconds tick by in silence. "You came back for me."

She nods, no words required as she presses her lips together, and all I can think about is sinking my teeth into that same flesh.

"Sugar," I start, preparing to warn her exactly what that does to me when she leans up, her hand leaving my foot as she slams her lips against mine.

We're a tangle of teeth and tongues as she wraps her arms around my neck. I pull her closer, not a fuck given that I'm literally dragging her through the mud as her hot body presses between my legs. *Fuck.*

I groan into her mouth, hoisting her up by her waist as I stand. Instinctively, her legs wrap around my hips, and I open my eyes long enough to find the closest tree to press her up against. Her nails rake over my skin, goosebumps breaking out as I grind against her, a whimper tumbling out between us.

"If you need me to stop," I pant, keeping my eyes closed and pressing my forehead against hers, not ready for the real chance she might actually say no. "Now is the time to tell me."

"I thought you were…" Her lips come to mine again, tasting the copper where my lip is bleeding again. "Don't stop."

I dare to open my eyes, praying to whatever God is out there that this isn't a dream and I'm not really just knocked the fuck out.

"Don't stop," she repeats resolutely.

She unhooks her legs, dropping to the ground as I

unfasten my jeans and she loses her pants and underwear in one fell swoop. There's no time to savour or enjoy her, both of us sucked into the moment as I push my boxers down and she practically climbs me, wrapping her arms and legs around me before I line up and slide into her slick heat.

"Hold on, sugar," is all I manage to get out before her lips are back on mine and I'm fucking her quick and hard against the tree. Her heels dig in against the backs of my thighs and I can't help but think of the dints and marks they'll leave, a physical reminder of the way she bucks and grinds, mewling against my lips.

I pull her up further, pressing her shoulders against the rough back and adjusting the angle, hitting her deeper as I hold her ass with one hand and shove two fingers in her mouth. Her tongue swirls around them before I remove my lips, confusion flickering in her eyes as I pull back.

Heat creeps into that gaze as she wraps those lips around them, and that look alone is enough to almost be my undoing. A wicked glint must register in my eyes as I push them further, making her gag and squeeze around both my dick and my fingers before I pull them out and shove them between us, finding that hot bundle of nerves that I know will tip her over the edge.

"You like it a little dirty, sugar?" I rasp, pushing her closer and closer to the edge. "You like it hot, fast and painful, huh?"

"Yes." The admission tumbles from her as she throws her head back, her nails biting into my skin.

"You gonna come for me? Scream my name into the fucking woods for everyone to hear?"

"Yes. Fuck, yes." I have no idea if she's answering me or just reacting to the pleasure as her body trembles in my hands. "Don't stop," she snaps, her eyes flying open, her desire on full display. "Don't you dare fucking stop."

I couldn't even if I wanted to.

Whatever magnetism that's been pulling us together and pushing us apart is finally working in our favour as I bend, bringing my lips to hers again, just in time for her to fall apart, swallowing her scream with my kiss.

She grips and shakes as I drag out every last second of her orgasm, until she's boneless in my arms. Gripping her ass in both hands, I pound into her, finally letting myself get swept away in the way she feels. *Mine.*

I come hard with her fingers in my hair, her tongue in my mouth, and her heels in the backs of my legs, our foreheads pressed together as we both attempt to get our breathing under control and come back down from the high.

"Wow," I finally manage to get out, sliding her back onto the ground and shimmying out of my jeans and boxers, using them to gently clean us both up before shoving them in my jeans pocket as I slide them on.

"Yeah, that's one word for it," she replies, sheepishly looking for her discarded trousers. "Sorry, you're bleeding again."

She swipes at my lip, brushing away the blood when I grab her thumb, sliding it in my mouth and cleaning it off. Her eyelids flutter and she stutters out a breath before pulling back. "Okay, I get it now," she whispers. "We should…" she says, gesturing in what I assume is the direction of the house.

"Ah, yeah. Sure, thanks," I agree, looking over the pair of us.

Her hair is a mess where it's been smashed up against the tree, her trousers and jacket are covered in dirt that I do my best to brush off as we head back, knowing there's no further excuse needed for the state of me, but her they're going to notice.

"Look, Ivy," I start, reaching for her hand.

"No, it's fine. I'm fine," she cuts me off, pulling her hand away. "Let's not make this into something it's not."

"Excuse me?"

"We've scratched the itch, now we can just go back to being friends." She brushes me off, pointing out the pink mark on the tree before stepping out at the side of the house, hurrying her steps to the door whilst fishing her keys from a bag I didn't even notice she was carrying.

"What?" I ask, stepping out from the cover of the trees and quick-stepping over the gravel to the door she's opening.

"Let's get you cleaned up or whatever," she says, quickly stepping through the door, rushing to get away.

"I put your ice cream in the freezer," Tamsin calls as I follow her down a corridor, turning the corner to their open-plan living and kitchen space, all eyes coming to us.

Ivy opens a door and pushes me inside, offering a wave to the rest of her stunned silent friends before she steps in and slams it closed behind us, closing her eyes and resting her body against the back of it.

"I don't have any guy clothes here," she comments, waving her hand at another door in the room. "But the shower's through there."

She leans there, eyes closed as I shuck my jeans, leaving them on the edge of her perfectly clean desk before heading to wash the day away.

# EIGHTEEN

## Ivy

I'm not ashamed to say I watch his fine ass strut across my room as if he owns it.

It never occurred to me that he wouldn't change in the bathroom, and the amount of control it takes to keep my eyes closed as the buttons rattle and the zip drags down is unbelievable. I'm surprised he doesn't catch me ogling that walk when the door closes and the sound of running water echoes in the silence.

"Uh, Ivy," Tamsin says from the other side of the door, knocking twice. "Are you okay?"

*Isn't that the million-dollar question?*

No, I'm pretty sure I've just lost my damn mind, but hey, why don't you come in?

"Sure," I reply, pulling the door open for her to step inside.

Whatever film they settled on continues in the room, the rest of them not daring to peek a look, but I know for certain the second this door closes, they'll be speculating.

"Don't even attempt to deny something is going on. Look at you." She smirks, looking me over and no doubt seeing exactly what we've done.

Self-consciously, I un-pin my hair, heading to the vanity to grab my brush and attempt to do something with the twigs that are probably stuck in there.

"You know how they had stuff for us at theirs yesterday, I don't suppose you know if there is any of their stuff here, do you?" I ask, completely avoiding the obvious.

"Not that I know of."

"Guess he's putting these dirty pants back on then," I comment. "He can't sit around here naked whilst they're washed and dried."

"You could fill a couple of hours with him naked, I'm sure." She smirks.

"Tamsin," I hiss, looking at the bathroom door and listening for the running water. "Nothing is going on. He's fine, just hiding out from the guys for a bit. He... I... We fell. Okay?"

"You fell?"

"Yes."

"On your knees?" We both look at my trousers. "And the back of your top... your hair?"

"I fell," I repeat. "He helped me. That's all that's going on."

"Sure." She rolls her eyes. "You fell on his cock. Don't worry, girl. We all do eventually. Enjoy it!"

"Tam," I grumble as she grins, the sound of the water shutting off having panic rushing through me.

I was supposed to get changed and hide the evidence whilst he was in the shower. Instead, I've wasted the time trying to argue some point with Tamsin. Not that it worked.

"Please," I plead, looking at the bathroom door. "Just

drop it."

She smiles, watching intently as the bathroom door opens, and like some ridiculous rom-com film, Nick appears in a cloud of steam, water dripping from his hair and casting shadows and rivulets down the artwork on his chest.

"Nick," Tamsin comments, snapping me back into reality as I close my mouth and glower in her direction, her phone in her hand as she types furiously. "You want a glass of wine?" she asks him, looking up.

"Sure," he agrees, his gaze locked on mine as he marches straight for me. With his back to Tamsin, he drops the towel, grabbing the rough denim and sliding them up his legs.

I can't hold that stare, everything in me is desperate to look down and absorb all that glorious skin, and his dick. I've felt it, the heat, the burn, and I know he's packing something good. But I've not seen it, and I'm not going there, not again. So, instead, I watch Tamsin watch him, whilst his gaze burns through me. It's awkward, but not nearly as bad as it would be with Tamsin in here whilst we eye-fuck each other.

And without a shadow of a doubt, I know that the second my gaze lowers, that's what's going to happen. That itch we scratched isn't nearly scratched enough. It's barely taken the surface edge off. I want him, still, and I'm not sure I'd be able to hide it right now either.

"Come on then, lover boy. Red or white?"

He drops that hot gaze over me one last time before turning to acknowledge she's even here, her gaze no doubt cataloguing each mark and bruise, much like I have been doing.

"Red."

"Ooh, a man with good taste." She winks. "I've just opened a bottle. Let's go find you a glass and give my girl a minute. Looks like she needs one."

She's not fucking wrong, but he hesitates. That magnetism coils in my stomach when it looks like he's going to close the distance between us and kiss me, until he sighs and follows her out, his shoulders dropping.

It's like I've been holding my breath this entire time when the door closes behind them and I sink onto my bed. I don't even know what the hell I was thinking. *I wasn't.* He's a controlling jerk. *Way too much testosterone.* But, fuck, when I thought someone had hurt him, when I thought he was in pain, the panic that gripped me was ridiculous, unreasonable, and completely undeniable.

I drop onto the edge of the bed, finally facing myself in the mirror opposite and seeing exactly what Tamsin was talking about. No there aren't any leaves sticking out of my hair, it is brushed after all, but the post-sex glow is irrefutable, the tear in my jacket sleeve uncounted for, and the mud caked into my trousers without justification.

If I thought there was any chance Tamsin, or anyone else, was going to believe that I fell over, I was living in some fucking dream world. *Never going to happen.*

With a defeated sigh, I unfasten my heels, refusing to acknowledge the state of them, and slide into a pair of skinny jeans and a clean top, after a proper clean up in the bathroom. The steam is just starting to tease an edge of frizz in my hair when I make a swift exit, doing my best to not think about Nick, naked, in my shower, or sitting wearing my body wash right now. *Fuck.*

Grabbing my phone from my bag, I steal a breath. It was just sex. It meant nothing. I nod my head once, like that fortifies the thought in my mind, dumping the dirty clothes and the memories hidden with them in the wash basket and heading into the living room.

It looks like the film has been completely forgotten as the girls rally around Nick, fussing over him unnecessarily.

"Seriously, guys? He's fine," I say, heading into the kitchen and grabbing a wine glass.

I can feel the heat of his stare following me as I pull out a bottle of wine from the fridge and fill my glass, agreement tumbling from the girls. "He sure is," and, "Uh, hmmm."

His smirk is front and centre as I dare to look through my lashes at him. The couple of hours that have passed and the decent lighting in here show the myriad of bruising coming out, but it hasn't held him back so far, why would it now? His gaze drops to my glass and back before he idly comments, "Heathen."

"Oh, she doesn't often drink white wine," Tamsin says over the rim of her glass. "Must be just to piss you off."

The front door slams, male voices carrying through as everyone pauses, Tamsin placing her glass on the table as Taylor and Wyatt round the corner, a handful of clothes and a case of beer in hand.

"Of course you called for backup," I grumble, watching the girls abandon Nick for the new shiny entertainment.

"Not my doing, sugar," he replies, coming up behind me and placing his hands on either side of me on the counter, his heat at my back and his cologne intoxicating, something altogether just Nick that can't be washed off, apparently.

Tamsin and Taylor are already making out when Stephanie and Charlotte usher Wyatt past the kitchen. He drops a stack of clothes on the counter before plucking Nick's phone from his back pocket with a wink, Aimee and Penelope fluffing up the cushions and pulling out blankets.

"I guess that means you guys are staying."

"So it would seem." The rough tenor of his voice hits me in places I really wish it didn't, his lips brushing the shell of my ear as he reaches for his stuff, pressing his cock against my back. And it would be so easy to let this roll, to scoot up on the counter and pull him between my legs, to devour him much like Taylor is with Tamsin right now, and no one would even care.

But I can't. I won't.

Not only because Wyatt just turned up and I can still remember the whisper of his lips against mine, but because Nick is not the type of guy built to sit back and let his woman run the show. And I am not a trophy wife. Not now, not ever.

"You can change in my room," I reply. "But you'd better be quick before they take this shit up a level."

His dark chuckle rolls over me before he steps back, making his way to my room without looking back. Avoiding all thoughts of him stripping off, muscles rippling and abs contracting, I drain half the glass of wine and refill it before closing the fridge loudly and heading to the living room.

Our place was not made for a dozen people. Wyatt attempts to avoid being harassed, making himself comfortable on one of the armchairs, but as Aimee perches on the arm, I know he's out of luck.

She's sweet, one of the nurturing ones of this mish-mash family; he could do worse. And yet his plea comes to me as I sit at the far end on one of the sofas.

"So, what are we watching?" I ask.

"Nothing girly," Taylor comments, dropping into the armchair beside me and pulling Tamsin down into his lap. "If I wanted to watch that we could have stuck it out at the house."

"And leave your friend here with six women and a cellar full of wine? I think not." Charlotte grins.

"Touche," Wyatt intervenes. "What have you got?"

They begin the tedious process of attempting to agree on something while I pull my phone out, scrolling through social media and waiting them out. They'll decide eventually.

I have no idea what they pick as the opening sequence starts, seriously wondering what's taking Nick so long in the bedroom, he was only changing, for God's sake. But just as I'm about to jump up, the door closes behind me and an awareness prickles over my skin as I look around the room.

It's dark outside, nothing to be seen against the glare of the lights in here as I look from one full armchair to the other, the sofa full too.

"I'll grab you a chair," Aimee comments, getting up from beside Wyatt.

"No need," Nick replies, significantly closer than I anticipated as he places his wine glass down beside mine and scoops me up in his arms, taking my seat and placing me possessively in his lap.

I could get up and move, but there aren't any other seats, and I'm not following Aimee's lead as she grabs a cushion and throws it on the floor between Wyatt's legs, leaning back against the chair.

Wyatt looks from her to me, raising an eyebrow in question as I shake my head. I can totally sit here unaffected, it's fine. I continue scrolling, doing my best to ignore the hard planes beneath me as I get comfortable.

"Are you going to ignore me the whole time?" Nick whispers, pulling me closer.

"Yes," I reply, attempting to shuffle out of his embrace and failing.

"What are we watching?"

I shrug, a squeak coming from Tamsin catching my attention before he plucks my phone from my fingers, opening a new message to a number I don't know and texting it. "Hey, hot stuff."

The vibration from his phone under my ass signals exactly whose number it is as he saves it in my phone. Another noise beside me has me on alert, sneaking a look at Tamsin and Taylor from the corner of my eye.

I type out a message, not pressing send as I know he's looking over my shoulder anyway. **Are they...?**

Nick nods.

Totally having sex in the living room while we all sit right here watching a film.

**Skirts for the win.** He types back.

Tamsin shuffles again beside me, and I can't work out whether I'm more surprised they thought nobody would notice or that they're actually giving it a go, but I don't say a thing, and neither does Nick. After what we just did in the woods not fifty feet from the house, who am I to say anything?

**You don't fancy it?** He types slowly with one hand whilst the other slides beneath the edge of my shirt. **The chance of getting caught doesn't turn you on?** His fingers slide along my waist and lower back as a shiver ripples over my body. *The treacherous bitch.*

"Deny it all you want," he whispers. "But your body can't lie."

I swallow thickly, knowing he's not wrong.

Standing up, I grab my glass. "I've got work to do," I declare before heading to my room and closing the door behind me.

I'd apologise to Tamsin, but it's not like she's using the room anyway, instead choosing to do whatever it is they're doing right there in the room alongside everyone else. I'm not sure whether it's brave or stupid, and whether I'm more annoyed she's doing it and I'm not.

Pulling out a couple of workbooks and a notepad, I make myself as comfortable as I can, doing my best to ignore the aching in my core. It was good. *He* was good. But now I need to forget it, and him.

And eventually, I manage it. Well, enough to get some work done, at least. It won't be perfect, but it's better than nothing. Someone knocks quietly on the door, and Wyatt comes in when I reply to say it's open.

"We're heading back," he says from the doorway. "Thought I'd better check on you before we leave."

"I'm good, don't worry about me." I brush him off,

dropping the pen on the pad and turning to take in his long strides closing the distance between us. He places a bottle of water on the desk, rubbing his hand comfortingly against my shoulder.

"He can choose you, but you've got to choose him back," he admits. "And you've got other options." He places a kiss on my cheek, gentle but intentional.

"Oh, I've got your jacket from the other night," I say, placing distance between us as I move to the wardrobe and pull it off the hanger.

He's sweet and kind, he's been gentle with me this whole time, and then I go and do that with Nick. Not even a dirty little secret that I was trying to hide, because we were more than out in the open. Wyatt should be the one I'm strung out on, but he's not.

"You could have kept it." He shrugs. "You never know when you might need something warm and comforting," he comments with a smile before leaving.

The smile doesn't meet his eyes, and Nick doesn't come to say goodbye, neither does Taylor, but the house goes quiet after the commotion of them leaving and I can't work out my confusion over the whole thing.

On one hand, this is what I wanted, isn't it? For Nick to leave me alone, to not be in my face and propositioning me every hour of the day. On the other, he didn't even bother to say goodbye.

Giving up on the work with a disappointed sigh, I head into the bathroom and turn on the hot water, throwing a handful of salts in the bath. I'm still not ready for people, and I guess Tamsin knows it as I close the world out, load up an audiobook, and hide in the bathroom.

# NINETEEN

## *Nick*

"Hey," Jacob says, quietly closing the door behind him. "Missed you at breakfast this morning." He takes a seat on my bed, grabs a book from the nightstand and flicks through the pages.

"Don't lose my page," I clip, finishing up the section I'm working on before turning and giving him my full attention. "If you're here to get me into shit again, I'm just going to say no now."

He holds his hands up in surrender, shaking his head.

"How's the head?"

His fingers automatically go to the strips above his eyebrow, wincing when he catches a sore bit. "It's fine, no walk-in clinic needed. Olly found these butterfly things in the first aid kit and they did the job just fine."

"Good." I nod.

"Are you going to stay pissed at me forever?"

"Are they going to hate me forever?"

"Don't be so dramatic. Nobody hates you."

I raise one eyebrow.

The tension was palpable when Wyatt, Taylor and I

finally made it back to the house last night. I skipped dinner and hid out up here, grabbing some snacks later on instead of stirring the pot with the rest of the guys.

"He knows it was my idea, knows it was just an accident. These things happen."

He. Not they.

No, because we aren't talking about the other seven people that live here, we're talking about Leopold Windsor. The man that seems intent on getting with my girl, or my brother.

"Sure."

"Hey, you were the one that wanted to come here and do this. You can't bail out now. It's barely started."

"That was a leap," I comment. "Projecting much?"

"Whatever."

"I'm not skipping out of anything. I'm just giving everyone a bit of space and getting ahead with this work. In case you hadn't noticed, this schedule is pretty hard going."

"Okay, I get that," he admits, dropping the book on the table as I wince—there's really no need for that. "Ooh, I learnt something this morning. It turns out that not everyone knew about The Sect before we turned up in the church."

That gets my attention as I tilt my head, waiting for him to continue.

"I was talking with Emmerson at breakfast and he was grumbling about the fighting and whatever, but yeah, he said it was ridiculous that we had no idea about any of this stuff before we were dumped in the thick of it."

"Well, we don't."

"Well, we at least knew we'd been requested before we

turned up here. Sure, we're figuring the rest out as we go, but we were one step ahead of some of these guys, apparently."

"That's something, I guess."

"I thought so." He shrugs, throwing the stress ball at me.

"What are you hiding up here for?" I ask.

"I'm checking on you." He rolls his eyes. "Not hiding."

The bell rings, signalling dinner as I throw it back to him. "I guess that means it's time to face the wolves," I grumble.

"Give over, it's not that bad." He chuckles, following me out and down the hall. Almost everyone is there as we take our seats, just in time for the food to be served.

"Is George not coming?" Jasper asks, looking at his empty seat.

"I can't see why he wouldn't be," Emmerson replies. "He's not in a class or anything from what I can remember."

"Is he in the games room?" Leo asks, looking around. "He wasn't in the den."

"Master DeLuca won't be joining you," one of the cooks states from the doorway.

"Why?"

"He's been removed from the challenge."

"What?"

"This can't be right," Emmerson says, standing and making his way out and up to their room. We all wait, the food going cold on the table as his furious steps thunder through the house. "It's... gone. Everything is gone. His clothes, books, stuff. It's like he was never here in the first place."

"Well, shit." I sigh, dropping back into the chair.

At what point I stood, I don't know. The entire table seems to draw breath at the same time.

They've just removed him and all trace of him, and we never even saw, didn't notice. And it's not like there are a lot of points in the day we aren't here. There's always someone milling around doing something, even in the early hours of the morning.

"Do we get a reason, an explanation?" Oliver asks. "Was there a challenge we didn't know about?"

The cook, who's clearly more important than we gave him credit for, shakes his head, going back into the kitchen and leaving us to it, now he's delivered the news and we believe it.

Nothing in here is as it seems, and with the rug pulled out from beneath us, we sit at the table, picking at the food that's been made for us. Another one is gone. We're down to eight.

Nobody makes conversation, the mood sombre as the doorbell rings, two heavy knocks following. I look at Jacob, and he looks at me; I guess that means answers aren't as far away as we thought.

He's the closest, so he gets up and heads to the front door, returning with a masked guy and his two security. He takes a seat at the head of the table, and I can't help but wonder why he's masked, the other guys weren't, and it grates.

"What was the point of blood oaths if you're still going to hide?" I ask, the question tumbling out before I can catch it.

Not that questioning The Sect is the smartest move, and it certainly didn't work out well for George. But then, he was throwing some kind of man-tantrum at the time, and I'm not. The question is reasonable, even if the timing could be better.

"Hiding?" he asks with the tilt of his head, the gold shimmering in the overhead light giving him a much more menacing feel than it had the other night.

"That's what the masks are for, isn't it? Concealing your identity," Jacob muses, finishing my thought.

"And yet, more than one of my brothers has shared theirs with you all."

"But not you…" I continue.

"*This* is for your protection, not mine," he replies flippantly. "And that is not why I'm here."

*Of course it isn't.*

"I imagine you have questions regarding Mr. DeLuca."

"Did we miss a challenge?" Wyatt asks quickly.

"This entire enterprise is a challenge."

*Helpful.*

"What did he do, or not do?" Oliver asks.

"Two drinks, clear up after the event, and look after your angels." He counts them off on his fingers. "One strike. Two strikes. Three strikes and you're out."

The silence stretches out as we ponder his words.

"To be fair, clearing up on crutches would have been tricky," Jasper comments.

"Did he offer? Or make any attempt at all?" he asks, looking from one person to the next as we shake our heads. "No, I didn't think so. Those that remain at the end of this will be a team. You'll have each other's backs. And if you're not even willing to *offer* to pull your weight at this point, how can you be expected to be relied upon when it counts?"

I mean, when he puts it like that…

His shrewd blue eyes travel over each of us, taking in the awkward mood at the table and the mostly uneaten food. He knows this has upset us all, he can read the room.

"I have something to show you," he declares, standing from the table.

Silently, we follow—it's not like anyone was eating anyway—as we make our way through the hallway and into the changing room. He presses a button high on the wall, one I've never noticed before as one of the panels moves, a staircase coming into view.

We follow him down the stairs, whispers of what might be down there covering the sound of our steps echoing off the concrete as we descend into the darkness. He pulls a cord I didn't even see, strip lights flickering before bursting forth into life.

"Perhaps, instead of working out in your rooms and taking chunks out of each other in the entranceway, you'd be able to make use of this space."

He pulls a dust sheet off a rack of free weights, but the machines all look new, the ring matt clean and seemingly free of dirt as we make our way around the space. There are sparring pads and gloves, tape, and more than one comprehensive first aid kit.

"There's a telephone number in there for a doctor, if you need something that the kit doesn't have, but let's keep that for emergencies if we can."

He's more than perceptive, watching us as we make our way around the room, Jasper checking out the machines whilst Emmerson and Leo fuck about with the free weights.

"I can't believe this has been here the whole time," Oliver comments.

"We were waiting to see how long it would take you to find it," our masked leader replies, amusement laced through his tone. "But after recent events, it seemed better to show you."

No shit.

"You've proved you're capable of holding your own, and of working as a team when needed. There'll be more to come, so be prepared," he adds ominously. His security follows him as he heads back up the stairs, leaving us to our new discovery.

"So, these girls are important, huh?" Oliver comments. It's clear it's been running through his mind for a while as he continues. "Well, as much as we are, I guess. Did you guys know about the drugs?"

"Him and Charlotte have been at it since the mixer," Leo replies. "But it's not down to me to tell you guys how to live your life, or party, or whatever. Seems like other people have something to say about it though."

"This is not going to be the partying couple of years I was hoping it would be," Jasper admits.

"I'm not sure what part of blood oaths and black masks suggested party central." Wyatt scoffs. "But you can have a good time whilst not spending the whole thing trashed, you know?"

"Yeah," he replies. "I guess I need to take this a bit

more seriously. I don't want to disappear with no trace," he whispers.

And with that mood killer, the room goes quiet, until Jacob suggests, "Who wants to hit Nick?" *Fucking family.*

***

I still ache as I drag myself out of the rapidly cooling water, but I've got to admit, whatever the hell it was Wyatt slid into my bath helped. Not that I'd say it out loud to him, of course, but I'll be asking for it next time I unexpectedly go five rounds in the ring.

Drying off, I wrap a towel around my waist and smooth some face shit on my skin. I don't care for it, but Jacob gets pissy when I, and I quote, *'don't look after myself properly'*. Apparently, I don't want people to be able to tell the difference between us because of the wrinkles or frown lines. *Whatever.*

Wyatt's got his nose in a book as I come out, he's got his headphones on and is trying to forget the world, no doubt. Until I throw a stress ball at him.

"What was with you and Ivy the other day?" I ask as he slides the headphones off, glowering at the ball before throwing it back. "Not that I was paying that much attention."

"Clearly." He huffs. "I went to say goodbye. It's called being a decent human being."

"And the rest? Don't think I didn't notice the two of you have some kind of silent conversation." And I should know, Jacob and I are the kings of that game.

"Feeling left out?" He smirks.

"Not in the slightest." At the end of the day, it was me

that took her all the places she wanted to go. No amount of unspoken words and quiet goodbyes can compare to the feel of her sated and boneless in my arms.

"You know she gets a choice in this, right? You can't just demand her and expect she'll come running."

"Oh, she'll come all right." Like a fucking banshee screaming my name into the night air, again. "You fancy your luck with my girl?"

"I think technically she's *our* angel."

"So, I can keep her satisfied and you can keep her happy. Is that the plan?"

"I didn't realise you could share." He huffs out a laugh, catching the ball as I throw it back harder than anticipated.

"No?"

"No, I have a feeling that you're used to getting what you want, and spoilt little rich boys don't often play well with others."

A tension that wasn't there before sizzles in the air between us. I'm not above taking what I want, and destroying anything in my way if needed.

"I'm not the only spoilt little rich boy here though, am I?"

I don't know enough about him, enough about his background. Small talk has never been my thing. But there are plenty of other guys in this building who prance around like God's gift to the world.

"I wonder what Jacob would think about you sharing *your girl* with me, but keeping him under wraps."

"What's that supposed to mean?" I seethe.

Talk shit about me all you like, but don't you dare talk

shit about my brother. Why he's waited until now to bait me, I'm not sure. Maybe it's just because he needs me on the back foot, and spending all that time fighting on the back of finally getting Ivy where I want her has me something akin to tired, and happy.

"Look, I'm not here to get in the middle of whatever relationship you think you're going to have with her. I'm more than sure your caveman bullshit will do that just fine all by itself. But your brother isn't going to be picking one of the girls out of that house, and you're making it very hard for anyone to get close to him."

"I'm…" I say, my eyebrows raising in disbelief as I point at my chest. "I'm doing nothing of the sort," I argue.

Yeah, I'm not happy with Leo and how he's always hovering around him. The guy is a dick, and Jacob is better off nowhere fucking near him. There are plenty of other people he could be interested in. Plenty. Aren't there?

I drop heavily onto the edge of the table, catching my weight with my hands. So, there are six girls and eight of us left… one of those is my brother, and he's gay… how many more options does he have?

"I'm sorry to have to put it to you like that," Wyatt admits. "But he's a good guy, I like him. I don't want to find him up and gone one day because he couldn't find his place."

I nod, not willing to give him anything more than the confirmation that I've heard him, and that I understand.

"And I'm not walking away from Ivy either. When she needs me, I'll be there."

With that his final word on the matter, he slides his

headphones on, dismissing me completely. With my head reeling, I slide on some sweatpants and a shirt, heading for the game consoles, or a movie. Just something, somewhere that I can do without thinking too hard about everything currently going through my head.

# TWENTY

*Ivy*

"I think it's bloody ridiculous they give us two half days of peer training or whatever and then expect us to meet these girls. I mean, seriously? One day of setting expectations and peer management and we're supposed to know what we're doing." Stephanie scoffs. "Yeah, right."

"We're only meeting them for a coffee or whatever," Aimee brushes off, dumping a pile of towels on the kitchen counter before pulling out a couple of bottles of water. "Nobody is expecting life-changing affirmations on the first date, so to speak."

"And we'll have had two or three more by the time we see them again," I add, tying my sarong in the doorway. "There's plenty of time for you to have something important ready to share."

"I can't believe nobody thought a hot tub would be a good idea," Penelope grumbles as she ties her hair up, following us down the corridor and locking up behind us. "The pool is great and all that, but a jacuzzi would have been better."

"Ooh, and a sauna," Charlotte adds excitedly. "Or a

steam room."

"Hell, why not just make the place a spa and call it a day." I laugh, the sound echoing in the thick brush around the pool as we abandon our things on a couple of loungers.

Aimee lays out on a towel, catching the last of the late summer rays, weak as they may be, Stephanie and Penelope joining her as Charlotte and I step into the beautifully warm water.

I don't know how it's heated or who maintains and cleans it but I'm loving having this available whenever we want. I try and avoid looking at the spot Nick and Leo checked out, a shiver of fear attempting to take hold, but no one was there, and if anyone is watching us now, it's the guys in the house. Or at least, that's what I attempt to console myself with as the two of us swim from one side to the other and back.

"That changing room is all wood," I ponder aloud. "It could totally become a sauna."

"And nobody needs a games room anyway. It would make a way better steam room," Stephanie agrees. "Ooh, and you could totally split it and have half for mani-pedis or massages!"

"And this is exactly why we're in the pool house and not that ancient monstrosity," Charlotte says as we touch base on one side. "Can you imagine how badly we'd show them up? I mean, six of them rammed into our comparatively tiny space… it would be complete carnage. At least with a huge house like that, there's half a chance it won't look like a complete bomb site in twenty minutes flat."

"True," Penelope agrees. "Did anyone else notice how

they have on-site chefs? Sure, the groceries are done for us, but we at least have to cook it ourselves."

"And clean up," Aimee agrees. "I bet they have a cleaner too."

"Probably," I agree. "But then, we do too. Helen comes twice a week. Have you not seen her?"

"What? No, I have not! Well, I'll stop mopping up so much then." She chuckles, laying back on the bed as Charlotte and I restart our swimming; break over.

The glass doors slide back, the sound of voices carrying our way as some of the guys step out, heading to the pool. At least I can't blame this one on Tamsin; her and Taylor are off *getting coffee*, or whatever that translates to.

That's probably code for fucking in the back of his suped-up dick extension, but as long as she's not doing it in the middle of the living room, I don't really care. She totally denied it when I asked, and I'm reasonably sure nobody else noticed, they were way too interested in Nick and Wyatt. But they were doing something, I'm sure. Although, after what we were doing in the woods just half an hour earlier, I don't really have any room to question it.

Leo and Jacob glide into the water whilst Emmerson and Jasper leap into the deep end, water going everywhere and causing the girls to shriek and jump up, finally making their way to the water and joining us. Leo joins Charlotte and me going back and forth across the pool while Jacob lounges comfortably at the side.

"Oh, hey, Emmerson. Have you seen George today?" Charlotte asks. "He's been ghosting me for days."

"He's not ghosting you, honey. He's gone," Emmerson

replies from the other end of the pool.

"Gone? What do you mean gone?" I ask, leaning up against the side as Charlotte stops mid-swim, turning to give him her full attention.

"He wouldn't just leave without saying goodbye," she argues.

"I'm not sure he had much choice," Leo counters, carving a path through the water to her. "But don't worry about it, we didn't get one either."

"So, what? He just up and left without seeing any of you?" She looks from Leo to Jacob, Jasper and then Emmerson, her longing gaze going to the big empty house that suddenly feels like it's looming over us. "Not a single one," she whispers, the sound almost lost under the movement of the water.

"Sorry, chick," Jacob says as he heads towards her, wrapping an arm around her shoulders comfortingly as he moves her towards the shallower water and the steps.

I don't miss Leo's raised eyebrow, but I think everyone else does as they make small talk, Jacob attempting to console a confused Charlotte.

"You know this is all a game, right?" Leo asks, coming up beside me.

I nod.

"Well, George is now out of the competition. Gone. Ended. Left without a trace."

Because that's not obvious enough without being so callous.

"But how? Why?" I ask.

I always knew whatever *prize* we were being offered

would come with a catch, and after last week's revelations, I thought that was needing a man at your side. Unfortunately, it looks like there's more to this than I anticipated.

"He didn't follow the rules and he can't be relied upon." He shrugs. "I get he's probably a nice guy or whatever, but you can't count on a guy like that, not when it really comes down to it."

His gaze flicks to the pool steps where Jacob sits, gently rubbing Charlotte's back while whispering comforting words in her ear. Not that I can hear him from here, but that's what I imagine as a knot forms in the pit of my stomach. What if it's her next? Or him.

I didn't really know George that well, but Charlotte did. Well enough for her to be this upset about it anyway. And let's be fair, my reaction to Nick getting hurt at the weekend is testament enough to how quickly bonds can be formed in this place, under this pressure, and for her to have not known for however long must have been so confusing, and frustrating.

How long would it take for me to go and find him if Nick stopped replying to me? Would I just brush it off as life and lectures and the general state of things in this chaotic place we've found ourselves, or would I find him gone without a trace when I finally see people to follow it up with?

"Would you miss her if Charlotte was next?" he whispers.

"Of course," I reply, my indignation clear. But his raised eyebrow says exactly what he thinks about that. *Bullshit.* "Well, not as much as if it was Tamsin," I admit. "But then we've been friends since we were like six or something. It's not the same thing. That would be like waking up without my left arm."

"Yeah," he agrees, a sadness creeping in I wasn't expecting. "I guess we're lucky in that way, the only guys that have known each other a long time are Nick and Jacob, obviously."

Our gazes both head to him as I reply, "You're usually kind of stuck with family."

Conversation falls to the wayside as we start to swim again, keeping half an eye on Charlotte as she starts to pull herself together.

"Where's the rest of your rabble anyway?" I ask, catching up with him.

"They're busy taking over the world, one game map at a time," he replies. "They didn't want to break off world domination for something as trivial as swimming, although had they realised who was out here, they might have changed their minds."

"That games room would be much better suited as a spa," Aimee comments, joining us.

"Erm, we're gonna have to agree to disagree there, I'm afraid," Leo replies, an amused smile on his face. "And you know there's a sauna and steam room just over there… right?"

"What?"

"Yeah, if you follow that path, it takes you straight to it. It needs half an hour to warm up, but there are instructions on the door. It's not complicated," he explains.

"Next time we want to go for a dip, we're totally adding that into the plan," she replies with a nod.

I wait at the side, watching Charlotte, Aimee and Leo move through the water, the silent conversation happening between Leo and Jacob amusing as he joins me at the side. Leo's gaze flicks from Jacob to me, an interest there that makes heat sizzle under my skin.

He's hot, they both are, but I have a feeling that Jacob is less interested in me than he is Leo, and there's little to no chance that Nick is interested in sharing. Not that I'm going there again. No, now the itch is scratched I can put that behind me and work out how the hell to get through this year.

"Is Olly here?" Stephanie calls.

"He's inside," Jacob replies. "I can text him…"

"Yeah, would you mind? I left my phone back at the house."

"Sure." Jacob shrugs, jumping out of the pool and pulling his phone from the table.

"Are you ladies staying for dinner?" Leo asks, coming back to join me.

"I've got lasagne in the oven," Aimee replies. "But there's plenty if any of you want to join?"

"I'm in," Jasper replies. "But only if you've got garlic bread. I'm not here for that side salad bullshit that girls like."

The guy has a six-pack that even movie stars would be proud of, and I'm not the only one that's noticed, if Penelope's comment on it is anything to go by.

"I'm bulking, babe," he replies, flexing. "I didn't realise how scrawny I looked until I had to eyeball this lot on the daily." He laughs, mimicking throwing a ball to Leo, who catches it with a leap and a splash.

"Happy to keep raising that bar, brother," Leo jokes, throwing that same imaginary ball to Jacob.

He doesn't join in with them, instead shaking his head as he gets back in the pool, sending a tidal wave of water in his direction. Unsurprisingly, he returns it, and I make a swift move to get out of the way, hiding with Charlotte and Aimee at the side while they generally act like the overgrown kids they are.

The glass door bangs closed, catching my attention as Oliver comes out, a surprised smile on his face as he stalks his way towards us, throwing his shirt on the nearest bench and sitting on the edge of the pool. Stephanie swims up between his legs as the two of them start a conversation I can't hear over the water fight.

Not that I'd want to, whatever she needed him for must be private. Maybe she just wanted to check he was still here after the whole George revelation? I don't know. But as Nick follows him out of the doorway, he pauses, his eyes narrowing on Jacob and Leo before zeroing in on me.

With a shake of his head and a disappointed slump to his shoulders, he goes back in, regret a sinking stone in my stomach. He's doing the right thing, we need distance between us right now, but it still smarts.

"Say that again," Oliver says, his sharp tone catching my attention.

Stephanie must repeat whatever she said quietly enough not to carry, but Oliver's agitation catches Leo's attention as well as mine as he calls over, "Is everything okay?"

"It's fine," Stephanie brushes off with a tense smile as she attempts to intervene.

"Like fuck it is," Oliver says, cutting off anything else she had to say. "I'll bury the little fucker. Did Taylor not make it clear enough the other week? Off-fucking-limits."

He gets back up, starting to pace as I head towards Stephanie. She might not be someone I've known my entire life, but even I can tell she's worried and needs a friend right now.

"I've told him now, I'm sure there won't be any more problems," she placates. "Come and jump in, we can swim it out or whatever."

"That's not happening." He huffs out an unimpressed laugh. "He knows you're an Angel and he still thought it was okay to single you out and corner you. I don't fucking think so."

"What's this?" Penelope asks as we all go towards them. "Who did what to you?"

"It's nothing, just one of the guys in my math class caught me at the end. He wanted me to get a coffee and wasn't taking no for an answer," she attempts to explain, turning to face the rest of us.

"And…" Oliver seethes. "Go on, tell them." He drops down on his haunches behind her, his elbows resting on his knees as his fury ripples across the space, almost a physical embodiment of the demon he's supposed to represent.

"And he blocked the door and wouldn't let me out. See, it's nothing. Not like he put his hands on me or anything." Stephanie rushes out the explanation, doing her best to downplay it.

"Lucky for him," Leo says, clearly on board with whatever Oliver is thinking as the man stands back up, wringing his hands together and continuing to pace. "What do you want to do?" Leo aims the question at his friend rather than mine.

"Surely it's down to Stephanie whether she wants to do anything about it?" I intervene. "And she just said that she's fine, so I'm not sure it needs the two of you rolling through like cavemen and banging on your chests."

Oliver cracks his wrists, shaking his arms and rotating his neck, diverting my attention from where Stephanie seems to shrink in on herself. Or, that is, until he slides in the water beside her, pulling her to his chest and taking her chin in his thumb and forefinger, drawing her cowed gaze to his.

It's almost too intimate to watch, the way their gazes lock, his anger melting away as her confidence slides back into place. A transfer of emotional energy and power. Something intangible, and yet you can see it when he brings his lips to hers. It's brief but possessive, and very clear that he isn't going to leave this alone.

And neither is she.

"I'm in," she declares.

There's a wicked glint in his eye as he grins. "Oh, baby. That's cute, but let us handle this. I wouldn't want you to get someone else's blood under those nails."

She holds his gaze, her perfect eyebrows raising in challenge before bursting into laughter. "Okay, baby. It's on you," she agrees as Aimee's phone alarm rings from the side.

"That's our fifteen-minute warning, ladies and gentlemen," she explains. "I'll jump out when the next one goes off, ready to get that garlic bread on."

It's the ice breaker we all needed as the tension seeps from the air, the threat of whatever retribution Oliver has in mind put to one side, for now.

"You think he's being too harsh?" Leo asks, swimming alongside me as I head towards the steps at the far end, more astute than I give him credit for.

"I dunno," I reply, my feet hitting the bottom as the water slows my steps, its unseen pressure wiggling through my fingers as I move them through the water.

"What do you think would have happened if it had been you someone cornered?" he asks as I trip, catching my toe on the bottom step before landing heavily on one of the others.

"Mother…" I swear, clutching my foot under the water.

His fingers peel mine away as he lets the thought marinate in my brain. How would I have got out if someone cornered me? If they locked me in a room where no one else was likely to be coming through.

"Do you think Wyatt would take that laying down?" he asks, running soothing circles over my toes. The question is barely audible over the sound of the blood rushing through my ears, his familiar scent mingling with the last of the summer flowers and the chlorine from the pool, a heady combination when mixed with the way his skin smooths over mine. "What about Jacob, or Nick?" he asks. "What about me?" The last words fall from him on a rumble, an intense darkness in his gaze as he pulls back.

He would go to war for me, with me, if needed. He steps out, water cascading over his skin as he holds his hand out for mine. It feels poignant, this moment, like the second I lace my fingers with his a pact has been made. It's a promise that I know he would avenge me. Needed, or not.

And as I slide my fingers through his, the promise is made. For better or worse. He's got my back, he's on my side. Some of the tension seeps from his shoulders as we step from the water together, another alliance formed within the pressure cooker of The Sect.

"We still don't have clothes for you guys," Charlotte comments, diverting my attention. "So, if you're coming for something to eat, you might want to go get dried off first."

"Good point," Jacob agrees, jumping out of the pool.

Wrapping a towel around my chest and the sarong around my waist, I can't help the way my gaze follows his movements. It's uncanny how he looks like Nick. I know, identical twins and all that, but the interested one is sulking with me. Rightly or wrongly.

"I'll let Chester know we won't be around for dinner," Jacob adds, winking my way before heading back to the house, and I know I've been caught ogling.

With a chuckle, I shake my head, getting my stuff together.

"Can you make it back to the pool house in one piece?" Leo asks with a smile.

I'm sure he caught me too, but he was probably joining me in the ogling. He's worth a look, that's for sure.

"I'm sure we'll be fine," I reply. "See you at ours in ten."

He nods, rounding Jasper, Emmerson and Oliver up as

the four of them head back to theirs, dripping water along the way.

"I don't know where they found these guys, but they're hot as hell," Penelope says, wrapping the towel around her tightly.

"Girl, you are not wrong," I agree, watching the four of them disappear.

# TWENTY-ONE

## Nick

I was expecting it to be laughter that alerted us to them getting back, not the irritated slamming of doors and the loud thundering of feet on the stairs.

"What the…" Taylor says, pausing the episode as the three of us head to the doorway to find out what the hell all the commotion is about.

"Wyatt, you're a techie, right?" Jasper asks from halfway up the stairs. "Any good at hacking?"

"Depends on what you need, when, and why?" he replies cryptically.

"Someone messed with Olly's girl. He's got a plan, but we need a list of the male-only apartments on campus. Do you reckon you're up to the task?"

"Who the fuck is Olly's girl?" I ask quietly, clearly having missed something important.

"What kind of messed with?" Taylor asks, ignoring me completely.

"The kind that's going to end up messy," he replies. "Are you up to this or not?" he repeats, looking at Wyatt.

"Of course." He steps out, following Jasper up the stairs as Taylor and I loiter awkwardly in the doorway, watching the rest of the guys come and go busily.

"I guess we'd better go find out what the fuck is going on," I grumble, the two of us heading up the stairs as I search out my brother. No doubt he'll have the info.

I knock twice as Taylor looks down the corridor, waiting for Jacob's reply before letting myself in.

"What the hell did we miss?" I ask, shoving him over and dropping onto the bed beside him. "You go for one fucking meal and it's all-out war or some shit."

"To be fair, the war talk started before dinner, we just didn't want to do anything until we had the cover of darkness," Jacob explains as Taylor pulls out a chair, flipping it around and dropping his arms over the back. "Some guy cornered Stephanie and made her uncomfortable, Oliver's lost it and is out for blood. He's down in the gym, attempting to take some of the edge off before we go do this."

"Who the hell is Stephanie?" I ask.

"She was their Angel at the party," Taylor says.

"Yeah, and they've been texting or whatever since," Jacob explains. "I know it doesn't sound like much, and it could have been a lot worse, but it's upset her and he's in full-on big, bad protector mode."

"To be fair, I was really fucking clear about it," Taylor comments. "If anyone went near Tamsin... heaven fucking help them. And you'd be the damned same if it was Ivy, don't even try and deny it."

The rumble that comes from my chest is all the confirmation they need as they look at each other and laugh.

"I didn't realise so many of you were coupling up," I muse, wondering what else I've been missing, Wyatt's words from the other day coming back to bite me on the ass. "George and Charlotte, Oliver and Stephanie, you and Tamsin." I reel them off, looking at Taylor, attempting to work out who and what else I'm missing.

I don't add that Wyatt thinks he's going to attempt some kind of claim on Ivy, but the numbers are stacking up and Jacob doesn't have anyone yet.

"Is Leo still sniffing around my girl?" I ask Jacob. "Do you have your eye on anyone?"

"You're not going to like the answer to that." Taylor whistles, raising his eyebrows.

"Look, we're in this to win it, and I'm not leaving him behind," I reply, gesturing to Jacob before turning and giving him my complete attention. "You don't want a girl, fine. Who else is there?"

His eyebrows raise, and I begin to wonder if being so straightforward about it has upset him in some way, until he answers, "Emmerson, Jasper, Leo and Wyatt."

"Well, Wyatt's not gay," I say with a roll of my eyes. "And Leo's whatever he said the other day, interested in the person, not the package."

"Oh, he's interested in someone's package all right." Taylor sniggers.

"Fuck off," Jacob replies with a small smile, amusement flickering over his face. "Emmerson and Penelope looked to be getting on well at the pool this afternoon, and I'm reasonably sure Jasper was quite happy consoling Charlotte whilst entertaining Aimee so… could be struggling." He grimaces.

Someone knocks on the door twice before it opens,

the only remaining anomaly sticking his head around the doorway.

"Oh, hey. I was just looking for Olly," Leo says awkwardly as he looks from Jacob to Taylor, and then me, stepping in as Jacob jumps up, crossing the room towards him.

"He's in the basement."

Leo's gaze flicks to mine over my brother's shoulder, dismissing me almost instantly before raising his chin in Taylor's direction.

"One of his handkerchiefs ended up in my washing," he says, handing the red cotton over.

Jacob turns it over, running it through his fingers before handing it back. "That's not Olly's. His are embroidered in the bottom corner with his initials, and they're a different shade."

"But these were your tell for the masquerade, right?" Leo confirms. "And I haven't seen anyone else with one."

"They were," he agrees. "But that's not his, and I have no idea where it came from."

Leo presses his lips together, cocking his head in question as he looks from Taylor to me, like either of us can shed light on the situation.

"Sorry, bro, can't help you there," Taylor says as I shrug, no idea what the fuck he thinks we can add to it. Who gives a toss about a handkerchief?

"Twenty minutes, boys," Olly says, his hands coming down on Leo's shoulders as he passes, a manic glint in his eye. "Masks at the ready."

"I'm going to go check on Wyatt," I comment, getting

up from the bed, the room feeling way too small with the five of us crammed in here. "See you downstairs in twenty."

Jacob nods as Taylor agrees, Leo moving so the two of us can get past. Irritation bristles under my skin leaving Leo and Jacob together, but part of me acknowledges that this would work in my favour. Not only would Leo bolster Jacob's potential position in the final three, but it also keeps him away from Ivy.

It might have been the two of them fucking about in the pool when I came out earlier on, but there's no doubt in my mind he's been making the most of getting her attention without me or Wyatt around. It's exactly what I'd do.

***

"Are you sure this is a good idea?" Emmerson asks, the mask doing nothing to hide his nerves. "Taking it into our own hands like this."

"Yes," at least three of us reply in unison.

"If you don't want anything to do with it, feel free to fuck off upstairs and leave us to it," Oliver clips. "But don't come crying to me when someone steps on your toes. You're in, or you're out."

And isn't that the feel for this entire damn enterprise?

"Let's go, we'll meet you all in building three as soon as you're done. Pair up and grab a list from Wyatt," he says.

Each pair of roommates grabs a list, heading out of the side entrance and through the marked path in the woods. I'm kind of glad to see that come in useful, but mostly, I'm just impressed nobody's realised the other direction takes you to the pool house. Oh, for the little wins.

"I'll be honest," I admit. "When he said things were

gonna get messy, this isn't exactly what I was expecting."

Wyatt holds open the door to the residential building we're allocated as I step through, arms full of supplies.

"Yeah, well, maybe not everyone got the idea that the Angels are off limits, but there'll be no excuses after this," he says. "He took some talking down by all accounts too."

"I guess that explains the limp that Jasper is currently sporting."

"And the black eye Emmerson has, not that you can tell right now," he adds. "Shall we start at the top and make our way down?"

Shrugging, I nod my agreement as he calls for the lift, grabbing a bunch of shit from my arms as we wait quietly. We work from apartment to apartment, sticking a picture of the girls from the masquerade party, minus masks, on each of the relevant doors with police tape.

If anyone manages to miss the fact that these girls are well and truly spoken for, I'd be surprised. No fucking excuses now. Nobody has seen us yet, and as we finish up the last door, I think we're in the clear, until a couple of girls come out of the door we've just done. Their giggling stops immediately as their eyes widen and they scurry away in the opposite direction.

I suppose two guys dressed all in black with our Devil's masks on is quite a sight, especially in the middle of the night.

"I guess there'll be no confusion over who left the messages now." Wyatt shrugs.

"Sure," I agree, checking over the list. "This is us done. Let's go find Jacob and Oliver."

To say I had concerns over Jacob heading out with him alone is an understatement. I get being pissed about the situation, I really do, but right now he's a loose cannon, and that's not safe for anyone.

"You guys done?" Leo asks as he and Emmerson join us at the doorway.

"Yeah, just coming to find the rest of you guys," I agree, noting the markings through his mask.

It's taken a little while to work out which mask is which person, and it's more than a little irritating to note that Leo was the one who helped me with the drunk guy last minute during the clear-up. I can't tell whether that pisses me off more because he's been helpful this entire time, or because I didn't realise it was him.

The four of us walk quickly to the building in question, keeping the conversation, and therefore noise, to a minimum so we don't disturb anyone. The buildings are easy to get into, the codes written down by Wyatt after less than three minutes in the system. And we could have had access to all the apartments, and probably a shit load more, had we needed them, but it seemed like a much higher risk of someone being up and about if we were inside the apartments; not worth the risk.

But for this guy, it's worth it.

Oliver rubs his hands together excitedly as the door lock changes from red to green, the handle giving way easily.

Wyatt takes one bedroom door, looking for the man in question but shaking his head as he waits there. I take the second one, still not finding the guy we're looking for as Jacob and Oliver pass, heading to the only place he could be.

Leo waits on the apartment door, keeping a lookout, as Emmerson waits downstairs for Taylor and Jasper to finally arrive. Time seems to slow as the two of them slip into the remaining bedroom, leaving the door open.

The commotion kicks off just seconds later, disturbing the rest of the guys in the apartment. One tries to burst past Wyatt, but he takes care of it, the same way the other two attempt to get past me, briefly.

The adrenaline kick is like nothing in this world as we go from the sacred silence of the middle of the night to all out war. I almost want one of these guys to kick off just so I can remind them who the fuck we are, but they already know.

Clearly not as mouthy as their housemates are, the two of them sit on the edge of their beds, anxiously looking past me and trying to work out what the hell is going on and why. The seconds tick on, the shouting dying down, and just when I think it must be over, Jacob's panicked voice calls out, "Bro."

A quick glance at Leo shows he's already moving towards me, ready to take my place as I move swiftly to Jacob. It turns out, commotion isn't quite the right word, chaos is probably closer. Jacob has the roommate pinned to the bed and going nowhere, despite his attempts, but it's the lack of movement in the guy below Oliver's rhythmic punches that is the concern as I follow Jacob's gaze.

"Woah, there," I call, wrapping my arms around his chest and hauling Olly off the guy. "I think he got the message, bro."

"You ever so much as fucking look at her again," he screeches. "And you'll be dead. Gone. Your parents won't even recognise you when I'm finished." *I'm not sure they would now.*

"Can you check him out?" I gesture to Leo with my head to the room I've just dragged Oliver out of while he's still kicking and screaming, raring to go back and finish the guy off. "Just tell me he's still fucking breathing," I say quieter as he passes.

The two guys come from the room as Leo moves away, taking one look at Oliver covered in blood and practically foaming at the mouth before they think better of it and head back inside. They don't know who it is, who any of us are, the masks doing their job and concealing our identities, but they know enough to stay the hell out of our way.

One of the guys from the other room peeks around Wyatt's shoulder before scurrying away quickly, the door closing behind him as I release Oliver and his pacing begins.

"I should…" he says, taking a step towards the room I've just pulled him from.

"They've got it," I placate, attempting to calm the raging beast as I block the way. "He understands."

"Yeah, sure." He nods, massaging the backs of his hands.

Leo stalks out, grabbing a hand towel from the side of the kitchen and throwing it at Oliver. "We need to move." Jacob follows him from the room, but he's not the only one as the roommate comes hurtling out after.

It's like slow motion as Leo grips Jacob, pulling him behind him and getting right in the guy's face, Wyatt's phone ringing. And as I stand in front of Oliver, attempting to keep him out of any further arguments, we come to a stand-off.

"If you're looking for a fight, I'll give you one, but you never sneak up on someone from behind," Leo growls.

"But it's okay to attack someone sleeping?" the guy snaps, getting up in Leo's face.

"That's our queue to leave, the boys are out." Wyatt intervenes quickly, the tension in the room amping up.

"He was more than awake," Oliver starts, ready to throw down again as he attempts to barge past me. "He knows exactly what the hell this is about."

Jacob nods, stepping out from behind Leo. "You were there just like I was, and you know damn well he was awake and with it. We're not sneaking up on anyone in their sleep or praying on women who are trapped and alone."

The sound of sirens nears, and we're all more than aware that's our queue to get the fuck out of here, but the roommate doesn't seem inclined to break Leo's stare or let this go. I pull Oliver back, pushing him towards the open doorway as Jacob takes another step around Leo, hitting the guy squarely under the jaw and snapping his head back.

He does down like a sack of shit as we all move towards the exit, quickly and quietly. Leo calls out, "Get some towels and get pressure on his nose," as we leave.

Taking the stairs, we power down them, sucking in air as we slide out of a fire door at the bottom and into the darkness at the back of the building. We're not inconspicuous as we make our way through the well-lit area, but as the first ambulance rounds the corner, we duck back into an alleyway, manic laughter falling from Oliver.

Luckily, we make it to the driveway and into the cover of the woods before anyone else appears. The rest of the guys are probably already back at the house, the silent tension building the further we get from the devastation we just caused.

A warning, for what happens when you mess with The Angels. A way to make sure every fucker knows who they are, that's what we set out to do. Not almost tangle my brother up in some kind of revenge beating.

"Have you still got the towel?" Leo asks, holding his hand out to Oliver, who throws it his way.

We come out of the clearing beside the garage, the motion sensors coming on automatically as the area floods with light. He pulls out a box of matches, setting the towel alight and dropping it to the ground. "I'll need the rest of your clothes."

Oliver shrugs, pulling the tee off his back and throwing it on the burning fabric, his trainers and jeans following before he heads back inside. "Get those knuckles sorted out too," Leo calls.

Jasper appears at the side door, looking at the half-naked Oliver and the fire before making the connection. "I'll grab any cloths we use," he comments before directing Oliver back to the basement to clean up.

"Did you get any blood on you?" he asks Jacob, kicking his footwear off and throwing them in the ever-growing fire.

Jacob shakes his head, throwing his trainers in too, knowing they both walked through whatever mess was left of the guy after I pulled Olly off.

"And you?" he asks, looking me over and pointing at a spot on my jumper. And that's another thing gone as the flames reflect off the red in his mask, the four of us stood silently.

It's almost like Wyatt doesn't want to leave the three of us alone as his words from the other day repeat in my head.

"Can you give us a minute?" Jacob asks, his gaze locked on the fire at our feet. "Go follow up on those cloths or whatever. I'll come find you in a bit."

Hesitantly, I nod, Wyatt and I go in the side door and head straight to the kitchen. *What a fucking night.* Grabbing us both a beer, I hand one over. "Well, I never knew you could do that."

"What? Hold a doorway, or get you the codes for just about anything?" he asks, taking his mask off and placing it on the island as I lean against the countertop.

The freedom that comes as I pull the plastic off and take the first swig of the crisp lager is surprising but welcome. "The computer shit," I answer. I'm more than sure he's capable of holding his own, second-round survivor or not.

His shaggy blonde hair is just slightly on the side of too long, the surfer boy attitude and laid-back commentary potentially nothing more than an act he's absolutely perfected, if the snippets of the man I've seen beneath are anything to go by.

"Well, things are not always as they first appear to be," he comments cryptically.

And he's not fucking wrong.

"Have you got five minutes?" he asks.

"I can have." I shrug, following him out of the kitchen

and upstairs.

My eyes wander to the front door as we pass, knowing Jacob isn't alone, and as much as it irks me to admit it, Leo's got his best interests in mind. He'll find me when he's ready.

"It looks like the pressure is on," he starts, perching on the edge of the desk as I drop onto the bed. "Leo and Jacob, Stephanie and Oliver, Taylor and Tamsin, Charlotte and George… if you want to keep hold of Ivy, then you're going to need to pull out all the stops."

"What exactly is it to do with you?" I clip, rolling my eyes.

Like I'm not aware things are heating up. Like I don't know she's a flight risk right now.

*I'm more than aware of that.*

She's pulling away, attempting to convince herself that she doesn't want this, doesn't want me. And I'm sure Leo's taking advantage of that.

"I spoke with my father. I've got an idea."

"I don't need your help."

"Do you want her safe or not?" he asks, way too calmly for it to be normal as he crosses his arms over his chest. "You can flounder around here, pissing her off and driving her into the arms of someone else, that's fine. I'm going to do my best to make sure that person is me, by the way, or you can accept some fucking help and know I've got her best interests at heart. She's special, and you know it."

As much as it pains me to admit it, he's right.

We piss each other off almost as much as we turn each other on, but time is running out, and whilst the noose tightens around both our throats, I'm not willing to let her be the one to fall with it.

"What did you have in mind?"

# TWENTY-TWO

Ruby

"**D**o we really need to do this today?" I grumble as the four of us pile out of the back of the black SUV. What I don't say is that I'm not ready. It wouldn't matter even if I did.

"You could at least pretend to be excited," Amy says with a roll of her eyes. "Everyone else is."

As we head into the little coffee shop, she's not wrong, each of the other girls fluffs up their hair, checking in their tiny mirrors and giggling away with each other. *Fucking ridiculous.* If we were meeting with The Devils, then maybe I'd consider going the extra mile, but for their bitches? I don't fucking think so. But then, I'm not like the rest of these girls. *Understatement of the century.*

"Cheer up, Rubes," Maggie calls. "At least you'll get a free coffee out of it."

*Bitch.*

"Ladies, grab your tables. They'll be here in ten minutes," Amy intervenes, cutting off any retort.

The SUVs have already disappeared, probably on their way to collect the princesses so they can shower us with their wisdom, or however the hell this is supposed to work. I grab my phone, tapping words out into a message, only to delete them again. *He doesn't want to hear from me anyway.*

Fancy coffee arrives and huge portions of cake that no self-respecting person would attempt to eat in front of a stranger, clearly some kind of test as I pull one towards me and grab a fork. The not-so-hushed intake of breath draws my attention to the cars as they pull up and the unfazed group of women climb from it.

Whoever their coordinator is greets Amy outside, the two of them doing that fake air kiss thing that makes me want to smash their heads together. I ignore them completely, only aware they've come in by the waft of expensive perfume and the tittering of the girls that came with me.

"Hey, you must be Ruby." I look up at her through my lashes, her perfectly pleasant smile front and centre as she takes the seat opposite me. "I'm Ivy. It's nice to meet you."

She doesn't offer her hand out for me to shake, instead grabbing the other slab of cake and a tiny fork and taking a delicate sliver from the edge before nodding her appreciation and taking a bigger piece the second time around. *Well, at least she's not a complete priss.*

"I knew the coffee was good here but I hadn't considered the baked goods might be worth trying," she admits. "I guess that could be the diet going straight out the window."

Diet. *Eye roll.* Yeah, she looks like the kind of girl who spends her entire life on a diet.

Her hair falls perfectly over her shoulders, her makeup light and natural as she smiles at me, waiting for me to engage with her in conversation probably. She shrugs her blazer off, draping it over the back of the chair, her sleeveless chiffon blouse a display of not only the money she throws on clothes but the amount of work she puts into keeping those arms toned and her physique in check.

Carefully placing the fork on the empty plate, I push it to the centre of the table, tugging the sleeves of my cardigan down and wrapping my hands around the large ceramic mug and letting its heat seep through my fingers and into my hands.

"I'm not sure how long we've got together today," she continues. "But I think the idea is that we get to know each other a little."

She doesn't bother to look around at the other tables, but I know she hears the conversation flowing easily, the laughter. But none of that is going to come easily with us, it would be too obvious if it did.

"So, I guess that means that I'm starting." She smiles, taking a sip of her coffee. "I'm hoping to become a psychologist. I have big dreams of running my own practice and being available to celebrities at any given time, hour, or day. Hoping to give those people with high powered jobs and huge pressures an alternative release to the ones they usually go to."

"You mean drugs."

"Yes, I mean drugs," she replies. "Or alcohol… sex. People turn to many different things to seek out the support and connection that they're missing in their everyday lives."

I nod, like any of this interests me or will affect me in any way.

"But I'm hoping to only be at Pendleton Prep for this

one year. Next year I'm hoping to be at University and taking the first steps towards that dream."

"Aren't you old enough to be there now?" I ask.

"I am."

"Then why aren't you?"

"It's complicated."

I scoff out a laugh, raising my chin in her direction.

Oh, I know all about complicated.

How complicated must it be for her to be here *supporting the next generation* whilst spending a year at a fancy as fuck preparatory school where the tuition fee is more than most people make in a year. Most normal people anyway.

It ain't that complicated.

Daddy threatened to take her credit cards away and she stomped her high heels and toddled along like the good little girl she's been trained to be. She'll make the perfect Angel, but which Devil is she linked with, and how do I get closer to them?

"Two minutes, ladies," Amy calls brightly.

"Well, it was nice to meet you." Ivy smiles, I guess hoping I'll fill her in on my name or some small detail that she can hold on to until we're shoved together in the next session.

I almost feel bad for her. Everyone else got a *nice girl*, someone easy, someone who wanted to be here. But poor little Ivy got me, and I'm not going to make it easy on her.

"We can swap numbers if you'd like?" she offers, looking at the phone I fidget with, turning it on its side, back, side, and front, and then repeating the sequence. "Then we can talk before we meet up next time?"

"I'm good, thanks." The smile I give her is forced and she knows it.

"Ruby, it's time." Amy's hand comes down on my shoulder, and I just about manage to hold in my startled reflex, clearly too interested in the woman opposite me and not paying enough attention to everyone else. Next time, I'll sit where I can see the rest of the room.

"Well, Ruby, I look forward to seeing you again soon," Ivy says, picking up on the name drop.

I nod, getting up and sliding the phone back into my pocket, following Amy to the door and waiting for everyone else to finish up their overly exciting conversations. Ivy's gaze lingers on me, I can feel the heat of it trickling over me as she analyses and catalogues.

Average height, average build, average mousey brown hair.

Everything about me is average, nothing special, nothing worth writing home about, and yet, I know she's going to be thinking about me. Wondering why I didn't respond to her as the other girls have done. Wondering what has happened to make me shy away.

With the right clothes, the right makeup, and the right confidence, I could be much more than mousey, much more than average, and she knows it. But does she want to pull that out of me, or is she more interested in getting to the bottom of what's going on here?

# TWENTY-THREE

## Ivy

"**S**o, how did you get on?" I ask, closing the bedroom door with my elbow and placing the two mugs of hot chocolate down on the small coffee table. Dragging a blanket from the end of the bed, I take the second chair by the bay window, wrapping myself up.

"Brooke seemed really nice," Tamsin replies absentmindedly. "I'm not sure I'm going to be able to impart my couture knowledge on that pink look she's got going on, but I guess time will tell. What about you?"

"Honestly?" She nods. "It was like getting blood from a stone." I sigh. "I thought these girls were supposed to be excited about being part of the programme and wanting to take the next step in their lives, and yet this girl seemed like she couldn't wait to get away."

"Sounds like you're going to be having fun."

"And she's not the only one," I continue. "At least two people moved away from me in classes today, and then the whispering in the corridors. We had to get to this meeting with the Little Sister thing, so I didn't have time to dig into it too deeply, but what the hell is going on? Do I smell or something?"

"Only of that flowery perfume you like," she brushes off. "But did you not hear? The Devils have put out some kind of warning to stay away from us. All the male apartments on campus woke up with our pictures taped to their doors in police tape."

"Well, it's not quite what I was expecting from them, but I guess that would do it," I admit.

"Pretty much," she agrees. "Doesn't help with your little sister issue though."

"No, I guess I'll have to figure that one out on my own. Did you have a good time on your date with Taylor the other day? It feels like we never get five minutes to catch up anymore."

"Things are a little busier than they used to be, I'll give you that." She chuckles. "And I'm doing my best to keep the boys from crowding around you all the time. I swear, every time Taylor suggests hanging out here, half the house wants to come along."

"I bet they do," I grumble. "Unfortunately, this place isn't equipped for that many people." And thank God for that. It's been hard enough adjusting to having five other people in my space, never mind boyfriends too.

It's a weird place to find ourselves.

I mean, we're literally having a conversation because we've barely seen each other all week. Even though we share a room, one of us is always just on their way out as the other comes in. When we lived at home, we made time and space to catch up, always five minutes on the phone before bed, or a lunch date.

Now, we're in each others space but barely in each others lives. And it's the same with the rest of the girls. They're just there, present, around. It's oddly comforting and irritating all at the same time.

"True. Oh, are you free Friday night? Taylor asked if we wanted to go to a party at one of the residential buildings. It's not supposed to be anything massive, and I think it's just him and Leo from their house, so you'll be free of the tangled menagerie thing that's going on."

"I've got an assignment due before Monday that I really need to work on," I say, whilst I'm sat in my pyjamas drinking hot chocolate, catching up with my friend and most definitely not researching or doing work on any kind of assignment.

"No bother." She shrugs. "I just know you had a thing for him or whatever, thought that might help you get this bug out of your ass about Nick."

"There is no bug in my ass about Nick," I bluster. "He's not even on the radar."

"Sure." She elongates the word, her eyes widening in clear disbelief. "You run off down the road after him less than a week ago because he's bleeding and whatever, fuck him, and now you're giving him the cold shoulder."

"I never—"

"Don't even attempt to lie to me. I can see through that shit easier than the sheer blouse you wore this afternoon," she interrupts, cutting me off. "It's fine, you're supposed to be enjoying yourself and letting your hair down this year. That was the deal, remember?"

Oh, I remember all right.

I remember my father demanding I put my dreams on hold for a year. And for what? Some stupid game that's going to force me to choose a man to get ahead in life.

I don't think so.

But then, I think of Charlotte, of George.

No calls. No messages. He's not been to his classes, and everything is gone from his room. Disappeared without a trace.

Would that happen to me? To us?

"I'll think about it," I reply reluctantly. "I've got a spare hour tomorrow to get some research in and get the last section planned out. If all I need to do is pad the thing out over the weekend, then I'll come." She grins. "But I'm not drinking."

"Deal." She nods, holding her hand out for us to shake on it.

***

God, how did I let you talk me into this?" I ask, looking around at the complete car crash of an apartment. There are people everywhere, music pumping at a seriously obnoxious volume from God knows where, and the not-so-familiar smell of weed in the cramped overcrowded space.

"I'm sure it'll be fine," she brushes off, checking her phone before grabbing my hand and making off through the crowd.

Interestingly enough, these guys are either too drunk or too stoned to care too much about the apparent warning handed out recently, the sea of people not parting at our very presence for the first time in days. It's both comforting and confusing.

Until a whistle rings out from somewhere and a path appears, Leo and Taylor holding court at what was seemingly a dining table long before it became an impromptu bar.

With much more enthusiasm than I can muster, Tamsin sashays her way to Taylor, dropping into his lap, their lips meeting almost instantly. Leo's amused expression catches me unaware as he dismisses the guy sitting beside him, pulling the chair out for me.

He watches me as I close the distance between us, his interest confusing. "Fancy seeing you here," he comments as I take the seat.

"Does that line work often?" I ask with a smile.

"Never." He laughs, the music seemingly quieter, the people further away. It's almost as if the rest of the party sinks into the background. So similar to how it did that first night by the pool, and I can't help but think back to the solidity of his body beneath mine, the darkness that overcame his eyes when he told me all I had to do was ask…

"So, are these two going to spend the entire night sucking face?" I ask, barking out an awkward laugh and attempting to think of anything other than the way he's looking at me right now. Like he can read exactly where my mind went.

"I heard that," Tamsin replies, raising an eyebrow in my direction before locking lips with her lover once again.

"I'm pretty sure you were supposed to," Leo replies with a smirk. "So, what do you want to do? There's beer pong, and some kind of dancing, I think…"

"Or we could just hide here while these two fuck on the chair… again."

"That's not what was going on," Tamsin says breathlessly as she pulls back from him again.

"Sure, sure."

"Huh?" Taylor's confused gaze goes from her to me and back again.

"The film, on Sunday, at our place," I prompt. "The two of you having sex in the chair, like, right there."

"Oh, that." He laughs. "We weren't fucking, just playing around. Totally harmless. And you can't have disliked the show that much, you came in a skirt tonight and everything."

Leo throws out a laugh, attempting to cover it with a cough and failing.

"I left, thank you very much," I reply sulkily. More than aware that was much more to do with Nick and everything we'd done, very publicly, not long before and less to do with whatever they were up to. "And I didn't wear a *dress* for anyone but me."

"Well, it looks very nice," Leo intervenes as Taylor opens his mouth to reply, something else cutting on the tip of his tongue, no doubt. "Why don't we go see what else is going on?"

He stands, holding his hand out for me as his appreciative gaze sweeps over me. I'm not wearing anything fancy, silver heels and a little black dress, the scoop neck probably lower than it ought to be considering our height difference, but the cross back is delicate and allows the searing heat from his touch to burn through me as he guides us away from Taylor.

"Sorry about him," he apologises, popping the top off a beer and handing it over. Not my drink of choice, but I'm not willing to risk anything not in a sealed bottle here. "He likes to play with his toys."

"And that's how he sees me, is it? Like one of his toys?"

"At the moment, I'm not sure he sees anything past Tamsin," he replies with a smile. "But we're all more than aware the stakes for the game we're playing are high right now."

The two of us move out of the busy kitchen, through the even busier living room, and find a quiet space down the end of a corridor, someone's study fitting the bill just nicely.

"I'm sorry about your friend," I finally say, accepting the seat as he leans against the table, his dark jeans pulling tight across thick thighs just inches from my fingers.

"George?" he confirms as I nod.

"Yeah, I didn't get a chance to say it the other day with everything else going on but that must have come as quite a surprise."

"Oh, it did. But there's no need to apologise to me, I didn't like the guy, but that's not to say I won't like the next one. And there will be a next one."

"What about us?" I ask, hoping and praying he knows more than we do about The Angels and is willing to share it.

His head tilts to one side, a smirk starting to kick up one side of his lips as that darkness creeps in again. "What about us, angel?"

"I meant The Angels." I blush, attraction buzzing in the air between us, and I can't help the confusion it creates. "Will we go one by one too?"

"Oh, I'm not sure about that. I have a feeling your positions are more linked to The Devils than we've been led to believe." I'm more than aware they are. "I think some misogynistic old man thinks he's going to be able to control us, with you."

"And you disagree…"

"I'm not interested in being led around by my dick." He takes a swig of the beer, placing it on the table beside him as he leans back.

It's an easy and comfortable position, and I can't help the question that tumbles from my lips, needing to clear the air and find out exactly where I stand. "Now, don't take this the wrong way, but is there something going on between you and Jacob?"

"What makes you ask that?"

"The way you watch him, the way he responds to you. I don't know, it's just a feeling," I admit, not quite able to put my finger on it.

There's definitely something there between them. What, I'm not sure, and how that fits in with the obvious temptation that crackles between us I'm even less sure of. But before I attempt to push Nick out of the back of my mind with Leo, I need to be sure I'm not diving out of one frying pan and straight into another.

"I'm not gay, if that's what you're asking."

"You're not straight though, either, are you?" It's a leap, one I'm not entirely sure I can back up.

"I'm not," he admits.

"And do you want there to be something between you and Jacob?"

"Do you want there to be something going on?" he asks, throwing the question back in my direction. "You're awfully interested in this for someone so obsessed with his brother."

"I am not obsessed," I refute.

"No?" The silence stretches out between us as I refuse to acknowledge his words. "He's obsessed with you." His words tumble out nothing more than a whisper. "He's jealous, possessive. I can't imagine him becoming so enamoured by someone without any encouragement. He's got that from somewhere."

"Nonsense."

He grips my chin, dragging my gaze to his as he dissects every thought flickering through my mind, like he's watching it all play out right in front of him.

"He's willing to do anything to get you, to keep you. And you'd be willing to do anything to be free."

"Free?"

"Free of expectation. Free of commitment. Just… free."

"You don't know what you're talking about," I dismiss, pulling my chin from his hand and tearing my gaze from his.

"What did he do to you?" Leo asks as he leans closer, close enough for me to feel the tickle of his breath against my cheek as I wait for some whispered admission that never comes.

"What did he do to make you want to take the woman he's obsessed with, and his brother from him?" I ask.

"Oh, I don't want to *take* anything," he rasps. "I want it to be given, freely and willingly."

His words or his tone hits me somewhere I wish it didn't as my stomach coils and need pools deep in my belly. I do want him. Not like I want Nick, not with that otherworldly connection that draws us willingly, or otherwise, together.

No, this is different. This is somewhere between the gentle touches and whispered words from Wyatt and the harsh taking with Nick, it's illicit.

"You only have to ask," I admit, returning his words from that very first night.

Because right now, I'd give him anything, and I'm not really sure why.

The door barges open, a couple tangled together apologising as they knock into Leo, forcing him to his feet and breaking the spell we found ourselves under. They apologise as the two of us get up, heading back into the party without a word and leaving them to do whatever the hell they wanted the privacy for.

The girly laughter is what catches my attention as we head back to find fresh drinks, ours forgotten about in the heat of the moment as we find the rest of the girls laughing in the kitchen, clearly turning up at some point after the two of us disappeared.

"You guys good?" Tamsin asks, taking in the awkward tension between us that certainly wasn't there when we left.

"Yeah, totally good. I'm going to head back though if you've got a lift to the house?" I check.

"Yeah, there's space to slide in mine." Penelope smiles, waving her keys. "Might be a bit of a squeeze, but we can do it."

We say our goodbyes and Leo offers to walk me safely to the car.

The dark evening wraps around us as he leans in just before closing the door and drops to his haunches. "It's okay to want what you want, it doesn't need to fit into anyone else's box of propriety, just remember that."

He closes the door, walking away and back towards the party, leaving me more confused than ever.

What is that supposed to mean?

# TWENTY-FOUR

## Ivy

"**Y**ou have got to be fucking kidding me," I grumble, grabbing the phone from the nightstand. There's only one person in the world that can get through my Do Not Disturb and I thought I left her safe and sound with the rest of the girls.

The text message suggests otherwise.

**T:** *Help!*

After what felt like a million years of attempting to get to sleep when I got back, all that flies straight out of the window. I've never in my life felt so awake so quickly as I throw on a pair of trainers and drag my ass out of the door, heading round the house for the cars.

Except, mine is blocked in. Penelope's stupid sports car in my way.

Legging it back through the house, I grab the key off the hook, apologising as I take it, slamming the door and flying back to the car.

In less than two minutes, I'm up the driveway and back outside the building I left her in, praying to whatever God is out there that she's okay, calling her as I wait for the elevator. What if they're not here? What if something happened and she ended up somewhere else?

The music blares as I get out on the right floor and part of my panic subsides. The party is still going on, she should be fine, right?

The door is unlocked as I get there. The music is still loud but the rooms are practically empty as I go from one to the next, still waiting for her to answer.

"Hey, girl. What are you doing here?" she calls drunkenly from a sofa where she's curled up with a much more sober-looking Taylor, and Leo.

"I got your message…"

"What message?" she asks, looking from her phone to me and back again, like the fucking thing sent it itself. And yet, she's not in any state to send anything like a coherent text message, one word or not.

My gaze flicks to Taylor's, a smirk on his face as Leo's gaze sears over my exposed skin, suddenly more than aware of what I left the house in; my trainers and less-than-covering silk pyjamas. The shorts barely cover my ass and the chamise top is half lace. *Fuck.*

Shit. This was a mistake.

They've been drinking and I look like brunch.

"Well, if you're okay, I'll just…" I say, gesturing to the door and hoping to make a swift exit before anyone else notices me and the amount of skin I'm currently sporting. Sexy pyjamas or not, this was not made for public consumption.

Leo attempts to get up, probably to walk me out safely again, but I wave him off. Whether he was in this with

Taylor to wind me up and piss me off, I don't know, but I've had more than enough of his irritating cryptic bullshit right now.

I just want to go to sleep.

The elevator takes half a lifetime to get to me, my irritation tapping out on the floor beneath me as I wait impatiently for it to haul ass down the stairs.

Gravel crunches under the tyres as I spin Penelope's pride and joy around, chips flying every-fucking-where, but who cares? Doesn't matter to me who's in the firing line. Maybe I'll care tomorrow, but not right now. *Why the hell did I bother dragging my ass out of bed for this shit?*

Because that's what you do for friends, isn't it? You haul ass when they call you in need. Fuck. She's not safe here, even I can see that, but if she thinks she is, whatever. It ain't my call.

A bush scrapes down the side of the car as I head back down the driveway, imagining the bright red paint being left behind. Part of me acknowledges that's probably going to be expensive to repair, but I guess I'll just have to pay her back. It's three in the morning and I've had barely two hours of sleep. Either way, I slow slightly.

The headlights flick as I fly over a bump, a silhouette outlined as I slam my foot on the brakes, hard. The car skids as I turn the wheel, attempting to avoid the encroaching forest surrounding me, fuck knows what waits for me in there, and not hit the person standing in the middle of the road.

"Shit," I yell into the night, holding on to the steering wheel as I manage to stop, barely three feet from whoever is still there.

My chest burns as I attempt to drag air into my lungs, but it's not enough, it doesn't matter how fast the blood pumps in my ears, my heart rate thunders as he stands there. Waiting.

I don't know how I know it's a man. It could be a woman, I suppose. But there's something about the way his head tilts, the side of my headlights illuminating the gold scar that runs left to right across the dark mask, the highlighted flecks reflecting in the darkness.

I slam my hand down on the emergency lock, but knowing there's no way he can get in and I just have to wait him out doesn't stop the rising panic, or the adrenaline still coursing through my veins, especially not when two others step into the light, one waiting either side of him.

The scars run in different places and are different colours, and my panicked gaze goes from one to the other as they stand there silently. *They didn't look this frightening before.* My head runs through a million and one scenarios, none of them good. But I'm safe in here, they can't get in.

The dirt road is too narrow for me to turn the car and head back to the rest of the campus, and I stopped too short, too sharp, to be able to manoeuvre it safely. *Fuck.*

Glass rains down on both sides of me as I scream, covering my head with my arms for whatever help that will be. I don't have time to process whatever the hell is happening before the safety of the door disappears from my side, something making light work of the seatbelt holding me in place and dragging me up by a fistful of my hair.

Pain rips through me, glass embedded in my skin as

whoever holds me drags me from the car, throwing me to the dirt in front of the car, in front of the three of them. But, no, there's the one who pulled me out, and another one; two of them, as they crowd around behind me, one from each side.

Tears pour down my face, streaking through the dirt.

What the fuck is going on?

The Devils of Pendleton Prep are here… for me.

The one in the middle. Gold. He steps forward. Silent like the night, and instinctively I know who this is. Not a single word is said by any of them. It's just two steps, but he might as well be on top of me breathing down my neck as I scrabble backwards. If I'm going down, it's not without a fight.

"Help," I scream, looking around, hoping for something, anything, anyone.

But there's nothing other than thick trees surrounding me. Death by wolves, or hyperthermia, might be preferable to what's to come, but the second the thought flits through my head and my foot hits the ground, he's on top of me, pushing me back against the corner of the car.

It's one single movement but it's purposeful and painful. Heat still resonates from the engine, despite it now being stalled, and it burns along the back of my exposed legs, a million miles from the chill that creeps through my blood, the autumn air kissing my skin.

My eyes close tightly, too afraid I'll be looking into the cold, dead gaze of the man that's come to kill me, at best. Every muscle in my body tenses, and my hands tighten into fists at my sides as his come down on top of them. His hands are huge and hold mine in place easily, pulling them together to hold them in one hand as the edge of his mask scrapes against my cheek, and I know that looking at that face will seal my fate, so my eyes stay closed as my body trembles uncontrollably.

Heat caresses the side of my face, his tongue lapping both the dirt and the tears still pouring from me. His entire body is pulled back from me, there's no comfort to be found here, no heat to ease the panic, just one long, slow taste of my fear.

I can almost feel his excitement, or is it enjoyment? Maybe it's just my mind playing tricks on me? But his words can't be mistaken. "You're mine now, sugar." They're rasped out on an exhale before a cloth comes to my mouth.

I fight, push against his hands on mine and attempt to twist my head from his hand, but it's no use. I'm trapped, stuck, held. The darkness doesn't creep over me like the night comes, it doesn't slowly edge its way over. No, it slams into me with the force of my car stopping mere feet away from him in the middle of the night.

And just like that, I'm his…

To be continued

Thank you for reading Her Devil, I hope you enjoyed it.
Get ready for more in His Angel:
www.goodreads.com/book/show/139457174-his-angel
Can't wait for more? Keep in touch with me here
https://authorhlpacker.com/keep-in-touch/

# ACKNOWLEDGEMENTS

Okay, here we go again.

Brand new series, brand new set of acknowledgements, and I'm going to do these ones a little differently.

As seen as they've been the stars of the show, let's see what our characters would have to say?

Nick – So, I'd like to take this opportunity to thank the author for finally getting around to putting my story on the page; it's taken her long enough. Without her help though, the readers wouldn't have got to enjoy this amazing story, or be left dying to see what comes next. So, yeah, thanks for that.

Ivy – I really have nothing to thank anyone for here, did you even read the story? I appear to be the only one doing the work, as always, aside from Tamsin. I might consider thanking the author in the next book, if we don't have so much of this awful back and forward going on. I think I'm going to die from the tension.

Well, that was fun.

So, for me, the author, I have to start with thanking my husband. He's still here, picking up the pieces of the housework that's been ignored for three days because I've been deep in story-land, and sorting out the children, and listening to me ramble about characters and the weird and wonderful things they're getting up to. Thanks, babe!

The team; Angela, Karen, Fay, Aliana, Christina, LeeAnn, Donna, Adina. Thank you all for the multitudinous things you do and the feedback you provide. You're an essential part of the process and I appreciate everything you're here for. You're all amazing!

A massive thank you to anyone who picked this book up and read it; whether you're a blogger, a reader, a reviewer, and it doesn't matter if you got this as part of the book tour, if you're in the street team, or if you purchased it at your retailer of choice, thank you for taking the chance on this book and the insane characters that live inside it, they're driving me a little crazier each day LOL

# About the Author

HL Packer is quite frankly, a busy bee.

When she's not running around after her free-spirited three children, and husband. You can find her tending to the dogs, bearded dragons, and snakes that also reside with them.

When she finished her office job for maternity leave, her husband purchased a Kindle E-Reader to give her something to do, and oh what a journey that has been. From reading to reviewing, then blogging and creating Romance Readers Book Box UK. And now, her own words being put out into the world.

When she is not coordinating her worlds, you can find her soaking in a bubbly bath or enjoying a glass of wine, often still with a book in her hand.

Newsletter: https://bit.ly/3rdYAny

# Also by H.L. Packer

**Fated Series**
Home
Within Reach
Within Hope
The Shadow
Amore
La Familglia
The Ties that Bind
The Bonds That Break
Broken Lies
Fractured Truth

**Pendleton Prep**
The Sect
Her Devil

www.ingramcontent.com/pod-product-compliance
Lightning Source LLC
Chambersburg PA
CBHW050744190726
48285CB00005B/1518